BALANCE OF

MAYHEM

MAYHEM WAVE SERIES

FROM THE
BESTSELLING
AUTHOR OF UNHAPPENINGS

EDWARD AUBRY

Balance of Mayhem
Mayhem Wave Book 4

CONTENTS

[PART 1]
WOMEN

[1]

ASSASSIN

*S*ister.

Light returned, sluggishly and as little more than a gray blur.

Child. We're in a pickle here. You'd best wake up.

Strontium. Dorothy's hidden second voice spoke to her in a hushed but urgent tone. She lifted her head, dimly aware of the rest of her body. Sitting? Her limbs did not respond to a cursory probe from her mind, and her heart accelerated at the accruing evidence of her helplessness.

Sister.

Dorothy reached back to her last memory. School shopping? Yes, her son, Ian. He needed a tennis racquet? Football shoes? Both, perhaps. Something uncharacteristically athletic. He had only been her son for five years, but his seventeenth birthday approached, and his childhood already raced away at the speed of adolescence.

That's it. Hold on to that.

Something happened. A fight? No, an argument. Hurt feelings. Strontium had made a joke about Ian, once her son, now Dorothy's. She laughed. Claudia, Dorothy's life-partner and co-parent, didn't like being left out. Sometimes the complicated nature of their family overwhelmed them all.

The conflict came back to her. Bitter words exchanged. Dorothy needed space. She went for a walk. Bought a chamomile tea. Something stung her neck.

Dorothy blinked, her eyelids heavy and confused. A black figure appeared in the wash of gray before her, the silhouette of a person. Sitting? Crouching?

Dorothy, you need up now.

The hazy form coalesced, surely now a woman. A vision of Strontium, perhaps? Her one-time mentor and best friend, ancient and beautiful, but ethereal now, trapped in the depths of Dorothy's consciousness. If the person before her represented a hallucination of her witch-sister, that could mean dire circumstances indeed. "Mm here." The words issued like cold syrup from numb lips. She shifted her hands again, this time rewarded with the sensation of pain, but no movement.

"Take your time," came a smooth voice, feminine and businesslike. Not Strontium. "Are you thirsty?"

"Mmm." Dorothy closed her eyes, searching for the word. Please? Yes? Help? She licked her dry lips, looking for the answer to the question. With a deep breath, she nodded, the motion triggering a drunken rush to her brain, followed by a plummeting sensation in her belly. Her heart rate picked up again.

Steady, child. You're all right. Shake it off.

Strontium's words caught her like a net, easing her fall to a halt. She sucked air through her teeth, opened her eyes, and nodded again with less vigor and more purpose. The woman before her extended a hand and poked her in the lower lip with something light and hollow. She opened her mouth, confirmed the presence of a straw with her tongue, closed her lips around it and drew. Tepid chamomile tea flooded her palate. She held it briefly in her cheeks, restoring the moisture there, before letting it trickle down her throat.

"Good," said her… nurse? Bystander? The specifics of her situation resisted analysis, and she struggled to organize them into a coherent picture. "Slowly. That's it."

Dorothy cleared her throat, took another sip, and swallowed.

"The dizziness and dry mouth will pass soon," said the woman. "Which is good, because we have maybe half an hour. Can you speak yet?"

The silhouette continued to come into focus, now a woman in a black cloak with curly hair. Dorothy attempted to rub her eyes. Something bit into her wrists, cruelly keeping her hands from her face, and bringing to her attention their bound position behind her back.

Not nurse. Not bystander. Captor.

"Yesh. I can shpeak." Dorothy's words came out more clearly than she expected, still struggling past the numbness of her mouth.

"More tea?"

"Pleashe."

Dorothy took the straw and filled her mouth again. She blinked several times, then held her eyes tightly shut. A tear ran down her cheek. When she opened her eyes again, the figure before her included a face. Black locks contrasted pale skin with tiny features, a strikingly girlish visage, but for the angry pink scar down her cheek. A scar Dorothy herself caused.

Adrenaline yanked Dorothy close to full alertness. She snapped her eyes wide.

Her captor nodded. "That's good. Your head should clear in a minute or so." Familiar, nemesis eyes stared back at her.

"Agent Kestrel."

"Not for quite some time," said her captor. "Do call me Felicia."

The sight of Felicia's facial scar triggered an involuntary twitch in Dorothy's shoulder, where she bore a similar mark, courtesy of Felicia's dagger. Both wounds had been acts of deliberate cruelty. Dorothy had sliced Felicia's cheek open as a warning; Felicia had thrown the knife at Dorothy to take her down, then twisted it to hear her screams.

Dorothy took in her surroundings. Cement floor, short windows close to the ceiling, room furnished with only a furnace and an assortment of pipes. She sat in a folding metal chair, hands bound behind her back, a prisoner in her own basement.

"Claudia will be so disappointed you're not dead." Dorothy punctuated this bravado with a coughing fit.

Felicia shrugged. "She won't be alone there, I'm sure. You can tell her my right ventricle still hurts from time to time, if you think that will help."

Dorothy frowned. "I can tell her? Aren't you going to kill me?"

"Not at all. I'm here to make a business proposal."

Dorothy stared at Felicia's eyes and lips, looking for any sign of her cruel cat-and-mouse sense of humor. "I have no idea what to say to that."

"That's a simpler reaction than I expected. I assume we can skip past the dance of whether I'm joking or mad? You're too sharp a tack for such prevarications, I would hope."

"That's fine," said Dorothy. "Perhaps we should also skip past the dance of me hearing you out? Whatever you want, the answer is no. I would like to proceed now to the matter of what happens now that I've refused. Shall we negotiate? I'd rather not die, please. You'll also find there is an especially vindictive wizard who will avenge me, so please take that into account."

Felicia sighed. "I am aware. He will be here shortly, if that makes you feel any safer. As I said, we don't have much time. Here's my bargain for your life: Listen to my offer. Then you can go, with or without answering."

"I said no."

"So you did, but I won't consider that final until you've heard me out. You're welcome, by the way. Now, unless you are prepared to repeat, 'La, la, la, not listening,' for the next fifteen minutes, I will present my case to you, then go."

Dorothy closed her eyes, and let her mind drift. Foreign words leaked from her mouth in a near whisper.

"If that's an incantation of unbinding, you're wasting your time," said Felicia. "The tranquilizing agent I used diminishes frontal lobe function. At your level, you won't be able to cast a spell of any value for the rest of the afternoon."

Dorothy opened her eyes and glared at Felicia, whose face offered signs of nothing beyond patience. "I suppose you have my attention."

Felicia straightened from her crouched position, standing little more than five feet tall. She shifted her weight and cocked her head, a look of intense concentration on her face. Her gaze drifted to a cellar window, and lingered for a few seconds. Sunlight cut in at a low angle, indicating late afternoon. Dorothy last saw her son and co-parent several hours ago, then.

By now, Claudia would have mobilized her resources at the New Chicago Security Agency, where she served in part-time capacity as a telekinetic special agent. Felicia's statement about their time limit accurately described the situation. With agency help, Claudia would find her in short order. Felicia would have to release Dorothy soon. Or kill her.

"There's a witch trapped in your mind," said the assassin.

Dorothy's heart picked up. She probed for a sign of Strontium's awareness, and came back empty. "I have a witch trapped in my mind? What's that supposed to mean? I *am* a witch."

"You are a wannabe witch." Felicia tilted her head to establish eye contact. "I don't have time for this game. An elderly witch named Strontium sacrificed her physical form to save you and your two brats five years ago. Her spirit took refuge in your mind. She hoped to reform her body and reenter it, but that hasn't worked out so well, has it?"

Dorothy inwardly acknowledged the truth in Felicia's question. As dear as she held Strontium, her mental stowaway had caused Dorothy no small amount of grief as she attempted to navigate both parenthood and a committed relationship. Though her adopted son Ian regarded her as his true mother from birth, he only did so as the result of a brainwashing spell whose effects had never dissipated. Intellectually, he understood Strontium had raised him from an infant after finding him alone and vulnerable after the Mayhem Wave. That both his mothers occupied the same body had brought its share of emotional confusion, and regrettable conversations in which he or Dorothy found the exact wrong ways to express their feelings about it. His adolescent inclination toward personal drama only aggravated the situation.

Her relationship with Claudia posed an entirely unrelated set of challenges, most notably that since shortly before their first kiss, and extending all the way to the present, they had never been alone with each other. Dorothy longed for an emotional privacy she had yet to experience, and though Claudia had never once complained about their invisible eavesdropper, she surely felt something similar.

Whatever Felicia intended to offer, it had the potential to liberate her entire family from the web that currently trapped them all. Dorothy looked down. Further denial would be pointless, even as a stalling tactic. "No. It hasn't."

"Mmm." The sound came out like a purr, and when Dorothy lifted her eyes, Felicia looked back with a smile that gave her chills. She spoke in a drawn-out, cat-like tone. "I can fix that for you."

Blood rushed to Dorothy's head. The sound of her pulse resonated in her skull. "I don't believe you."

"Yes, you do." Felicia's businesslike manner returned. "This is too good an opportunity for you to let yourself believe I'm lying. Your hope will sustain you far beyond what reason alone would allow. As it happens, you are in luck, because I'm telling the truth, though we both know you'd hear me out either way."

"You talk a lot for someone in a hurry."

Felicia shook her head. "No, I just cut past four rounds of negotiations. This is what I do, witchling, and we are on the clock."

Dorothy inwardly growled. "All right, how will you fix it for me?"

"That's better," said Felicia. "See how directness moves things along? There's an artifact that will solve your problem. An item of immense magical substance and power."

"And you want me to help you steal it," said Dorothy. "Am I close? Because if that's where you're taking this, I'm not quite that stupid."

"You are close, but no, not steal it. I need you to help me find it, and once we have it in our possession, I will need your magical expertise and intuition to unlock its power."

Despite her circumstance, Dorothy laughed. "Even better. I help you activate this weapon, probably dying in the process, and then you go on a magical killing spree? How am I doing now?"

The smile drained away from Felicia's face. She closed her eyes and slumped her shoulders. "Damn it. Why is this so hard?" She looked up. Her pale cheeks had taken on a pink hue, and moisture glistened in her eyes. "I'm so good at deception! What is it you honest people do to make people believe the truth? If I could just lie about this, you'd have agreed to my every suggestion by now!"

Dorothy frowned. "You're trying to confuse me."

"No!" shouted Felicia. "I'm trying to do the opposite of confuse you! I don't know how to make this happen if the bona fide truth won't penetrate!" She crouched again, staring at Dorothy with cold, steely eyes. "I can help you. All you have to do is want my help, and agree to help me in return. There is no weapon. The object I seek is a single dragon scale. It has no power beyond the power to heal. That is all I intend to use it for. There is no need or reason for me to betray you. Once we have it, your problem is solved, and I will have a tool for healing, not violence." Over the course of this declaration, Felicia's eyes softened. She wiped a tear from one with the back of her hand, and looked again to the window. "Believe me or don't."

Dorothy sat in silence, as much to absorb this tale as to buy her time. "A dragon scale?"

"That's right."

"I have never met a dragon, apart from Basil, if he counts," said Dorothy. "I am in no hurry to break that streak. What makes you think I can help you steal a scale from a dragon?"

Felicia stood again, and walked to the window. "We won't be taking it from a dragon. Someone did that already. I seek the Scale of Hypatia, last remnant of the White Wyvern." She paused there.

Dorothy sighed. "You know I don't know what that is, right?"

"Yes, I know that," said Felicia. "Hypatia was one of the most powerful dragons from my world. A snow-white firedrake from the isles of the Mediterranean. She ruled an entire continent for a thousand years, reigning over a time of unparalleled peace and progress."

Dorothy frowned. "That... I'm sorry, a dragon did that? I didn't know dragons were in the business of peace and progress. Not to mention governing."

"She was unique. She also had her detractors. A band of rebels, aided by a pair of less progressive dragons, attempted to seize power in a coup. They were all killed, of course, but not before prying a single scale from her armor. The wound never healed. Her integument broken, Hypatia's strength waned. By the time she finally fell from power, her empire had shriveled to nothing." Felicia gazed out the window again. "She did not survive when the worlds merged."

Dorothy waited for more, and got nothing. "How do you know all this?"

"It is common knowledge," said Felicia. "Ask your pixie pet. Or anyone else you know from the so-called imaginary world. Or... You're the scholar. Look it up."

"All right," said Dorothy. "Assuming any of that is true, why do you need her missing scale? What happened to it?"

"The Scale was imbued with only a small fraction of Hypatia's power, but even that was enough to make it highly sought after. Hypatian clerics kept it safe until the Sicilian Thieves Guild infiltrated their monastery. It changed hands a few times after that." Felicia turned to face Dorothy, and leaned her back against the cement wall. "None of which matters now. Your Mayhem Wave redistributed a lot of possessions, at least the ones it didn't erase. I have reason to believe the Scale of Hypatia survived, and I have a lead on its possible whereabouts."

"That doesn't answer my question. Why do you need it?"

Felicia folded her arms across her chest. Her face went one degree darker. "That is none of your concern. A better question is why do *you* need it, and the answer to that lies in the catacombs of your own mind. The Scale has certain powers that will allow you to free the witch from her discorporate state, and restore you both to your own separate bodies, in good health and of clear minds. You should be grateful. I could have brought this venture to any number of mages, but I wouldn't know what to offer them for their services. Sorcerers tend to play their desires close to the vest, which makes for endlessly frustrating negotiations. As it happens, your needs dovetail neatly with my own."

"How very convenient," said Dorothy.

"I respect your cynicism, but I think you know your fellow magicians well enough to understand the truth about them. You have skills I require and a problem I can solve for you in return. That makes you the obvious choice for this offer. Your concern I will use the Scale as a weapon is misplaced; it cannot be used in such a fashion. I tell you all of this freely, and back its truth with the vow of an assassin's guild contract."

Dorothy offered a deadpan stare.

Felicia frowned. "There exists no stronger bond." She drew a small dagger from a hilt on her forearm. "I can swear it in blood, if that would persuade you."

"While I'm sure I would enjoy watching you cut yourself, that won't be necessary."

Felicia pushed the knife back into its sheath with a *click*. "Very well. We find the Scale together, and restore Strontium to her rightful form. I keep the Scale as payment for services rendered, and vow it cannot and will not be used for any purpose of violence. Do you agree?"

"No."

Felicia watched Dorothy closely for a few moments, then closed her eyes and turned her head away. "I won't hold you to that. Please discuss this with Strontium. Assuming she heard any of this, you may find she feels entitled to some say in the matter." Felicia reached into a hip-pouch, and produced a small, obsidian vial. Removing the stopper, she moved behind Dorothy's chair. "Consider it a standing offer."

Dorothy flinched as something wet splashed onto her wrists. The cool liquid tickled her skin.

"I should add, if you consult with your wizard about this, or that lockpick ass you consider your father, the offer will be rescinded immediately. No one can know about this but you and I and your unconscious passenger. When you feel ready to consent to this partnership, I will find you."

Microscopic pins nipped at Dorothy's skin at the point of moisture. She wriggled her arms, serving only to accelerate the sensation. "What are you doing to me back there?"

No reply.

As the burning on her skin intensified, Dorothy's heart rate picked up again. Her fear, so tenuously kept at bay during this entire exchange, flooded back, and she jerked her arms forward. Her bonds fell away, and she pulled her wrists into view. Traces of a pale foam lingered, fizzing away on her skin. It smelled of vinegar, rosewater, and hops. She wiped it away with her sleeves, and probed for injury. Her skin showed no sign of redness or irritation. Behind her, a heap of waxy, yellow twine continued to dissolve into white foam.

She stood, now the room's only occupant, and shut the window Felicia had opened for her egress, but not before looking outside for signs of her captor she did not find.

[2]

LEGENDS

A dim house greeted Dorothy when she emerged from her basement. Felicia had left the lights off when she brought her home, somehow, the whole way from the mall, unconscious. She entered her kitchen, on guard, though aware of the low probability of a trap. Arranged in a neat row on the counter lay her shoulder bag, her phone, and her wallet. She counted her money, vaguely confident none of it had been taken.

She inventoried the contents of her bag and found tissues, breath mints, pads, an assortment of crystals and herbs, pens, a memo pad, and a miniature, petrified tortoise skeleton preserved in an acrylic brick, all apparently untouched, and nothing missing. Her mentor, the wizard Aplomado, had yet to disclose the purpose of the tiny fossil, and Dorothy put even money on it being the physical component for some new spell she had yet to learn, or a random and bizarre trinket meant to test her patience. The game of question-chicken now in its second week, she would probably break down in the next day or two and ask for an explanation.

Most importantly, a small, gray, clamshell box lay undisturbed in the bottom of the bag. Opening it revealed a narrow palladium band holding a single, dark amethyst surrounded by a dozen tiny emerald chips in a leafy pattern. The elven jeweler who sold her the ring had given her a deal on it when she declined the offered enchantment of élan. Whatever joy Claudia found in this token would have to come from its intent and natural beauty, not from magic.

Dorothy snapped the box closed and held it to her lips. She had not yet refined her plans for the marriage proposal. In truth, though they had discussed the possibility on several occasions, she and Claudia had managed to evade any direct expression of that goal.

Growing up, Dorothy had never contemplated sharing that life with another woman, but with five years to weigh the idea, and with post-Mayhem norms so little resembling the social environment she grew up in, she had long since leapt that hurdle. For the past three months, Dorothy had worked up the courage to admit to herself she yearned for the comfort of traditionalism. She had never, as a child, fantasized about domestic happily-ever-afters. What few relationship experiences she had prior to Claudia had not inspired her to imagine growing old together with anyone.

Claudia did.

They had met as young teens, and found an attraction there Dorothy misinterpreted but Claudia understood all too well. The two of them spent their entire adolescence in a state of vaguely defined frustration, as Dorothy pined for a friendship she could never earn, and Claudia pined for something more.

Though it took them half a lifetime, they eventually figured it out.

Claudia's boldness and spontaneity complemented Dorothy's reserved intellectuality. She brought out Dorothy's sense of humor, otherwise largely dormant. Dorothy admired and envied Claudia's free-spiritedness, while marveling such a person could respect and adore her in return for possessing virtually opposite qualities. Claudia taught Dorothy things about herself that made her feel like a better person, while never asking her to change.

Living with her these past five years had given her a wonderful life, and a partner who made everything easier to do, and every trial easier to bear. As much as she cherished that, Dorothy wanted more than joy and convenience. She wanted family. She wanted Claudia's name. She wanted to stand tall and declare to all the world she had found *the one*.

Apprehensively, she hoped Claudia would want the same.

Felicia's proposition threw all of this into disarray. It forced her to confront the reality Strontium's continued—and potentially permanent—residence in her mind would influence her life goal in ways she could not properly define. If Strontium could live independently, if they could exist separately, that would make her connection to Claudia all the more valuable, and a marriage to her all the more real. Until then, if ever, this fantasy would have to wait.

She took the box into the bedroom she shared with Claudia, and tucked it into a dresser drawer under two layers of neatly paired and folded socks. It would wait for her until this crisis passed, one way or the other.

Returning to the kitchen, Dorothy picked up her phone and found the expected icons for missed calls and text messages, three of the former and twelve of the latter, all but one from Claudia. The messages provided a rough narrative of the effects of her disappearance several hours earlier.

11:23 Dotty? Sporting goods?
    11:29 Hello?
    11:34 Wtfru
    11:38 Answer your damn phone
    11:46 WHERE THE DUCK ARE YOU???
    11:46 *fuck
    12:02 Did you hear the page? Starting to get worried
    12:30 Very worried now
    12:30 Are you mad at us? Please answer. Ian is frwaking out
    12:30 UGH *freaking
    12:52 I dont know whats going on. If you need space fine. Please text. We can talk later. Ian and I had lunch. We're going to poke around the mall. Tell us whenever you're ready to go home, and we'll meet you at the car. Is that okay?

Dorothy opted to pass on listening to her voice messages. Apparently, Claudia's response to her abduction did not even approximately match Dorothy's claim of imminent rescue. She couldn't decide whether to be horrified her disappearance caused her lover so little distress, or flattered by Claudia's obvious faith in her ability to keep herself safe. She typed.

    4:38 I'm all right. Please come home.
A few seconds later, her phone chirped back at her.
    4:38 WHAT HAPPENED
Dorothy laughed lightly.
    4:38 Not over the phone. Sorry. Please come home ASAP.
It took more than a minute for the reply this time.
    4:40 On our way. I LOVE YOU
The phrase, which had become something of a rote salutation over the past five years, tugged at Dorothy's heart in that moment. She wiped the corner of her eye.
    4:40 I love you, too. See you soon.

Dorothy set her phone down on the counter. She planted her palms there, closed her eyes and took a deep, slow breath. Finally allowing herself to believe no immediate threat to her life loomed over her, she took a moment to regroup, mentally and emotionally. Felicia's offer, while horribly executed, presented a temptation she only now began to absorb. Assuming Felicia could be trusted at all—a seriously risky assumption, to be sure—the thought of freeing Strontium from her captivity, and regaining sole occupation of her own mind, held appeal beyond measure.

Strontium? Dorothy reached into her subconscious, searching for her friend. *Are you there? Did you hear all of this? Can we talk about it?*

Nothing. Communicating with Strontium rarely proved a simple or easy task. She would emerge in her own time, or not at all. Counsel would not come from those quarters, at least not yet. Thankfully, Dorothy had many resources.

She opened her bag, and rummaged through a cluster of tiny, color-coded drawstring pouches. After extracting pouches of white, greenish black, and lavender, she set them on the counter and pulled a small, clay dish from a cabinet. She wiped ashy residue from it with a dry paper towel, then filled it with a handful of straw from a jar near the stove. From each pouch, she drew a pinch of the herbs stored there and sprinkled them over the straw in the dish. From a drawer, she produced a box of matches, struck one, and laid it atop the pile of herbs and dried grass.

Flames slipped into the mixture, releasing a sweet yet pungent smoke. Dorothy took a bag of confectioners' sugar from another cabinet, and sprinkled some of it over the fire. It sparked and crackled, adding the scent of caramel into the mix. She closed her eyes and whispered a brief chant over the tiny blaze.

Several minutes later, a rap came from Dorothy's kitchen window. Outside hovered a nude, frowning pixie, with fair skin, bright orange hair, and butterfly wings. Dorothy smiled at this, and opened the window.

"Hello, Sparky."

"Hey," said the pixie. "Um, should I come in?"

"Please do."

Sparky flitted into the room, settling on the counter, her usual chipper smile nowhere to be seen. "So, yeah. Awkward question, but… did you just summon me?"

Dorothy sighed. "I did."

"Oh," said Sparky. "I didn't know you could do that."

"Yes. *Summon pixie* was one of the first spells I asked Aplomado to teach me."

"Right. Okay, cool." Sparky bit her lip and scratched the back of her head. "The thing is, you probably didn't know this, but summoning a pixie… It's usually considered kind of rude. I mean, I'm not, like, mad at you or anything. I'm just saying. As a friend. You really shouldn't oughta do that."

"I am sorry," said Dorothy. "Truly. I wouldn't have done this, but I needed to speak with you right away."

"You know Esoteric has phones, right?"

Sparky worked for the Department of Esoteric Affairs in their research and development wing. She also worked for the New Chicago Security Agency as a magical agent. Dorothy could have reached her through either avenue of contact, but secrecy trumped convenience, or, as it turned out, courtesy.

"This isn't something we could have done over the phone," said Dorothy. "Please forgive me. Thank you for coming, even though I didn't give you a choice. It still means a lot to me."

"Yeah, okay, sure," said Sparky. "What can I do for you?"

"What do you know about the dragon Hypatia?"

Sparky's eyebrows shot up at this. "Whoa! Where is this coming from? Is she alive?"

"No," said Dorothy. "Clearly you have heard of her, though, which is helpful. What can you tell me?"

"Wow," said Sparky. "Yeah, I've heard of her. Everyone has heard of her, I think. At least, everyone from my world. I'm not exactly an expert, though. You'll want to talk to someone on Esoteric's dragon staff. They mostly deal with live dragons, though. Not legends."

Dorothy frowned. "Legends? Are you saying she wasn't real?"

Sparky shrugged. "Don't know. Everyone says she was real. I never met her personally."

"All right," said Dorothy. "Then what was the legend?"

"Oh. Um, let's see." Sparky scratched her head. "I'm a little hazy on the details, but I know she was a queen, and there was a war. She had some sort of talisman. A scale? Something like that. I think the war was about that thing. Maybe she created the thing to help with the war." She shook her head. "I'm really not the right pixie to be asking about this. If you want, I can poke around Esoteric and see if anyone has the answers you're looking for. Why do you want to know about this, anyway?"

At Sparky's mention of the scale, Dorothy's pulse picked up. Though not qualifying as a corroboration of Felicia's story, it did add an edge of verisimilitude. "A personal matter. For now, I would like you to keep this conversation confidential. You can keep a secret, can't you?"

"I can if it's boring enough," said Sparky. "This one should be easy."

"That's good to know. What can you tell me about this scale?"

"Not much. I'm not even sure it was a scale. Supposedly it was something that could grant wishes."

Dorothy blinked. "Wishes? What kind of wishes?"

"The wishy kind, I guess. Tell it you want something, get the thing, right? There was a catch, though."

"What kind of catch?" Dorothy narrowed her eyes.

Sparky shrugged. "Beats me. There's always a catch. That's like Wishing 101. Be careful what you wish for, and even then, you're gonna screw it up."

"Could this object be used as a weapon?" asked Dorothy.

"Probably not," said Sparky. "Totally guessing now, though. You really should bring this to the dragon lore guys where I work."

"Perhaps later. For now, let's keep this between us. Thank you, Sparky. This has been very helpful, I think."

"I would ask you what this is about, but I think I'll save you the trouble of making up a cover story. Thanks for trusting me. I won't let you down."

"Let me down?" said Dorothy.

Sparky grinned. "Every quest needs a pixie. We come in very handy."

Dorothy avoided eye contact. "I never said anything about a quest."

"Yeah, that's cute. When you're ready to roll, give me a ring. Oh, and ixnay on the ummoningsay. That gave me the willies." With that, Sparky offered a whimsical salute, and zipped out the window.

Dorothy had enough time to change into her slippers and brew a pot of chamomile tea before Claudia and Ian returned. The sound of the front door latch stirred her from her ruminations.

"Dotty?"

"I'm in the living room," said Dorothy.

Claudia entered the room with a cautious gait, Ian trailing behind laden with several shopping bags. When a white-bearded man in a gray cloak entered behind them, Dorothy stood.

"Aplomado," she said to the wizard. "What are you doing here?"

Claudia took advantage of Dorothy's standing position to run into her arms. "We were worried about you," she said softly into Dorothy's ear.

"I'm all right." Dorothy returned the hug, drawing strength from it.

Claudia pulled back. "When you didn't call back after two hours, we went straight to Gerry's." She nodded in Aplomado's direction. "He couldn't tell us where you were, but he said you were in distress. I've been on the phone with Harrison all afternoon. He was getting ready to shut down the Worm station and coordinate with the police when I got your text."

So. Claudia had been mounting a rescue after all. Dorothy smiled inwardly, her faith in her life-partner restored.

Claudia turned to Ian. "This would probably be a good time for you to find something else to do."

He nodded, but Dorothy held out her arms. "Come here, you." She gave her son a tight hug, and a kiss on the cheek. "I'm all right. I'm so sorry you were worried. Everything is fine, I promise."

He nodded again. "Okay. Good."

"Claudia is right, though," said Dorothy. "We do need a little time to talk about this alone. Are you okay?"

"Sure. I'll... I guess I'll go for a walk. Is an hour long enough?"

"I think so." She gave him another hug.

Ian departed, and Claudia led Dorothy by the hand back to the sofa, where she sat with her. Aplomado remained standing. When the front door closed behind Ian, Claudia asked, "What happened?"

Dorothy opened her mouth, then looked up at Aplomado. "We're going to need some time alone, please."

The wizard frowned. "It's my job to protect you from harm. I cannot do that without all the information."

"It's your job to teach me how to use magic. Protecting me from harm is just something you like to do. Right now, I am safe. If that changes, you'll be the first to know. Now, git. I need to have a moment with the love of my life."

Aplomado bowed, and exited without further argument.

"Love of your life?" said Claudia. "This is bad, isn't it?"

"I'm not sure," said Dorothy. "Before I tell you what happened today, I need you to understand this has to stay between the two of us for now. No one can know what I'm about to tell you, at least not yet. You can't take this to Harrison, even though I know you will want to. I will bring it to him myself when I am ready. Can you agree to that?"

"You're scaring me now."

Dorothy took Claudia's hand. "Don't be afraid. I don't think we are in any danger at the moment. I may be mistaken, but that's what I believe. I need you to trust me on this, even if you find some of what I am about to tell you upsetting."

Claudia frowned. "How about I promise to keep this to myself until at least tomorrow? If it's really bad, that still buys you a day to convince me it will be okay. Deal?"

"I can work with that." She cleared her throat, and took Claudia's other hand, squeezing both gently. "The first part will upset you, and I'm sorry about that. Are you ready?"

"Bring it."

"Felicia Kestrel is alive."

Claudia's eyes narrowed. "Where is she? Did she hurt you? Tell me everything she said to you."

Dorothy sat up straighter. "That's not surprise. That's anger. You knew."

"I'm NCSA, Dotty. Of course I knew. Bitch's body disappeared from the morgue the day after we brought her back. Alec thought it was stolen at first, but there were signs of a break-out, not a break-in. Aplomado says—"

"Hang on, Aplomado knows?" Dorothy released Claudia's hands. "You all kept this from me for five years? After what she did to me?" Her hand went to her shoulder to rub out a new phantom pain under the scar. "After what she did to Harrison? You don't think I deserved to know she was still out there?"

"I'm sorry, okay? Dotty, you didn't have the clearance for that information. I could've gone to jail for telling you."

Dorothy's lips thinned. "What a convenient and uncharacteristic respect for the law."

"Dotty, seriously, can we get back to what happened today?"

"I don't know. I think this changes my feelings about what happened today somewhat."

"Damn it, Dotty," said Claudia. "Don't do this. I thought I was protecting you, okay?"

"You really think I need that kind of protection?" asked Dorothy.

Claudia rubbed her face with both hands. "I need you to tell me what happened today, please. What did Felicia do to you?"

Dorothy paused, in a failed attempt to bring her feelings of confusion and anger to some level of stability. "She drugged me. Some kind of tranquilizer. I woke up in the basement tied to a chair."

"Did she ask you any questions? If this was an interrogation—"

"She asked for my help."

Claudia's jaw hung open for a few seconds. "Your help with what?"

"Finding an artifact. A dragon scale. She says in exchange for my help, she will provide Strontium with a new body so she can be free again, and I can have my mind back."

Claudia stared at her with wide eyes, then looked away. "Don't trust her."

"You're not very well positioned to advise me on trust today, Ms. de Queiroz."

Claudia looked back at her, steel in her gaze. "Do not trust her! I don't care what you think about me. That woman is a murderer and a snake, and she will kill us all as soon as look at us. Even if she's telling the truth…"

The pause dragged out longer than Dorothy's patience. "Even if she's telling the truth…?"

"Strontium is safe now, right?" said Claudia.

"Safe? I suppose so. There's no way to know if that will always be true," said Dorothy. "The Council of Mages hasn't made any progress on freeing her in the five years since I asked them. I think if she were in any danger they would have warned me by now."

"Well… maybe for now we're better off leaving her in there. Just, you know, until we have a better plan than trusting an evil person to help her out." Claudia's eyes drifted around the room, landing everywhere but Dorothy's line of sight.

"Oh, my God," said Dorothy. "I expected you to be upset about Felicia, but I thought for sure you would jump at the chance to have Strontium out of my head. This conversation was supposed to be about you trying to convince me to take the chance. Now I don't know what to think."

Claudia shrugged, still avoiding eye contact. "This is a lot to process all at once, is all. If Felicia's back in town, Harrison needs to know. I won't tell him today, because I promised. Let me sleep on the rest of this, okay?"

Dorothy put her hand on Claudia's knee. "I told her no, flat out. I probably should have started with that, and I'm sorry. But I have to consider it. If she's telling the truth, this venture could end up with Strontium freed. Don't you want that? You have never seemed comfortable with that part of me. Just this morning we had a fight about it. Isn't it worth considering the remote possibility? You and I could be together without an extra passenger along at every turn."

Claudia hesitated. "What if it doesn't end up that way?"

"If she fails to free Strontium? We're no worse off that way."

"That's not what I mean," said Claudia. "I mean, what if she does free Strontium, but we don't end up together?"

Dorothy shrank back. "I don't understand. Why would you say that?"

"C'mon, Dotty. I can do the math. You avoided me for eight years. Then as soon as that witch got in your head, you kissed me. What if she's the reason?"

Dorothy pushed past the tightening in her throat. "You mean what if she's the reason I love you? How can you say that? I love you because I love you." She took Claudia's hand. "How long have you had this worry?"

Claudia shrugged. "I dunno. Five years?"

"So, the entire time we've been together."

"Maybe not the entire time," said Claudia. "I can't exactly point to a date."

"You were afraid to tell me?" said Dorothy.

Claudia took her hand back. "What was I supposed to say? I think you're only with me because some witch I never met has the hots for me? You'd tell me it wasn't true, but you'd say that either way. I didn't see any point in bringing it up."

"You can tell me anything. I'm so sorry you carried this pain without sharing it. Please believe me. Strontium likes you, but nothing more than that. I'm the one who loves you, and I don't need her whispering in my ear for that to be true."

"Yeah, but what if having her in your head changed you in ways you don't know about? You have to admit you've been different since Fenway. I mean, not in a bad way, but more... I don't know. Worldly? Intense? I can't explain it right."

Dorothy laughed lightly. "Of course Fenway changed me. I'm a witch! And a mother!"

"And a lesbian."

Dorothy shook her head. "I'm not a lesbian. I love *you*. It's not about an identity or a label. It's about my heart. That didn't start at Fenway. I had weeks to process your little slip over the phone."

Claudia blushed at the reminder of accidentally exposing her years-long crush on Dorothy in a casual conversation, but kept quiet.

"The whole time Melody and I traveled in Strontium's cabin, I couldn't stop thinking about you," said Dorothy. "Also talking about you, apparently. Strontium figured out how I felt long before I did. I felt it without her in my head, even if it took me a long time to piece it together."

"Yeah, okay," said Claudia. "I believe you. Just... leave that alone for now, okay. I need to think about it. It's a pretty big fear to let go of just because you say so. Maybe we can give Strontium her own life, and maybe I can trust it will all be okay. Just give me tonight to get used to the idea. Tell me what Felicia wants you to do. Tomorrow morning we take this story to Harrison and see what he thinks. Then you and I can decide together."

"If we take this to Harrison she will withdraw the offer," said Dorothy. "I'm taking a terrible chance even telling it to you. I don't know any more details than I already shared. She wants help finding a dragon scale, the Scale of Hypatia she called it. It supposedly grants wishes, and it supposedly can't be used as a weapon."

"You believe all this?"

Dorothy spread her arms in a wide shrug. "I think so? I don't know. She could have killed me, but she didn't. Maybe that's worth something. Give me the night to think this over. If I decide not to trust her, I will bring this to Harrison myself. If not… we will need to have another conversation."

"I'll settle for that," said Claudia. "For now."

"Thank you." Dorothy leaned in and gave Claudia a kiss, though she barely reciprocated. "I think I need a little time alone now. Strontium hasn't said anything to me since right after I woke up tied to a chair in the basement two hours ago. I need to get her thoughts on all of this."

Claudia stood. "I understand. I'll be in the kitchen figuring out what to feed you and Ian when he gets back."

Dorothy waited for Claudia to leave her sight, then probed again. *Strontium? I need you. We might be able to get you into a proper body, but there's a risk. Please talk to me. I can't make this decision for both of us by myself.* She waited for a response, but it didn't come.

[3]

UNEASY ALLIANCE

Shortly after dawn, Dorothy slipped out of bed. While Claudia slept, Dorothy cast a sedative spell on her to deepen her slumber. Without an alarm, she could count on Claudia sleeping until at least nine o'clock, probably much later, and she would wake up groggy and out of sorts, in no shape to question Dorothy's absence. A note on the kitchen table would greet her, an apology for leaving without telling her, claiming Dorothy needed some time to sort things out, and asking Claudia to hold off saying anything to Harrison until Dorothy had a chance to organize her feelings. With luck, by the time Claudia's head cleared from the spell, and she figured out Dorothy wasn't coming back, she and Felicia would have enough lead time to evade pursuit.

Before exiting the house, Dorothy made a sandwich for Ian, and left a second note for him, telling him to look in the refrigerator. He required no further assistance to get himself to school, and even the sandwich represented Dorothy's desire to nurture him more than his own needs. She stood by his closed bedroom door for a long while, debating whether to sneak in and kiss him on the head while he slept. Brushing her fingertips against the wood, she sighed. If she did this right, she would reunite Ian with the woman who raised him from a toddler to a young man. The sacrifice of her temporary abandonment of him would pale in the light of that gift. She kissed her fingers before touching them to the door one last time, and departed.

Dorothy reached the Pre-Mayhem Memorial around six o'clock, and settled in on her favorite bench with a novel. Immersion in literature provided her go-to source of stress relief, and today she called on *Pride and Prejudice* to serve. She welcomed the light tone of the prose, by contrast to her current, fraught state of mind. It rose beautifully to the challenge of distracting her from the consequences that would surely follow her decision to throw her lot in with the worst criminal of her acquaintance. It did, however, draw her thoughts in another, less relaxing direction.

Marriage.

The conduct of these characters with respect to their life choices came across as absurd by any modern sensibility. Even in Austen's time, these elaborate social acrobatics, equal parts intricate maneuvering and rash spontaneity, reflected a hyperbolic version of societal norms, played for comedy and dramatic effect. Nevertheless, scene after scene, Dorothy found herself in those pages. Her relationship with Claudia sprang from a history of mutual misapprehensions about their feelings for each other.

Dorothy's mind wandered to the image of the ring hiding in its box at the bottom of her sock drawer. Her attempts to plan the perfect circumstance to present it now felt foolish. How could she ask Claudia to commit to a lifetime with her when she couldn't even commit to a single day of careful consideration before casting her own life to the wind with this mad scheme? Would Claudia still want that life once Dorothy returned? Did Claudia even want that in the first place? Did Dorothy? How much of her intent in this proposal lay in an unrealistic assumption of what marriage meant? How much of it came from an ingrained need to follow some unwritten set of expectations?

In the middle of a passage describing Elizabeth's displeasure with Mr. Darcy, Dorothy found herself unable to recall what particular (or most recent) offense he had committed, and flipped back to find the last page that had still held her attention. Random paragraphs offered familiarity, but inconsistently. She flipped back two chapters, inserted her bookmark, and set the book aside to clear her head.

Dorothy checked her watch. Forty minutes had passed since her arrival at the memorial. She had no sense of how much time it would take Felicia to find her there, if she even would, but suspected it would be more than an hour. Without an agreed upon meeting place or time, Dorothy gambled Felicia had some way to surveil her, and coming to a place she visited often, but at a time that differed from her habits, would send the proper signal. If this risk did not pay off, she would have to return home before Claudia woke up, and in all likelihood, lose this opportunity for good.

Though Felicia had not yet found her, a small child and her

grandmother did. The little girl, clutching a large stuffed rabbit with floppy ears, ran to the bench where Dorothy sat as the woman moved to the wall to find the name of her lost husband. Her dark blonde hair bounced as she sprinted, highlighting an infectious smile. She climbed onto the bench and planted the rabbit there between her and Dorothy.

"Hello, Ruby," said Dorothy. "You're here early."

"Gramma wanted to say goodbye to Grampa before we go on vacation," said Ruby. "We're leaving today."

"Vacation? Where are you going?"

"The ocean!"

That word could mean any number of beaches, as expeditions had reached both the Pacific and Atlantic coasts in recent years, with dozens of settlements and several full colonies established along their shores. To Ruby, the specifics would not make a difference. The ocean meant waves, and Ruby had spent the summer cutting her surfing teeth on the shores of Lake Michigan.

As one of the natural developments of becoming a regular at the Pre-Mayhem Memorial, Dorothy had come to know several other regulars whose engraved names of lost loved ones shared this section of the structure with Dorothy's family. Ruby's grandfather adorned a spot on the wall a dozen or so feet to the left of Dorothy's sisters, and a few feet higher. Her grandmother and mother came to pay to their respects frequently, often with Ruby in tow. The little girl herself, at only seven years of age, had come into this world well after her grandfather departed it in the Mayhem Wave. She, and the children of her generation, could only understand this loss in abstract terms. Ruby would grow up in a world that had always included magic. Dorothy envied her simple acceptance of that, with no need to adapt.

"The ocean!" said Dorothy. "That's wonderful! Are you going to surf it? Are you ready for that?"

Ruby shrugged, but her smile did not fade. "Maybe. Dad says we have to see if the waves are safe. I hope I can."

Dorothy nodded, perhaps aware with more clarity than Ruby of the nature of her father's uncertainty. As a long-standing side effect of the Mayhem Wave, weather patterns remained difficult to predict. Usually, the atmosphere and oceans behaved in ways that resembled their pre-Mayhem counterparts, but occasionally they dealt wild cards, such as abnormally large waves that could threaten a beginning surfer. Fortunately, Mayhem also brought technologies that allowed for safeguards against such surprises. Dorothy hoped Ruby would experience her first trip to the seashore without disappointment on that count.

"I hope that, too. You'll have to take lots of pictures to show me when you get back!"

Sister.

Strontium's intrusion startled Dorothy out of her conversation with Ruby. She nodded through Ruby's response to her request for photos without fully processing it.

Ruby's grandmother, having finished her visit, approached. "Is Ruby talking your ear off?"

Dorothy laughed politely. "Yes, and it is delightful, as always."

"Are we going?" asked Ruby.

"Yes, we should get a move on so we don't miss our train."

Ruby leaned over and gave Dorothy a big hug before grabbing her bunny and hopping off the bench. She dashed down the path ahead of her grandmother, running her fingers along the thousands of names carved into the wall.

Once the two of them left earshot, Dorothy whispered, "Strontium? Where have you been? Do you know what's happening?"

Where have I been? Lands sakes, child! Where do you think I've been? Roaming the territories? What the hell happened yesterday? Are you still in trouble?

How to answer that? "I don't know. Maybe? Not the same trouble I was in yesterday." Dorothy glanced around her, furtively. In five years, she still found it easiest to communicate with Strontium's consciousness by speaking aloud. It rarely mattered whether anyone noticed her doing that. Today, she kept her head down and spoke softly, alert to eavesdroppers.

Don't hedge, woman. Spit it out.

Dorothy sighed. "I really wanted to talk about this yesterday. I could have used your advice. As things stand now, I'm pretty well committed."

Committed to what?

"I may have found a way to get you back into your own body." Dorothy waited for a reaction, until the silence drew out beyond her patience. "Are you still there?"

What's the catch?

"What makes you think there's a catch?"

Life is a tradeoff, kiddo. Magical fixes don't come cheap. It's the balance of mayhem. That's a powerful good take, so what's the give?

"I had to make a deal with an assassin," said Dorothy.

After a pause, Strontium said, *That doesn't sound like you.*

"Tell me about it. I haven't agreed to anything yet, but I have a plan. She swore on an assassins' guild contract not to betray me. Does that mean anything?"

Do I look like a lawyer?

Dorothy laughed. "You don't look like anything, sister. I mean to correct that."

Don't risk yourself on my account. I smell a bad idea here. I'm not worth it, child. Be patient. Find a better way. Or don't. I won't make any trouble in here. I can stay buried so deep you won't know I'm here.

"No!" Dorothy caught herself, and looked around, grateful no one heard the outburst. "No. It's not about me needing you out. This is about you. And Ian, who frankly deserves his mother back."

You're his mother.

"We both are, and don't play that card. Trust me to do this."

You're not the one I don't trust.

The silence in Dorothy's head went deeper, as Strontium dropped out of consciousness again. After a minute or so of waiting for the witch to resurface, she returned to her book. Once again, she read a full chapter without a single word registering, and turned the pages back to start it over for a third time.

"Who were Lorraine and Fiona?" asked Felicia.

Dorothy looked up. Felicia stood with her back to her. In place of her usual black, knife-laden garb, she wore a hooded sweatshirt, jeans and sneakers. They likely concealed fewer weapons than her standard arsenal, but not much.

Felicia had beaten her tightest estimate for the amount of time it would take her to read Dorothy's appearance at the memorial as a signal. That would give their head start a convenient boost, but the timing, following on the heels of Dorothy's aborted chance to properly explain the situation to Strontium, rattled her.

"Sisters," said Dorothy.

"Younger or older?" Felicia continued to face the wall. Tens of thousands of names covered this section of the memorial, arranged in order of submission. One would need to know exactly where to look to find any specific loved one, or have phenomenal patience and stamina in the search.

"Younger."

Felicia turned around, uncharacteristic softness in her eyes. "I'm sorry for your loss."

Dorothy closed her book. "Save it. That's not why you're here. I assumed coming somewhere predictable would make it easier for you to find me."

"I would have found you anywhere, but that's very considerate. Are we on?"

"Conditionally, yes."

Felicia narrowed her eyes and smiled. "Is this where you tell me we only have a matter of hours before the NCSA starts looking for you? I assume Special Agent de Queiroz is the wild card in play at the moment, yes? I am curious: how did she react when you told her?"

Dorothy sat up at this. "How did you know?"

Felicia shrugged. "I didn't, but it seemed likely enough. What did she say?"

"Not to trust you. Obviously." Dorothy paused, lips parted.

"And...?" said Felicia with a smirk.

"And nothing. For the record, she was right. I do not trust you, but I am willing to entertain the possibility you are telling the truth. I owe it to Strontium to try."

"How noble."

"Yes, well, you should be advised if at any point I even suspect you are playing me, my pixie will execute you."

An orange streak of sparks arced over the memorial wall and came to rest on the bench beside Dorothy. Seated, Sparky crossed her arms, crossed her legs, and nodded without smiling. "Howdy do."

Felicia laughed. "I wouldn't have it any other way. Have you ever killed anyone, little imp?"

"Yes."

Felicia's smile diminished by a degree. "All right then. Well played. Happily for all of us, it won't come to that. You have my word no harm will come to you by my hand, nor by any agent of mine, in perpetuity. I would be grateful for similar assurances, but I understand your reticence on that count. I shall simply have to rely on your good nature."

"No promises," said Dorothy. "I will need your vow not to harm my loved ones as well. Revenge against Claudia is off the table forever. Understood?"

Felicia shrugged. "Done. Your lover, your boy, your so-called father and all their ilk are safe from me."

"Claudia stabbed you in the heart. Are you telling me you can let bygones be bygones over that?"

"Yes, I am," said Felicia. "Revenge is a meaningless concept in my field. Grudges serve no one, and what de Queiroz did was business, not personal. You may rest easy."

"All right. Before this goes even one step further, I need to hear your plan. All of it. If I don't like what I hear, I am walking. If you follow me, you get a pixie through the heart. Will you survive that? I gather from what happened in Fenway your heart is not exactly your vulnerability. Do you even have one?"

"That's uncalled for." Felicia no longer smiled. "No, I would not survive. The spell that resuscitated me only works once."

"Spell?" said Dorothy.

"Prophylactic resurrection," said Felicia. "Assassin apprentices of great promise are gifted the spell when we turn twelve. It is meant to be our one and only escape, should things ever go badly for us."

A knot formed in the pit of Dorothy's stomach. "Twelve? They... twelve? My God. How old were you when you joined?"

"Less than twelve. Your lover activated the spell with that mortal wound. I never technically died. Stasis and repairs typically take a day or two. The lucky ones don't wake up in graves. You should speak to the NCSA about their morgue security, by the way. You know those drawers don't even lock?"

Dorothy shrank back. "How do you turn a child into a murderer? What did they do to you?"

Felicia nonchalantly flicked her wrist. A dagger sprang from her sleeve. She used it to clean under a fingernail. "Please don't mistake this joint venture for an opportunity to get to know me, Dorothy Brigid Eileen O'Neill, PhD. The short answer to every question you could imagine to ask me about my history is it doesn't matter. I am who I am. I like who I am. Under any other circumstance, I would relish killing you, not because I desire your death, but because my work brings me great joy. Whatever preconceived notions you harbor about the nature of childhood mean nothing to me."

Dorothy frowned. "I'm sorry."

"Well, that's a waste of your sorrow. Shall we discuss business?"

"Yes, that's fine. What's your plan?"

"I'm still working out some of the details," said Felicia. "Before we can use the Scale to regrow Strontium's body, her consciousness needs to be transferred from your mind to a temporary vessel."

"How do we do that?" asked Dorothy.

"I know a guy. Once we secure that transfer, we need to meet with my contact regarding the location of the Scale."

"I assume we have an appointment?"

"Not at a designated time, no, but he is expecting the visit. That meeting could prove the trickiest part of the mission. Assuming it goes well, we launch the expedition proper. If the Scale is where I think it is, we should count on two days travel." Felicia indicated Dorothy's feet. "I see you brought your hiking boots."

"Proper footwear is essential for a woman on a quest," said Dorothy. "I learned that lesson at fourteen."

"I hope that bag of tricks you wear is fully stocked," said Felicia.

"I have what I need. I assume you're carrying at least a hundred knives under that hoodie?"

Felicia laughed. "Give or take. On that topic, we do have one business item that needs to be taken care of before we can leave town. I need you to go to NCSA HQ and get my swords."

"What?" Dorothy stood. The NCSA vault contained, among many other dangerous items, a set of matching katana and wakizashi, both formerly Felicia's, both enchanted, and both sentient. Dorothy had only seen the katana up close, after incapacitating Felicia during her escape from Fenway five years earlier. At that time, she nearly made the mistake of wielding it, before detecting magic on it and shying away. Had she taken it in hand, it likely would have killed her and anyone who stood with her by hijacking her motor functions. Thankfully, she did not learn this detail until much later. "No! Absolutely not. Was this all a ruse to get your weapons back? Should Sparky kill you right now?"

Felicia rolled her eyes. She retracted the dagger into her sleeve. "We really don't have time for this. No, the weapons were not my only goal. Yes, I need them for the mission. I swear this to you on the same oath as my promise not to harm you. At this point you can either accept my word or bow out. The only question before you is how badly you want to help your witch-sister, and I can't answer that for you." She turned to Sparky. "Imp, magic sword versus pixie, who wins?"

Sparky glared back at her. "Best of seven? Pixie, hands down."

"Best of seven?" said Dorothy. "What about sudden death?"

"Could go either way," said the pixie. "I'll do my best."

"That really won't be necessary," said Felicia.

"Thank you, Sparky," said Dorothy. "All right, I will get you the swords on one condition. Once we have the Scale, you surrender them back to the NCSA."

"No deal."

"It's the only deal you're going to get. I told you if I didn't like what I heard I would walk. Take this deal or I take my first step."

Felicia held her hands up. "All right. Agreed. I don't like it, but we don't have time to argue about it. We need to get the swords and get out of New Chicago in the next two hours. Your clearance will get you in the door, but you're going to need my help getting past vault security. You'll need to use your eye repellant spell, and I can teach you how to hack into the vault. Once you have them, you'll have to sneak out through the tunnels. Do you know where the access points are?"

"Whoa, whoa," said Dorothy. "Back up. I'm not going to burgle the NCSA, especially to help you. I'm sure the fugitive life suits you, but I plan to return home when this is over, not go to prison. We have to do this my way, or you can forget the swords right now."

Felicia cocked an eyebrow at this. "You think you have a better plan?"

Dorothy smiled. "I know a guy."

[4]

VAULT

NCSA Headquarters stood near the center of the city of New Chicago. A pre-Mayhem office building, its conversion to government use had been one of the first projects after the founding of the city-state, made convenient by the curious variety of interior functionality. The seventh floor hosted a block of hotel-style bedrooms once, before their destruction in a fire Felicia helped start. The building also housed a barber shop, a swimming pool, and in a sub-basement, Dorothy's destination this day: a bank vault.

At a little after 8:00 on a weekday morning, much of the city continued to rise from its slumber, diners and coffee shops populated with people not yet ready to face their days. Streets offered their first hints of the rush hour to come. Much about life in post-Mayhem New Chicago had come to resemble the world of Dorothy's childhood, or at least what she remembered of it. That humans had reestablished a comfortable routine stood as testimony to their resilience. That they did so alongside elves, centaurs, and any number of creatures from their own fairy tales spoke of their adaptability.

Dorothy entered the NCSA lobby and strode through the metal detector without hesitation or concern. That represented only one tier of entrance security, however, and as she approached the magic detector, her heart rate picked up. Though designed to identify magical weapons, the detector occasionally returned false positives, particularly in cases of people who had recently cast common spells, such as a sleep charm, or summoning a pixie. With Claudia's induced doze likely to run its course in the next few hours, Dorothy would not welcome the delay this day. She slid her bag onto the side counter, took a deep breath, and stepped forward.

The detector tickled her with its probing enchantment. Not everyone experienced this sensation passing through it, and she normally found it soothing. Not so today.

"Morning, Miss O'Neill," said a uniformed security officer stationed at the detector. The satyr who worked this station most days Dorothy came into the building took a later shift. Though she typically pretended to find his flirtations annoying, in truth they amused her, and the unfamiliar guard here now did little to put her at ease.

"It's Doctor O'Neill now." Though her original ambition of teaching mathematics at the University of New Chicago had been sidetracked by her new career in magic, the hard-earned PhD credential still mattered to her. Moments after saying it, she regretted the additional attention it brought to her. Every second spent in this conversation brought her one second closer to mission failure.

"Hmm," said the guard, apparently less impressed. He opened her bag and inspected the contents. "Is that a turtle skeleton?"

"Tortoise," said Dorothy.

He frowned and held it closer to his eyes. "How can you tell?"

Dorothy inwardly kicked herself for prolonging this interaction with the correction, dreading her compulsion to educate everyone around her might now create even more delay she could not afford. She offered her best vapid smile and shrugged. "I have no idea. It was given to me by my mentor for safe keeping."

"What's it for?"

"I'm sure I don't know. You would have to take that up with Magical Agent Aplomado. If he does answer your question, please pass that along to me, would you?"

The guard furrowed his brow, and for a moment Dorothy feared her objective would fall victim to a variable outside her control, specifically a meaningless suspicion over an irrelevant object. He shrugged and handed her the bag. "You here to see Cody?"

"I am," she said.

The guard pulled a PDA from his pocket and looked at it for a few seconds. "I don't see an appointment."

"I didn't make one. He is my father, after all. Is that a problem? Should I come back at a better time?" Dorothy strained to conceal the adrenaline dump she experienced at the question. Her security clearance should be sufficient to get her to Harrison's office, but if this uniformed bureaucrat turned her away now, the entirety of her plan would fall to ruin, and she would need to fall back on Felicia's burglary instructions.

The guard shook his head. "No, you're fine. Head on up."

Dorothy smiled, and her thanks came out as a mumble, hopefully an innocent-sounding one. She proceeded to the elevator with a deliberate calm, fighting her drive to flee.

A minute or so later, she found the door to Harrison's outer office open, and an agent seated at the desk there. For an instant, she pictured Felicia in that chair, carrying out the role whose fictitious nature only she knew for an entire year. How many times had Dorothy walked past a desk like this one, and heard Felicia's polite, businesslike greeting? How many times had that assassin given Dorothy an entirely unwarranted sense of security? Presumably this new assistant had experienced a more thorough and unforgiving vetting before being assigned to the Assistant Director of the NCSA, but if it could happen once…

"Can I help you?" The agent stared at her, unsmiling, one hand conspicuously unseen under his desk. His words startled her out of her ruminations.

"I'm Dorothy O'Neill. Is Har—Is the Assistant Director in?"

Simultaneously, his shoulders relaxed and his eyes widened. "Dr. O'Neill. Are you here to debrief? You're not on my schedule."

"Debrief?" Dorothy struggled to keep up.

"After yesterday's excitement?"

"Oh! I…"

The agent punched an intercom. "A.D. Cody? Dr. O'Neill is here to see you. Can you take the meeting right now?"

"Absolutely," came Harrison's voice.

This first element of familiarity put Dorothy at ease, and she strode to the inner door with a touch of confidence. He rose from his seat as she entered.

"Come on in. Close the door behind you, please." Harrison's smile and pleasant tone, surely meant to comfort her, instead triggered doubts about the wisdom of this plan, and its likelihood of success.

She pulled the door shut, and took a seat across from him. "I hope this isn't an inconvenient time."

"No, no," said Harrison. "Of course not. Are you all right?"

Dorothy looked down. "Yes, I'm fine. I'm so sorry about yesterday."

"What happened?"

"That's... not why I'm here," said Dorothy. "I'm sorry, truly, but I'm afraid you were dragged into something very personal. I really don't feel equipped to talk about it yet."

Harrison frowned. "Hmm. I respect that, of course. Unfortunately for both of us, agency personnel and resources were engaged. Alec needs a report, even if it was nothing. Can you give me anything at all?"

Dorothy bit her lip. "It's about Strontium. We had something unexpected happen yesterday, and I did not handle it well. She and I are going to have to work this out, probably in consultation with the Council of Mages."

Harrison nodded. "Okay, that's a start. I can refer you to Aplomado in his capacity with the agency. That should satisfy the bureaucratic requirements. I do need to ask if whatever this thing is with Strontium poses a threat to you or anyone else."

Dorothy intended to get through this meeting without telling Harrison any straight-out lies. She did not consider this question cooperative on that count. "To the best of my knowledge, she and I do not pose a threat."

"All right. I'll need a written report to that effect. Can you and Aplomado write something up for me before the end of next week?"

Dorothy smiled. "Yes, I'm quite certain by the end of next week you will have a full explanation. Thank you for that latitude."

"You're welcome. If that's not why you're here, why are you here?"

Dorothy took a deep breath, with as much subtlety as she could muster. "I need something from the NCSA vault, for a study I'm conducting."

"For Esoteric?" asked Harrison.

"No, this is for some research I am doing on my own."

Harrison drummed his fingers on his desk. "We have a requisition procedure for pulling vault items. I'm not even part of that chain. You should have gone through Esoteric instead of coming to me." He paused. "I'm guessing you already know all that, meaning you need me to pull strings for you. How am I doing so far?"

"Very well," said Dorothy.

"Okay. Depending on what you want to borrow, I might be able to take care of that. What object do you need?"

Dorothy cleared her throat. "A pair of Samurai swords."

Harrison sat back in his chair. The color drained from his face.

"I won't be handling them directly," said Dorothy. "If that's your concern."

Harrison reached across the table with his right hand, and pulled up his sleeve. He had lost the middle finger of this hand on the Static Mayhem bomb mission, and while the scar from that injury had long since smoothed over, a more recent and jagged line around his wrist still showed in raised, vivid pink. He turned his hand over, emphasizing the scar ran the whole way around, forming a complete bracelet of ruined tissue. "I would say this still hurts when it rains, but the truth is it just still hurts."

He stood, and untucked his shirt to expose a similar streak across his midriff. "This one still hurts, too. My sister says the pain should fade away in another year or two." He tucked his shirt back in and sat. "Those are scars from one of those weapons. One. You are asking me to give you both of them."

"I understand your misgivings," said Dorothy. "As I said, I won't be handling—"

"No," said Harrison. "I'm sorry, but no."

"Harrison, please—"

"What do you need them for?"

"I told you," said Dorothy. "It's a personal project. I understand the danger, and promise I will not be wielding them. I only need them for a few days."

"There is no way I can sanction turning those blades over to someone outside the agency," said Harrison. "I know that's not the answer you wanted—"

"I will be operating under the supervision of an NCSA agent," said Dorothy. "Does that make a difference?"

Harrison narrowed his eyes. "What agent? Why didn't he come to me with this himself?"

"Magical Agent Sparky."

"Ah. That answers both questions." Harrison's frown shifted then, to something more relaxed. "Wait a minute... You and Sparky need the swords for a personal project?"

"That's correct, yes."

"And you can't divulge the nature of this project to the only person who could possibly acquire them for you."

Dorothy shifted in her seat. "That's not how I would have phrased it, but yes, I am asking for your discretion here."

"Huh."

Dorothy waited. "Huh? What does that mean?"

"Nothing. Just thinking." Harrison picked up a pen and tapped it several times on his desk. "All right." He touched a screen on the surface of his desk, and typed something on a virtual keyboard there.

"All right?" said Dorothy.

"Yup. All right. I am sending a requisition override to the vault right now. Go ahead on down there. They will get you what you need."

Dorothy sat up. "Oh! I… Thank you. That's… very kind of you."

"It's not kindness. It's trust. What I am handing you is extremely powerful, but I believe you need it, I believe you will use it appropriately, and I believe you will return it." He tapped the final keystroke with great flourish. "You'll want to hustle. This is legit, but Alec is still going to be pissed when he sees the form."

Dorothy hopped to her feet, fighting off a momentary dizziness from an eagerness she hoped did not come across as too obvious. "Well then, I will be on my way. Thank you again."

Harrison stood, and extended his battle-scarred hand. "Be careful, Dr. O'Neill, and good luck."

Dorothy took his hand, shook it firmly, and made for the door with swiftness and grace.

<hr>

It took two minutes to get to the sub-basement that housed the magical artifact vault. Dorothy's journey down included two additional security checkpoints, neither of which posed any obstacle to her in the face of Harrison's requisition form. The fear of capture dogged her nonetheless.

The vault itself sat behind a cage. An elf with olive skin and spiky black hair, wearing the standard NCSA black jacket and tie, sat at a counter behind the lattice of bars. "Dr. O'Neill?"

"Yes," said Dorothy. "I'm here to pick up two artifacts?"

The elf tilted his head at this remark. "I have one artifact for you." He opened a small sliding door in the cage, and slid a package across the counter to the other side. A rod-shaped bundle, about two feet long, wrapped in canvas and tied with twine waited for her to snatch it and abscond.

"Oh," said Dorothy. "There were supposed to be two. Are they bundled together? Or…?"

"No. This was the only object requested. Sign, please." A line appeared on the counter, and the elf slid a brass stylus through the door.

Dorothy took the implement and scrawled her name absent-mindedly. Her signature and the line beneath it faded to nothing, recorded magically in the stone material of the counter. "Then I suppose this will have to do."

She attempted to keep the bitterness out of her voice, still acutely cognizant of the risk of being detained if any part of her behavior aroused suspicion. Concealing that irritation proved the most challenging part of her mission here.

Apparently, Harrison's trust in her extended exactly fifty percent as far as she thought.

[5]

FLIGHT

With less than two hours before the sleep spell on Claudia would likely wear off, Dorothy made her way on foot to rendezvous with Felicia at a parking garage ten blocks from the NCSA building. A minute after getting to the street, she cast an eye repellant spell on herself. It would not shield her from technological surveillance, but it would expedite her walk as passersby unconsciously moved out of her path to avoid looking at her.

Sister.

"Strontium?" said Dorothy. A pedestrian winced and sidestepped to give her an extra wide berth. She ignored him.

Child, what are we doing?

"We're in a bit of a rush at the moment. Can explanations wait?"

You're carrying a weapon that thinks. You know that, right?

"Yes. His name is Pierre, and he is an enchanted wakizashi. I think."

Oh, hells. You went and did it, didn't you? Made a deal with that devil.

"I'm doing it for you," said Dorothy. "Can we not talk about this right now? I'm about to become a fugitive, and I would prefer doing so without distractions."

Well, isn't that just too bad? You do know if you end up in jail, I end up in jail too? Thought I'd mention that while we're on the subject of things you're doing for me.

"It won't come to that. Besides, by the time they arrest me, you'll be in your own body."

Sister, turn around. Give the sword back. Sic your friends on that assassin. If you keep going down this road, nothing good happens next.

"No. I'm sorry. I asked for your counsel on this, and you said nothing. I had to decide for us both, and this is the decision I made. You need your own body, and I need my life back."

Strontium paused. *I see.*

Dorothy stopped short. "Damn it," she whispered. "Sister, you know that's not what I meant. You know you mean the world to me, and you know I would host you forever if you needed me to. That doesn't change the fact that if there's a chance to free you, it's better for all of us. Please tell me you understand that."

Dorothy reached out, and found only silence in the background of her mind.

On the third level of the garage, she found Felicia astride a hoverbike, Sparky lounging on an identical ride parked alongside. The sleek, black vehicles resembled covered bicycle frames, each wheel swapped out for a cluster of five antigrav generators the size of a deck of playing cards.

Felicia tossed her a pair of goggles.

"Are you kidding me?" said Dorothy.

"They cruise at eighty miles an hour, with fantastic maneuverability," said Felicia. "If you've ever ridden a bicycle, you'll be fine, or so I'm told. I never had a bicycle growing up. You accelerate with the pedal; brakes are on the handlebars. We can take a spin around the garage if you want to get a feel for them before we head out, but make it quick."

"Did you steal these?" asked Dorothy. "Not that I'm judging, but it would be nice to have an accurate inventory of all the charges I can expect to be brought against me when I get home."

"What? No!" Felicia sat up. "What do you take me for? A thief? I bought these! Do you need to see the titles?"

"To be sure I understand you correctly," said Dorothy, "having committed countless murders for pay, you are now offended at the suggestion you would take something that doesn't belong to you. Is that right?"

"Do you have any idea how wealthy I am?" asked Felicia.

Confronted with that question, Dorothy replayed her own words. She had attempted to sting Felicia, but instead had simply described her. "Oh. I really didn't think that through."

"Well then, I suppose you have something new to think about." Felicia pointed to the package under Dorothy's arm. "That doesn't look like two swords."

"It's not. Harrison would only let me have one, which I didn't find out until I got to the vault. Consider yourself lucky to get anything." She lifted the wrapped sword. "Sparky, on guard, please."

"Yes, ma'am." The Pixie took flight and hovered near Felicia.

"You try anything I don't like with this, and we will leave you here with a pixie-sized hole in your head," said Dorothy.

"Charming," said Felicia.

Dorothy tossed the sword to Felicia, who caught it with one hand. "Open that slowly, and keep your hands where Sparky can see them."

"Yes, of course." Felicia set the bundle on her knee and picked at one of the twine ties. "You know, you shouldn't knock the money. Comfort is important to a full life. You should come by the lair sometime. See the rewards of my hard work."

"I think I would prefer my modest home, surrounded by people who love me," said Dorothy.

"What is this 'love' of which you speak?" Felicia pulled the first piece of twine off and dropped it on the garage floor before going to work on the second one.

"Love is a state of profound personal investment in the well-being and destiny of someone other than yourself. I'm so sorry you don't find that familiar."

"It sounds terrible. I can't imagine how—Ah!" Felicia interrupted herself with a shriek, and hurled the half-unwrapped bundle away from herself. It spun in the air, and landed a few yards away with a soft clatter. She sprang backward off the hoverbike, positioning it between Dorothy and herself. A dagger appeared in each of her outstretched hands. "Bitch!"

"Whoa!" said Dorothy. "What?"

Sparky growled. "Should I kill her?"

"Not yet!" Dorothy put up her hands. "Felicia, talk to me."

"I swore I would not harm you! I trusted you! Did you ever intend to work with me, or was killing me your plan from the start?"

Dorothy shook her head. "I don't know what you're talking about."

Felicia jabbed one of her daggers in the direction of the discarded sword. "That! That clumsy attempt on my life!"

"What? You asked me to bring you that!"

"I asked for my swords!" She pointed with the dagger again. "That's Bess!"

Dorothy gasped. "Stay there!"

"Which one of us are you talking to?" asked Sparky.

"Both of you!" Dorothy ran to the discarded sword and knelt on the floor beside it. The canvas covering lay half open, exposing the smooth, metal hilt and knobby, cylindrical pommel of a weapon she had heard of, but never seen in person. It bore a small cross-guard, and a straight blade wider than the hilt, partially extended from the scabbard in its collision with the floor. It in no way resembled the Samurai sword she thought she had been carrying. She reached for it.

"Don't touch that blade!" shouted Felicia.

Dorothy looked up. Felicia's stance shifted to a crouch. She would never have time to vault the hoverbike and stab Dorothy before Sparky could riddle her with pixie-induced puncture wounds, and she would surely know that. "Hush! Sparky, don't let her move from that spot."

"You got it!" said the pixie.

Dorothy brought her fingers close to the sword. At about three inches away, a tiny, green spark leapt from the hilt and tickled the tip of her index finger. "Shh. It's all right." She moved her hand closer, muttering an incantation to communicate her friendly intentions. She grasped the partially covered scabbard with her left hand, and wrapped her right palm around the hilt. Though she expected cold metal, the surface of the weapon warmed her hand, a sensation reminiscent of bare skin on skin. She drew the sword from its sheath, with a metallic scrape and ring.

The blade extended approximately eighteen inches from the cross guard, straight, double-edged, and unadorned with markings. A ridge ran up the center from the hilt to the tip on both sides, defining a diamond-shaped cross-section. Blade and hilt shared a uniform pale silver hue, revealing the sword to be a single, solid piece of polished steel.

Good morrow, Dr. Witch, said Bess.

Even expecting the words, Dorothy shivered at the sensation of hearing them in her head. By contrast to how Strontium communicated with her, the sword's voice resonated with a distinctly inhuman quality. "Good morrow, Bess. Do you know who I am?"

Aye. You are the Captain's daughter. He speaks of you fondly.

"He speaks of you fondly, as well." For a second, the sword's hilt grew a degree or two warmer. "Do you know why you are here?"

Nay. Are you in need of protection?

Dorothy looked up at Felicia, who had not dropped her guard. "I'll let you know."

I stand at your beck.

"Thank you. That's good to know. I'm going to return you to your sheath now. Is that all right?"

Aye.

Dorothy slid Bess back into her scabbard. She removed the remaining twine and canvas, exposing a leather belt wrapped around the sheath. "We need to go now," she said to Felicia as she unwound the belt.

"If you think I'm going anywhere with you now—"

"Harrison knows I am up to something. He gave me this sword to protect me, probably from you in particular given that I asked for your swords." Dorothy pulled the belt around her waist and buckled it. Holes ran the entire length of the leather strip, with clips at the edges to manage surplus length, making it suitable for any sized frame. She found the right notch, and let the belt settle comfortably on her hips.

"That doesn't make sense," said Felicia. "Why would he give you a sword at all if he knew you were lying to him?"

Dorothy paused, glancing to the sword at her side. "Because he trusts me." She looked back to Felicia. "I didn't lie to him, but I didn't tell him everything, either, and he saw through my half-truths. He's trying to protect me, because he thinks I'm in trouble." She looked at the daggers in Felicia's hands, still one swift toss from her throat. "He's probably right, just not the way he thinks. Will you put those away, please?"

"He may trust you, but I don't."

Dorothy threw her arms up. "Ugh! Then escape! Or set aside your trust issues and let's get moving. Lord knows I've set aside mine! Either way, we don't have time for this. Whatever head start I bought us keeping Claudia asleep is now spent. Harrison is probably calling Claudia right now, and when she doesn't answer, he's going to send someone to my house. We have maybe fifteen minutes before the full-blown manhunt starts, and if we're still here sniping at each other we won't be hard to find. Now put down the damn knives, get on your bike, and tell me where we're going."

Dorothy strode to the other hoverbike and mounted it. She took a moment to get a feel for the seat, the handlebars, and the pedal stirrups. Behind her, the soft whoosh of Felicia's bike lifting off the floor blew past her feet and rippled her skirt. She turned to face her partner.

"West. Keep up." Felicia's bike zipped out the broad opening in the side of the garage and dropped out of sight.

"Stay on her," said Dorothy to Sparky.

"Way ahead of you." The pixie shot away, leaving an easy-to-follow trail of sparks.

Dorothy took a deep breath and pushed her foot to the accelerator, her life as a fugitive now underway.

[6]

ON THE LAM

Like most examples of post-Mayhem advanced technology, the hoverbike proved as easy to operate as Felicia claimed. Obstacle detectors and deflector fields assured a safe ride, despite the speed Dorothy needed to travel to keep Felicia in sight and the density of trees along their route. Though extremely grateful for both the seatbelt and the googles she wore, it took four swallowed bugs for Dorothy to learn she could not open her mouth even slightly as they cut through the forest.

They traveled for about three hours. Apart from the general westerly heading, Dorothy had no way of guessing their destination. Given their speed, at some point they would have crossed the border of the city-state of New Chicago, entering either the newly founded state of Centauria or the state of Umbra.

Over its twelve-year history, New Chicago had grown from a single city to a nation comprising eight semi-independent states, each with its own demographic and culture. Centauria, the eighth state to be added to the union, rose from a settlement of centaurs, who made up more than three-quarters of its population, and occupied all but a handful of positions in its government. Umbra, the second state to be founded, and so named for springing up in the shadow of its parent state, New Chicago, represented the first major human colony to strike out from the homeland. New Chicago's expansion from a single state to a two-state nation marked a turning point in the evolution of post-Mayhem civilization. With that benchmark attained, the next six states cascaded in over a scant two years.

Felicia coasted to a halt. Dorothy pulled up alongside her, leaving at least ten feet between them. Sparky lighted on her handlebars. The trail of orange in her wake rained out as tiny sparks before vanishing.

"Are you tired?" asked Dorothy.

"I can do this all day," said the pixie. "Is this a pee break? Should I pee?"

"Do you in fact pee?"

Sparky shrugged. "I can. Never saw the appeal."

"Hey," said Felicia.

Dorothy looked over to her in time to catch the object she tossed, a protein bar still in the wrapper. She recognized the brand. It showed no signs of tampering or contamination. She looked up at Felicia, who ate a similar bar while studying a map. With Felicia's attention occupied, Dorothy slipped the protein bar into her bag and took out a granola bar.

"I wouldn't take you hundreds of miles into the forest just to poison you," said the assassin, her eyes still on the map. "I've had five clean opportunities to kill you since yesterday, four of which would have looked like accidents, and one of which would have destroyed your reputation and ruined your family. At some point, you'll have to recognize I have no interest in harming you."

"Isn't that what you would say if you wanted me to trust you, even if you did plan to kill me?" asked Dorothy.

"Honestly, I'm not that interested in your trust, just your help. You can keep looking over your shoulder and I'll go on not murdering you. Same end result for me, though I think you'll find it exhausting."

Dorothy crunched into her granola bar, focusing on the texture, and the sweetness of the honey. The small comfort distracted her from the insanity of her current course of action. It also gave her time to smoothly change the subject after she swallowed. "Where are we?"

"Umbra," said Felicia. "Still about three hundred miles from Kansas City. We should be there by midafternoon."

Dorothy sat up at this. "Kansas City? Is that where your contact is?"

Felicia shook her head, chewing a mouthful of protein bar. "No, that's where we get Strontium out of your body into a temporary vessel. Once we have the Scale we can make that permanent."

"You mentioned this earlier. What kind of vessel? Are we putting her in a jar?" Dorothy reached out to Strontium, but got nothing.

"That's really outside my field of expertise," said Felicia. "More up your alley, isn't it?"

"I don't know that spell. I don't even know what it's called." Dorothy held her hand up and concentrated. A small, red, leather-bound book shimmered into existence there. The longer she apprenticed with Aplomado, the less she needed the reference, but it remained a part of her, available on command.

Dorothy skimmed the table of contents, written in an alphabet she did not recognize, in a language she did not speak, its meaning clear to her all the same. A search for spells regarding transfer of consciousness yielded a reference to the spell Strontium used to place herself in Dorothy's mind five years earlier, but nothing about storing a consciousness in an inanimate container.

"This is beyond me," said Dorothy. "I hope your wizard knows what he's doing."

"And I hope whatever he uses is portable," said Felicia. "We'll still have a long journey ahead of us. If he puts her in a trunk, we're going to have a problem. I don't have any idea if the scale can be moved, so we should have her with us when we find it."

"How big is it?" asked Dorothy.

"Dragon scales vary from the size of a saucer to the size of a dinner plate," said Felicia. "I assume it's somewhere in the middle."

"Hold on," said Dorothy. "You don't even know what it looks like? You've never seen a picture of it?"

"My world had a shortage of cameras."

"What about painters? No one ever illustrated an object of that importance?"

"That's more common than you might think," said Felicia. "Some artifacts derive their power in part from the legendary nature of their stories. Locking them down by making art about them diminishes them. The Wand of Jarloth, for example, was so beautiful that many artists created replicas of it for decoration. By the time Jarloth understood that each replica erased a fraction of the wand's power, it was spent. It may be still out there, but the original is just a stick now, no more powerful than any of the fakes."

"So, what, you think you'll just know it when you see it?" asked Dorothy.

"I know it's white, and I know it's a dragon scale," said Felicia. "Once I know its location, I can't imagine I will need more information than that."

Dorothy closed her eyes. "Come on, Strontium," she whispered. "I need you here for this."

Sister?

Dorothy's eyes snapped open. "Don't disappear on me. Can you stay alert for a while?"

I don't exactly control it.

"You seemed in control when you vanished last time. No pouting, sister. I need you and I'm going to need you all day."

Where are we?

"Umbra. A forest. We are heading for Kansas City, to find a wizard to put your mind in a temporary vessel."

You better not be putting me in a bowl, said Strontium. *That never ends well.*

"Do you know how the spell works?" asked Dorothy.

"Are you talking to Strontium or Bess?" called Felicia. "It's going to get difficult to keep track now."

Dorothy held her hand up and looked away.

Was that the killer? said Strontium.

"Yes," said Dorothy. "Can we focus, please? Tell me about the spell."

You know, she wanted to kill Ian. When he was eleven.

"I'm aware."

Saw the whole thing through your eyes, said Strontium. *Took me a while to piece it together though. She would have cut up our little boy, right in front of you. That's who you work for now.*

"Work with," said Dorothy. "Not for. Don't change the subject, please."

What does she need you for, anyway?

"She needs my help to obtain something called the Scale of Hypatia. She says we can use it to restore your body."

A pause followed. Strontium broke the silence with a decidedly witchy cackle. *Child, you've been dragged into a snipe hunt. The Scale of Hypatia? I didn't think anyone was still fool enough to search for that. What did she tell you? That it would grow me a new body? Then what? She'll use it to rule the world?*

The sound of Dorothy's pulse in her ears threatened to overtake Strontium's voice. "She said it can't be used as a weapon."

Ha! Did she now?

"What do you know about the Scale?"

Same as everybody else, said Strontium. *Not a damn thing. If she told you what it can do, she's lying.*

Dorothy looked back to the other bike. Felicia sat there, patiently watching her. Dorothy glanced to her own hip, momentarily startled to see Bess gone, before remembering the sword turned invisible when not wielded. She patted her side to confirm the sword still hung there, and found the stiff, leather scabbard, perfectly camouflaged.

"What does your passenger have to say about our plan?" asked Felicia.

"She doesn't want you to put her in a bowl."

Felicia shrugged. "That's not my department, but I will pass it along."

"Why did you need your swords?" asked Dorothy.

"To kill monsters, of course. Now that task falls to you, oh blade mistress." Felicia bowed from her seat.

Dorothy frowned. "What monsters?"

"Not entirely sure, to be frank. One must always allow for unexpected monsters now and again. I didn't plan on troubling you about it. Things have changed now, naturally. Have you ever fought with that blade?"

"You know I haven't," said Dorothy.

"True," said Felicia, "but I wanted to hear you say it. Don't worry too much about how to use her. When the time comes, she will use you. "

"When will that moment come?"

"I won't know until tomorrow. You ready to get moving again?"

"I need to stretch my legs first," said Dorothy. "Do I have time to visit the ladies room?"

"You can have five minutes," said Felicia. "The nearest ladies room is at least a hundred miles from here, so you'll have to improvise. I recommend against wiping with anything poisonous, but I'll leave that up to you."

Dorothy reached into her bag and produced a new roll of toilet paper.

Felicia laughed. "I must learn to stop underestimating you. Is that bag bottomless?"

Dorothy peered into her bag, the only piece of luggage she brought with her before fleeing her home on a mission of undetermined duration and dubious legality, and its meager contents. "I wish."

[7]

TOUCHED

Sparky cut a streak of brilliant orange ahead of Dorothy's bike. The pixie paced Felicia, whose lead grew and shrank as Dorothy navigated the forest. They followed hiking trails when possible, and passed the occasional traveler, who paid them no mind.

The pixie light presented a potential danger in providing a signal so easy to track, but at any given moment in the nation of New Chicago, thousands of such trails decorated the landscape. All that noise allowed them to travel in secret, hiding in plain sight. At least, in theory it should. Dorothy did not count stealth among her areas of expertise. Felicia, who would surely have a better sense of their security, had voiced no concerns on the matter.

Dorothy had known the collective entity Glimmer for only a few months. She contained multitudes, a million pixies in vast variety all bound in a single, butterfly-winged form. Though Sparky always left orange in her wake, Glimmer's trails of light never bore the same color twice. Perhaps, at some point, Dorothy had seen Sparky's trail in there without knowing it. She smiled at her own recollection of Glimmer's charm and humor, probably colored to inaccuracy by years of nostalgia.

With a bright flash, the streak of light rained out to sparks, leaving behind a cloud of orange smoke. It dissipated as Dorothy closed in on it, and she passed through it while attempting to brake. It smelled of cinnamon.

Felicia, already traveling at a substantial lead, shot out of sight in a burst of acceleration.

Dorothy hesitated, torn between her need to stop and investigate what happened to Sparky and her need to pursue Felicia. An object clipped the side of her bike, taking the decision out of her hands. The rear of the vehicle rose under her, in the beginning of a tumble. In sickening slow motion, indicator lights for both the obstacle detectors and the deflector fields sprang to life. Without those, her seatbelt, ostensibly a safety feature, now virtually guaranteed the bike would crush her when it finished its flip.

A magnet-like tug yanked her hand to Bess's hilt. Clutching the sword, she drew, simultaneously slicing through the belt with the same motion. As the bike reached the apex of its vertical rotation, she kicked off from the sideboards with both feet, propelling herself forward. The bike acted as a sling, its angular momentum flinging her far outward. She completed the roll mid-air, and touched down sprinting. Alerted by the sound of the bike crashing into the packed dirt of the trail, she leapt to her right, and spun around in time to watch it tumble past her, veer to the left and slam into a tree, snapping three branches and its own frame.

It took her a moment to regain her bearings as Bess released motor control back to her. Harrison had described how Bess guided his movements when he held her in a fight, but none of those stories prepared Dorothy for the exhilaration of experiencing it firsthand. Bess had taken her hand and saved her from certain death before her brain had fully registered the danger.

Panting, she pulled the goggles from her face and looked down the trail to Felicia's last known heading. She had pulled far enough ahead to exit earshot. Dorothy looked behind her. The last few tendrils of orange vapor dissipated into the breeze. A smattering of debris lay strewn down the path among the scars gouged into the dirt by the tumbling bike, some of it pieces of the vehicle, and some of it articles from her bag, still hanging from her shoulder.

"Sparky?" she cried.

Predictably, no reply followed.

We cannot remain here, said Bess.

"Was that an attack?"

Likely. Your pixie is neutralized, and your companion has deserted you.

"I got all that, thank you," said Dorothy. "What do we do now?"

Pursue the assassin or return home, said Bess. *The latter is safer. The decision is yours.*

"Give me a minute, here." Dorothy sheathed Bess, and strode back down the path. She surveyed the scraps lying there, recovering a box of mints, a pair of scissors in a cloth cover, and a leather purse of polished crystals. The plastic-encased tortoise skeleton lay inverted in the middle of the path, dusty but otherwise unscathed. A quick inventory of her bag confirmed several items still missing, but none of consequence.

She returned to the bike, now cloven into two bent, ragged fragments. Near the forward antigrav generators, a silver lump no larger than a quarter stood out against the sleek, black metal. She pried it off with a pocket knife, leaving five puncture marks arrayed in a regular pentagon that matched claws on the underside of the object. It went in her bag.

Dorothy cast her gaze forward down the trail. If Felicia set this up as a trap, the wiser course of action would lead Dorothy away from the assassin, toward home. If this ambush had come from a third party, Dorothy would need Felicia as an ally.

Sparky's disappearance presented an unanticipated danger. She probably survived whatever spell whisked her away, pixies being notoriously difficult to slay. Without her, Dorothy's insurance against betrayal from Felicia also vanished. With luck, Bess would suffice as a replacement, especially in light of Felicia's belief she would be armed with enchanted swords of her own, which did not play out for her.

Dorothy double-checked the contents of her bag, confirming she still possessed the ingredients for *Summon Pixie*. Despite Sparky's admonishment on the appropriateness of the spell, Dorothy chose to reserve it as an emergency backup plan, should they become separated. Given the nature of this separation, however, she had no way of knowing how far away Sparky landed, nor whether she had fallen victim to any sort of binding. Summoning a pixie might draw one at random, which could create its own set of challenges.

The sun descended below the forest canopy, casting a broad shadow that anticipated the evening to come. This late in the afternoon, Dorothy's daily routine usually entailed welcoming Ian home from school, and engaging Claudia in discussion about what they should have for dinner. Claudia's day surely did not include that consideration right then, and Dorothy allowed herself the first full wave of regret over the consequences of her actions to the people she loved. Her expectation of returning home shortly to ask forgiveness now jabbed her as newly unrealistic. With luck, she would make it home unharmed. The probability of attaining her goal of a freed mind and a rescued friend now remote, she did not anticipate Claudia or the NCSA agreeing her risks to be justified.

Brush rustled behind her. She held still, taking care to gauge the wind, barely perceptible. The soft crunch of footfalls in the groundcover confirmed activity, and she drew Bess with deliberate caution. A growl followed this gesture. She turned and braced herself for Bess to assess her situation and deploy her as necessary.

Two ebony wolves approached her. They moved with purpose, but not stealth, fangs bared, hackles raised. In the pale light of the forest shade, their eyes glowed amber.

"That can't be right," said Dorothy.

It is not, said Bess. *Relax.*

Under full influence of the sword, Dorothy dropped her bag to the ground, took two rapid steps forward and sprang over the bodies of the advancing wolves. She landed behind them, and as she spun to attack from behind, they attempted to turn and scatter, newly energized with apparent confusion. The nearer animal could not retreat in time, and she swung broadly at its flank to disembowel it. The blade hit its mark, but did not fully penetrate, leaving only a shallow gash as she drew it along the beast's side.

It howled, stumbling in its rotation, but righted quickly enough to launch itself at Dorothy, jaws wide, seeking her throat.

She swung Bess to deflect it, striking the side of its snout with the flat of the blade. Its maxilla snapped, and a fountain of blood jetted from its nostrils. It tumbled to her side, yelping and gagging. She brought the tip of Bess's blade down into its throat. It pierced the tough hide there, and sank a few inches before becoming lodged. She tugged upward, to no avail.

Behind you.

Dorothy spun, releasing her grasp on the sword. The other wolf paced in front of her. It twitched as it moved, wasting the opportunity to lunge at its unarmed opponent. Dorothy took advantage of its hesitation, thrusting her palm outward to employ a concussion spell. She used this tactic for the first time fighting Felicia in Fenway five years earlier. It successfully propelled her several feet then, winding and stunning her.

The wolf responded to this affront with an angry bark. Its fur rippled as the wave of force passed over it, but it stood its ground.

Dorothy took a step back, then leapt upward, in an arc at least twenty feet high. This maneuver did not require Bess's assistance, being one of the first magical defensive tactics Aplomado taught her. She grabbed for a tree branch, and skinned her palm scrambling for purchase there.

The wolf crouched momentarily, then catapulted vertically, with at least as much force as Dorothy's magical escape attempt.

Her arms, not strong enough for the task before them, failed her. She fell, colliding with the wolf in midair. It snapped its jaws at her, and she screamed. In desperation, she kicked against the tree trunk on her way down, spinning body and wolf into position to break her fall on the animal. It lashed out with a front paw, carving painful, bloody trails through her midriff.

They landed together. The wolf absorbed the brunt of the impact, and something broke inside it beneath her. Shrieking, she grabbed its throat in both hands. White light arced from her body to the wolf's head, summoned lightning that scorched its fur before cooking its flesh. Dorothy did not release her hold on it until smoke drifted from its eye sockets. Her hands came away red and blistered.

She rolled off the animal's still form, panting. Pain assaulted her from her hands and belly. She probed her abdominal wound, barely able to confront the horror of its possible severity. It stung, but the gashes appeared neither wide nor deep. She looked up.

The first wolf, bloody snout dangling from its face, Bess embedded it its neck, sprang at her.

Out of ideas, magical stamina for the moment spent, she threw her arms in front of her face.

With a piercing yelp, the wolf crashed to the ground, grazing her side as it tumbled past.

Dorothy lowered her arms. Her foe lay on the ground, legs splayed, body wracked with spasms. An arrow, black as its hide, protruded from one of its eyes. The amber glow in its other eye faded as its motions ground to a halt.

Behind it, Felicia stood, bow in hand, arrow nocked.

Dorothy dropped her head to the ground, and lay there on her back, clenching her jaw, willing the sobs not to come.

After a few seconds, Felicia approached her and crouched beside her. "You did well there."

Dorothy closed her eyes and nodded. Tears rolled down the sides of her face.

"I need to dress that wound," said Felicia. "Please hold still."

New pain pricked Dorothy on the skin of her belly, and she cried out.

Felicia dabbed at the injury with a white cloth, rapidly turning red. "These are scratches. You'll be fine." She drew a small tube from a pouch at her hip, unscrewed the top and squeezed a trail of clear goo over each of Dorothy's wounds. It cooled her skin.

"What is that?" asked Dorothy.

"Glue. I'll need to hold your skin closed on the widest cut before it sets. Do you need a rag to scream into?"

Dorothy shook her head, a gesture that evolved into a nod.

Felicia produced a folded dinner napkin, and held it out.

Dorothy opened her mouth, and bit down as Felicia lowered the cloth. It absorbed the sound of her shriek as new fire consumed her abdomen.

"Almost done," said Felicia.

The pain faded. Dorothy spat out the napkin and panted, gritting her teeth.

"You'll want to lie there for a minute or two. The glue is already set, but if you stand too quickly you might tear it. Give the anesthetic in it time to numb you. When you think you're ready, I will help you up."

Dorothy nodded. "Thank you."

"I must say, as much as I hate your world, your medical science is fantastic. That ointment includes an antibiotic, by the way. Hopefully you won't get infected. Let me see your hands."

Dorothy held her palms up, one bleeding, both burned.

Felicia put a dollop of balm in each one, and wrapped them in rolled cloth bandages.

"I want to sit up."

"All right." Felicia moved behind her. Hands under Dorothy's arms, she gently pulled her to a sitting position. Leaving her there, she got up and walked to the corpse of the wolf.

"What are you doing?" asked Dorothy.

"I need my arrow back. You'll want to recover the sword yourself. I don't dare touch it." Felicia dropped to her knees. She poked the flesh around the wolf's eye socket, then took the shaft of her arrow in one hand, holding the wolf's head steady with the other. After rocking it back and forth a few times, she yanked. The arrow came out, spattering her with droplets of blood. She set it down on the dirt beside her, still looking at the slain animal. After a pause, she reached down and stroked its forehead.

Dorothy watched Felicia with caution. Something here did not track. "Felicia?"

"Give me a moment, please." Turning away from Dorothy, she wiped her eyes.

"What happened here?" asked Dorothy.

Felicia sniffed. She stood, pulled something out of her pocket and tossed it on the ground near Dorothy. The tiny disruptor chip matched the one Dorothy had pried off her own bike minutes earlier.

"Three-pronged attack, looks like. Take out the pixie, take out the bikes, send in the executioners." Felicia cast her gaze on Dorothy's slain attacker. "These wolves were ensorcelled. Cursed. Used. They never had a chance. It wasn't their fault." She looked back to Dorothy. "The people who abused these creatures were probably after me, not you, if you find that at all reassuring."

"Who did this?"

Felicia stood. She brought her arrow back to where Dorothy sat, and picked up the cloth she used to dab her wound. After using it to wipe the arrow clean, she dropped it to the trail. "I don't know. That's not the answer you want, but it's all I have right now. I'm sorry, but we can't afford to rest long. We now have a considerable walk ahead of us, and this carnage will soon draw predators." She brushed the side of her eye.

Dorothy scrutinized Felicia's countenance, strangely unfamiliar. "I will walk with you, but I still don't trust you."

Felicia smiled then, an edge of bitterness in her eyes. "Of course you don't." She returned the arrow to its home in the quiver on her back, and strode down the path.

[8]

ISTHMUS

The trail proved easy going, and Dorothy silently thanked herself for wearing the boots. With about fifteen miles to go, she and Felicia hiked until sundown, then made camp in a cozy clearing off the trail. Dorothy again declined an offer of food from Felicia, who let the slight pass without comment this time.

Dorothy retired to a relatively smooth patch of ground, a rolled sweater under her head. The possibility Felicia might kill her in her sleep nagged her, but not in any way she could justify given the events of the day, and exhaustion compelled her to give her partner the benefit of a doubt.

She woke to gentle prodding, the sky still dark.

"Rise and shine, little witch. It's your watch."

Dorothy sat up and rubbed her eyes. "What time is it?"

"It's three o'clock," said Felicia. "I let you sleep most of the night. You needed the rest. Wake me at sunup, please."

"Right." Dorothy nodded. "Got it. Sunup."

"We have at least four hours of hiking before we make it to Kansas City, so whatever you have to do to be ready to move, do it before I wake up." Felicia held her hand out. Dorothy took it, and winced in new pain from her burns as Felicia pulled her to her feet. As Felicia moved away, she drew a dagger. She sat at a tree, tucking the knife under her leg and propping her back against the trunk. She closed her eyes and went still.

Dorothy watched the assassin, looking for signs of slumber and finding none. Felicia did not snore, or fall into a pattern of deep breathing. In fact, her chest did not move at all, making it impossible to tell her state of wakefulness, or, for that matter, life. Creepy.

As she took a seat on the edge of a fallen tree, Dorothy held a bandaged palm up and willed her book of spells to come forth. The little tome shimmered into existence, casting a pale crimson glow that served to illuminate the pages as she flipped through them. She browsed for any method of compelling a person to answer any question truthfully, or, failing that, protection from violence with blades, but came up empty on both counts.

≡

Hiking to the outskirts of Kansas City took two hours longer than Felicia predicted. Dorothy's belly wound slowed her, the anesthetic having worn off overnight. Newly flaring pain in her hands distracted her further. Though it went against her better judgment, when they reached the city she would need to find a magical healer for her to have any hope of continuing this quest.

The hiking trail intersected an unpaved road. They followed this for less than a mile before the low-lying buildings became dense enough to resemble a town. They encountered other pedestrians, none of whom took any interest or exhibited any suspicion about the two women entering their community.

Sister.

Strontium?" whispered Dorothy.

You're hurt! What has that villain done to you?

"She saved my life. Long story, but Felicia didn't injure me. She saved me from a mad wolf, and treated my wounds."

Five'll get you ten she sicced that wolf on you herself. Don't let her lull you, child.

"It's not like that."

"She's right to keep you on your guard." Felicia. walked ahead of her without turning around. "Please tell her to stay awake today. We'll have her out of your head shortly, and she'd best be prepared. Oh, and if we have some time today, remind me to teach you a proper whisper. I could have heard you at twice this distance."

"Stay awake," said Dorothy in a normal volume. "We're going to free you today."

Is that what she told you? That will be quite a trick.

"How soon until we reach your contact?" Dorothy asked Felicia. "Strontium wants to know the details of how we're going to get her out."

That's not what I said.

"Hush, you. Felicia?"

"We have two stops to make first," said Felicia. "I know a healer who will take care of your assorted wounds without asking any questions. Then I need to see a man about a sword. I planned to have my own weapons on this trip, and that didn't quite pan out the way I hoped."

"Are we visiting a blacksmith?" asked Dorothy. "Won't that attract attention?"

"We're visiting an antique shop, and no. My weapons guy isn't a blacksmith, just a dealer."

"Does he deal in enchanted samurai swords?"

"He would if he could get them, yes," said Felicia. "I'm not setting my sights that high today."

Dorothy patted the invisible blade at her side. "See that you don't," she whispered.

Felicia clucked her tongue. "Let's make time for that whispering lesson as soon as possible."

———

The quaint bell over Dorothy's head jingled as she passed through the doorway. Archaic furniture and bric-a-brac surrounded her. Though not a connoisseur of antiques, she suspected most of it to be junk. She credited that assessment partially to Felicia's claim the store acted as a front for an illicit arms dealer, partly to her personal tastes, which ran decidedly in another direction than these wares, and partly to her overall poor mood, which left her inclined to pessimism and judgment. She picked up a mermaid-shaped bottle opener from a shelf and inspected it for any authentic signs of age.

Felicia sat in an upholstered armchair (whose must Dorothy could smell from a distance) and ran her finger along the scrollwork of the hand rest. From behind her, a man emerged from a back room. He wore a tie-dyed shirt, a shaggy salt-and-pepper beard behind a tan face, long dark hair tied back in a ponytail, and a smile.

"That's a little soft for you, isn't it?"

Felicia curled the corners of her mouth, and at first Dorothy did not recognize the expression. It vaguely resembled the bitter smirk Felicia employed right before discussing her joy at the prospect of a new murder, but this smile held something else inconsistent with her usual demeanor, and it took Dorothy several seconds to identify it: warmth.

"It's not quite as comfortable as the tree root I slept on, but it gets the job done." She stood and turned. "Hello, Eric. You're looking well."

"Likewise. Are you going to introduce me to your friend?"

Dorothy set the bottle opener back down and rubbed her hands together. Though the healer Felicia promised wiped the burns and scrapes away with little discomfort, the effect left a residual itching that had not yet faded. "I'm not her friend. I'm her nemesis."

Felicia laughed. "You flatter yourself. Don't get any ideas, Eric. This one's taken." She gave Dorothy a sly look. "And complicated."

Eric held his hands up. "I wouldn't dream of fraternizing with your associate. Just trying to be a courteous host."

Felicia sighed. "Eric Simon, Dorothy O'Neill. Not to skip past the small talk, but we are very much on the clock here. I need a sword."

The color drained out of Eric's face, and he took a step backward. "You know, it's funny, there's an apprentice witch connected to the NCSA named Dorothy O'Neill. I'm sure you're not that person, because there's no way Felicia would bring the NCSA to my shop."

"I'm not connected to the NCSA," said Dorothy. "At least, not anymore. I'm fairly certain I'll be in more trouble with them than you are when they catch up to me."

"Like I said, complicated." Felicia cracked her knuckles. "We don't have time for this either. I need a katana."

Eric hesitated, looking back and forth between the two women. "I don't have a katana at the moment. A shame about Maurice and Pierre. I may have a rapier that would serve your needs."

"Nothing with an ornate hilt. I can't have anything that slows down my draw."

"I know the perfect weapon. Ideal for stabbing attacks, obviously, but also sharpened along both edges for slashing moves. It has an enchantment of strength to keep it from shattering if you swing it too hard. You won't be able to chop a tree down with it, but a wrist or a neck should be doable. It will be a weak substitute for your isthmian blades, but it will get the job done."

"It would be nice to have those back." Felicia glared at Dorothy. "I suppose I'll have to make do."

"Is this where you got Maurice and Pierre?" asked Dorothy.

"I wish!" said Eric. "Of the fifteen, those are the only two I have seen in person. I've never had the good fortune to possess one."

"It's only good fortune if the blade likes you," said Felicia.

"The fifteen what?" asked Dorothy.

"Swords of the Isthmian Generals," said Eric. "You know about Maurice and Pierre, but you don't know what they really are?"

"I know they are both enchanted," said Dorothy. "And sentient, right?"

"Oh, they are so much more than that." Eric grinned. "The Flood Swords are a collector's dream. Easily the most significant relics of the non-real world, and easily the most dangerous. Felicia never told you the tale?"

Felicia rolled her eyes. "Honestly? Tick tock?"

Eric held up a hand. "Indulge me a minute, would you? This is a great story." He directed his gaze to Dorothy. "How well do you know non-real history? Are you familiar with the Tuscan wars?"

"No."

"I won't bore you with the long version. Suffice to say a series of progressively ill-advised invasions from a series of progressively dimwitted monarchs led to the downfall of a five hundred-year kingdom."

"Is this about Hypatia's reign?" asked Dorothy.

"Hypatia?" said Eric. "The Dragon Empress? No, this was well after that. Tuscany was one of the kingdoms that rose to fill the void after the fall of the Hypatian Empire. Without her wisdom to guide them, the peoples of Europe fell under the rule of various warlords, and the successful ones eventually established their own kingdoms. The line of Toscano ruled only a fraction of the lands under Hypatia's control at her peak. I'm surprised to hear you ask about her. Not many people from our world know much non-real history."

Felicia glared at Dorothy. "She dabbles. Can we stick to the point?"

Dorothy shrank back, fighting off regret and embarrassment over potentially exposing the nature of their quest to this third party.

"So sorry," said Eric. "Where was I? Ah, yes. Tuscany. After the inevitable coup, the last king fled to his stronghold on the Elba Peninsula."

Dorothy perked up at this. "1814, by any chance?"

Eric's grin widened. "By our reckoning, yes."

"I'm pretty sure you're thinking of Napoleon. Unless everything I know is wrong, Elba is an island, not a peninsula."

"It is now! Otherwise, yes, everything you know is wrong. It's a fascinating parallel, but a very different story. In the non-real world, it was the King of Tuscany who fled to Elba, not the Emperor of France. He didn't go there to live in exile; he dug in his heels to make a last stand. A coalition of nations Tuscany had wronged over the centuries sent a massive force of thirteen armies to wipe him off the face of the Earth. It was the grandest fighting force ever assembled, and it did not end well for them. Toscano's closest advisor, a dark mage of the seventh order, fled with him, and laid a trap of unfathomable proportions. When the armies attempted to cross the isthmus between the mainland and the Elban keep, he turned the entire strip of land to mud, and flooded it with tidal waves. Five miles of solid terrain were swept into the Mediterranean Sea. It took three days for the isthmus to dissolve completely. The casualties exceeded a hundred thousand, possibly twice that many."

Dorothy's face went cold. "That's horrible."

Eric shrugged. "That's war. Don't shed too many tears for those long-departed soldiers. Many of them were no better than the man who slaughtered them. They did exact their revenge, after a fashion. Several of those armies brought wizards of their own, and before they all perished, they joined together to cast a spell that would seal Toscano's doom. They probably could have saved themselves, if not the armies, but they chose revenge over survival. Wizards, right?" Eric grinned at Felicia.

"Move it along, please," she said.

"Right," said Eric. "So, the wizards enchanted the swords of the thirteen generals. They were gifted with extraordinary powers, granted minds of their own, and imbued with the singular desire to kill Toscano and any who supported him. When the isthmus vanished into the sea, it took the weapons with it, but they resurfaced on beaches and in fisherman's nets. The ill-fated souls who salvaged them became their slaves, and over the next ten years erased Toscano's influence from every corner of Europe. Maurice was the blade who removed the deposed king's head, ending the wars for good."

Bile rose in Dorothy's throat, and she swallowed. Silently, she thanked Harrison for preventing her from completing the task of stealing that weapon from the vault. She recognized the characteristics of the swords Eric described, and moved her left hand to her side with as much subtlety as she could manage. "You said fifteen swords, but only thirteen generals."

"The fourteenth was Pierre, my Wakizashi," said Felicia. "The general of the Gallian army carried two blades on his person."

"What about the fifteenth?"

Felicia nodded at Dorothy's hip. "You're wearing it."

Eric eyes went wide. "No way! Bess? Surely not Bess!"

Dorothy lifted her hand and glanced at her side involuntarily. The invisible scabbard rippled in her eyes for a moment.

Eric stared at her belt with an intensity and for a duration that made her uncomfortable, before finally whispering, "Oh, man."

Dorothy shook her head. "I don't understand. What's her significance? What… How is she different from the others?"

"If that really is Bess, the sword at your side is Toscano's own blade, cursed to rebel against him. She used him to murder what was left of his own royal guard, but refused to deliver the killing stroke herself. He chucked her into the sea, and she was the only blade never recovered. I assumed she didn't survive Mayhem. Are you sure that's her?" he asked Felicia.

"Pretty sure."

"Where did you find her?" he asked Dorothy.

"I…" She faltered, unsure how much she could safely reveal, and uncertain what consequences would follow withholding.

"Alec Baker burgled her from a goblin prince in late 2004," said Felicia. "He kept her as his personal weapon until his injuries forced him to retire from the field. Her usual handler now is Harrison Cody."

Eric's brows lifted. "The NCSA has had this sword since 2004? If you stole it from them, you're right, you're in a lot more trouble than I am. Can I see it?"

Dorothy took a step back. "What?"

"The sword. May I see it? I want to have one look before she walks out of my life forever."

"She's sworn to protect me," said Dorothy.

"If I posed any threat to you, I'm sure she would kill me, but I don't. I just want one quick look. From the invisibility spell and the apparent length of the blade, it could be Bess, or it could be one of two other swords. I want to know whether Bess was truly in my shop, however fleetingly."

"What does Bess look like?" asked Dorothy.

"A xiphos," said Eric. "Greek style short sword. A single piece of unadorned metal. At least if the legends are accurate. If there's a single jewel on the hilt, or if the pommel bears a royal seal, then you're carrying Hector or Gladys."

Felicia rolled her eyes. "Can we get this over with? Show him the sword. Let him drool. Just be quick about it."

Dorothy wrapped her hand around Bess's hilt and drew her slowly from her scabbard. As she lifted the blade vertically in front of her face, Eric giggled.

Do you need my protection?

"I don't think so," said Dorothy. "Not at the moment."

"Did she just ask you if she should kill me?" asked Eric.

"Something like that."

"Ha! Fantastic!" He clapped his hands once.

Child, what's happening?

Dorothy blinked. "Strontium?"

"Strontium?" said Eric. "No, steel."

"Hush!" said Dorothy.

You need me silent? asked Bess.

"No!" said Dorothy.

No, what? came Strontium's voice. *Something here doesn't feel right.*

"I'm holding Bess," said Dorothy. "Are you able to hear her?"

Able to hear whom? said Bess.

Bess? said Strontium. *The sword? She's talking to you? No, I can't hear that.*

"What's going on here?" asked Eric.

"Complicated," said Felicia. "Do pay attention."

"Will you two shut up?" said Dorothy. "Bess, I have a witch trapped in my mind. She cannot hear you. Strontium, yes, she speaks to me."

I don't think that's it, sister, said Strontium.

"Don't think it's what?" asked Dorothy.

Dotty?

Claudia's voice. The blood drained from Dorothy's head. She shook herself out of the sudden dizziness, propped up at least in part by Bess.

You are unwell, said Bess. *Did the witch do this to you? I cannot sense this foe. What shall I do?*

Whoa! said Strontium. *You pert near tumbled there! That sword messing up your marbles?*

"Both of you be quiet!" shouted Dorothy.

"We are being quiet," said Eric. "Is she usually like this?"

Felicia frowned. "No. Something's wrong."

"Not both of you!" said Dorothy. "Both of them! All of you! Claudia?"

"Claudia?" said Felicia.

Claudia? said Strontium and Bess.

This a bad time, Dotty?

Dorothy sheathed Bess, and pushed with whatever mental might she could muster. She waited a few seconds for any vestiges of Claudia's presence to make themselves known, but she remained silent. Unfortunately, the push also repressed Strontium, beyond Dorothy's reach for the moment.

"Get your damn sword," she said to Felicia, "and get us to our next stop. We need to do this now."

[9]

DOLL

Dorothy stormed out of the antique shop, arbitrarily chose to turn left, and marched down the street. A few seconds later, Felicia, still adjusting the scabbard on her back, exited the shop and jogged to catch up.

"Are you planning to pretend you know where you're going?" asked Felicia.

"Am I wrong?"

"Not yet."

They walked for a bit in silence. Dorothy watched for some sign she should turn, but did not otherwise interact with Felicia.

"Do you want to talk about what happened in the shop?" asked the assassin.

Dorothy stopped short. "Do I…?" She turned to face Felicia, studying her eyes. "What are you doing? Trying to console me? Are you that out of touch?"

"Do you need consoling? That's not an area of personal strength for me. I merely asked if you wanted to talk about it. Not being privy to your thoughts, I have no way of knowing if your sudden and obvious distress could compromise the mission. I will ask again. Do you want to talk about what happened in the shop?"

Dorothy looked down, and took a deep breath. Of course Felicia would take no interest in her feelings, except insofar as the risk they posed. "Don't worry about it. It's under control." She turned away, avoiding eye contact, and resumed her march.

"A psychic rapport is actually quite romantic, you know," said Felicia. "How long have you been connected?"

Dorothy halted again. Evidently Felicia intended to press the matter until Dorothy satisfied her sense of security. Dorothy wanted no part of that. She stared Felicia down. "What could you possibly know about romance?"

Felicia shrugged. "I know about seduction. How different could they be?"

Dorothy offered a churlish smile. "Now that's interesting. Tell me, how many men have you bedded only to get close enough to murder them?"

Felicia's eyes went a degree wider, and she looked away. The snappy retort Dorothy anticipated did not come. After a few seconds of surprisingly uncomfortable silence, Felicia said, "Four men. One woman."

A chill ran down Dorothy's spine. "Thank you for reminding me you are incomprehensibly terrible. To answer your question, the first time Claudia and I connected was right after I gave you that scar."

Felicia raised her hand to her cheek without breaking eye contact.

"Unfortunately for both of us," said Dorothy, "that means the memory of that moment will forever be connected to the memory of being locked in a baseball stadium basement, planning our escape and knowing failure would mean death. Thank you very much for that gift, Agent Kestrel. Now you know on those very rare occasions when Claudia and I share the most vulnerable of intimacies, including now, the image of you and your knives comes along for the ride."

Felicia crossed her arms. All signs of emotion drained from her face.

"There," said Dorothy. "I talked about it. Did you get what you needed?"

"Maybe. Did you?"

Dorothy scoured Felicia's eyes, searching for an indication of mockery or deception, without success. "I don't know."

Felicia nodded, then strode off, taking the lead.

Nestled between a café and a shoe store, Felicia's destination gave no indication of either importance or sketchy character. A worn, wooden sign hung over the door. Dorothy read it aloud.

"Alabaster's Magic Shack." She eyed Felicia with skepticism. "Magic Shack? Seriously?"

"Check your snobbery. Not everyone gets to apprentice with a member of the New Chicago Council of Mages."

Dorothy frowned. "I don't think it's snobbery to be concerned about trusting my friend's fate to some back-alley wizard."

"Really? You're trusting me. I didn't realize you had any standards left. Come on." Felicia entered the shop.

Dorothy looked around her, trying to gauge the seediness of the neighborhood. Everything she had seen on her walk through the nascent city reminded her of New Chicago's awkward phase as it grew from a makeshift town to a true metropolis. Dorothy, adopted daughter of a prominent figure, never wanted for safety or convenience. Would she recognize a dangerous part of town if she saw it? Felicia's snobbery comment bit deep, as much from the fact she had never given the question much thought as from its perceived unfairness. She took a deep breath, and followed Felicia inside.

Bulk bins of crystals, herbs, and assorted powders lined fixtures throughout the tiny shop, filling it with a pleasant, spicy aroma. Though familiar with the physical materials required for many incantations, Dorothy's experience with acquiring them thus far involved either collecting them from the wild or requisitioning them from the council stock room. The notion that a commercial market existed for these objects had not occurred to her. Handwritten paper labels displayed prices, some of which exceeded what she would pay to avoid the work of gathering her own ingredients, others prompting her to calculate how much labor she could save for so little cost.

"You're late."

Dorothy looked up to find a man an inch or two shorter than she, wearing a faded, charcoal grey cloak and a frown. "Are you talking to me?"

"You're the witch with the other witch in her head?"

Dorothy nodded. She looked around for Felicia, finding instead two other people she presumed to be customers. They paid no attention to her as they perused the wares.

"Then let's get this done." He strode away from her.

"Wait!" Dorothy followed him. "Is my friend here?"

"If you think she's your friend, you're in for some bad news."

Dorothy followed him through a beaded curtain into a cluttered back room. Felicia stood leaning against a far wall, inspecting the sword she had purchased earlier. At a wooden table in the center of the room sat a dark elf in a red Nehru jacket, her eyes closed, palms resting on the surface in front of her. Wavy, copper-colored hair partially obscured her face. At another seat to her side, a life-sized wooden doll mimicked the elf's pose, hinged fingers resting on the table, featureless face staring straight ahead.

"Have a seat," said the man. "We're way behind schedule here."

"Settle down, Cyrus." Felicia swished her rapier back and forth experimentally.

Dorothy stared at the naked mannequin. "You can't be serious. That's your temporary vessel?"

"Hey, you said you didn't want a bowl," said Felicia.

"How are we supposed to carry that?" said Dorothy.

The man Felicia called Cyrus harrumphed. "It's fully articulated. You're lucky I was able to find one of these on short notice."

Dorothy shook her head. "What does that even mean?"

"It means," said the elf, eyes still closed, in a gravelly voice barely more than a hiss, "it can walk."

Dorothy's jaw dropped. She turned on Felicia. "You never said anything about this! I thought we were going to put her in something small and carry her with us!"

"You think I'm happy about it? I thought that, too. This is what we have. We can run with it or we can scrap the mission. Besides, don't you think your friend will be happier in a form that moves instead of being trapped in a bottle or something?"

Dorothy crossed her arms. "I don't like it."

Child.

Strontium's intrusion startled Dorothy out of her funk. "Strontium?"

"Oh, good," said Felicia. "She's awake."

What's happening?

"We are in a magic shop, in the presence of an elf who plans to transfer your consciousness into a doll," said Dorothy. "I am trying to decide whether to let her."

Never been a doll before. Is it a pretty one?

"No. It's a full-sized mannequin with no face." Dorothy stepped closer to inspect it. "It appears to be vaguely female, at least. It might be an artist's model. The vendor here says it is fully articulated."

What does that mean?

"It means you will be able to walk. I can see movable joints at neck, shoulders, elbows, wrists and fingers. It is impossible for me to tell how tight or flexible they are."

Well that's a damn sight better than a bowl. Best get this show on the road.

Dorothy frowned. "You seem awfully eager for someone who didn't trust this plan."

You seem awful reluctant for someone who tossed her life out to make it happen. What's the problem?

"I haven't decided if this is worth the risk. We were expecting something smaller and more portable."

You mean something you can protect.

"Exactly!"

Child, I managed to take care of myself for ninety years before I met you. You think I can't manage without you now?

"I don't understand," said Dorothy. "I thought you didn't want to do this. Do you suddenly trust Felicia?"

"Oh, my," said Felicia. "I'd love to hear the other end of this discussion."

Dorothy glared at her. "Shut up! You stay out of this!"

I can guess what that was about, said Strontium.

"Don't worry about that," said Dorothy.

And don't you worry about me. Yes, I didn't want to do this when you were going to put me in some damn box. This is a body, or a kind of one, anyway.

"I'd hardly call it a body."

Will I be able to do magic in it?

"I have no idea." Dorothy addressed the dark elf. "Will my friend be able to cast spells in this form?"

"Impossible to say," said the elf. "Perhaps."

"Your answer is 'Perhaps.' Do you still want to try this?"

Yes.

"Strontium..."

Dorothy, you have been a kind host, but you and I both know I've outstayed my welcome. This is a chance for us both to be free. Let's not blow it, all right?

Dorothy rubbed her eyes with the heels of her palms. "All right." She pulled up a seat at the table across from the elf. "All right. What do I do?"

"Take the vessel's hand," said the elf.

Dorothy reached for the mannequin's nearest hand. The smooth wood felt cold to the touch. "Now what?"

A pop sounded in Dorothy's head, loud enough to cause phantom tinnitus. Simultaneously, a shock assaulted the hand holding the doll. She jerked away on reflex, to rub her sore palm, unpleasantly reminded of her recent burns.

"Ow! What just happened?"

The elf sat back in her chair, exhaustion in her eyes. "It is done."

"What? Already? Strontium?" Dorothy reached into the depths of her mind, searching for some sign of her friend, but meeting only dead silence. Her heart pounded, and an unexpected vertigo stirred.

The mannequin spasmed and sprang to its feet, toppling the chair under it in the process. It threw its arms out sideways, head pivoting from side to side, and attempted a step backward, only to stumble over the downed chair, and collapse to the floor with a loud, wooden clatter.

"Hell's bells!" it said in a muffled voice, as though speaking from inside a sealed crate.

"Strontium!" Dorothy knelt beside the fallen mannequin. "Are you in there? Are you all right?"

Strontium pushed herself to a sitting position, then rocked her head back and forth before turning it in Dorothy's direction. "Sister?"

Dorothy looked into the faceless block of wood before her. "I'm here." She stroked Strontium's new cheek with the back of her hand, and found it inflexible but warm.

"I can see you." Strontium's voice buzzed as she spoke. No obvious mechanism in her form to produce the sound presented itself.

Felicia stepped in and offered her hand. "On your feet, witch. I need to see if you can walk."

"Leave her alone!" said Dorothy.

Strontium shook her wooden head. "No, she's right." She took Felicia's hand and pulled, rising to her feet with surprising swiftness. Once standing, she rocked back and forth on the balls of her new feet, held her hands in front of her to inspect both sides, then slapped Felicia across the face, hard enough to send her sprawling to the floor.

Felicia rolled as she landed, fluidly drawing her sword in the process. In the cramped quarters, her momentum slammed her into a freestanding set of shelves, toppling it and all of its contents. Several artifacts hit the floor with the tinkling sound of fragile materials shattering, accompanied by the high-pitched shriek of Cyrus seeing his valuable wares instantly depreciate. Felicia attempted to regain her footing, and slipped on the fragments. Her bottom hit the floor with a graceless thud.

Strontium shook out her hand. "Joints feel flexible enough."

As Dorothy looked back and forth between assassin and mannequin, attempting to decide how or whether to intervene, Felicia threw back her head and guffawed.

"Fine! You get that one for free." Felicia pushed herself to her feet and sheathed her sword. She pulled a small purse from her pocket and tossed it Cyrus, who caught it with the unmistakable sound of coins jingling. "A pleasure doing business with you."

"What about the damages?"

"You'll have to take that up with the scrapper here." She pointed to Strontium, who shrugged, clearly not carrying any money.

A streak of orange light shot through the beaded curtain, terminating on the table surface. It faded to reveal a pixie. "Oh, good! You're here!"

"Sparky?" said Dorothy. "Oh, thank God! Are you okay?"

"Never better! Well, never much better, anyway. Honestly? A little bit traumatized. I'm okay, I guess. How are you?" Sparky's gaze fell on Strontium. "What's with the aura on that doll? Oh, wow! Is that your witchy pal?"

"Yes," said Dorothy. "Slow down. What happened to you? Where have you been?"

"No idea. Here and there. I have some great news!"

With the sound of rattling beads, Sparky's great news let herself in.

"Hey, Dotty," said Claudia. "Is this a good time?"

[PART 2]
WOODEN

.

BUSTED

C aught between the shock of being discovered and the joy of seeing Claudia, Dorothy froze.

"Ms. de Queiroz," said Felicia.

"Bitch," said Claudia.

Sparky held up her hands. "Hey, now…"

Claudia turned to Dorothy. "Is there somewhere we can talk?"

"What are you doing here?"

Claudia laughed. "What the hell do you think I'm doing here? We never finished our conversation about whether you were going to trust a hired killer to help you do something dangerous. I still vote no, by the way."

"I think that's still two to one in favor," said Felicia.

Claudia glared. "Dotty, seriously, can we have this fight somewhere without so many nosey murderers?"

"There's nothing to fight about," said Dorothy. "This wasn't your decision. How did you even find us?"

"I dropped a tracking device in your bag last night."

Dorothy's eyes went wide. "A tracking device? I take it back. We are fighting."

"Dotty, come on, can we do this at home?"

"We can do this right here!" said Dorothy.

"No offense?" said Cyrus.

All eyes in the room turned to the proprietor. Though already the shortest human in the room, he shrank under their gaze.

"N-no offense, but you can't. I don't want any more trouble here. You all… you all need to go."

Felicia slapped him on the back, and laughed as he wobbled unsteadily under the blow. "True enough! We should all withdraw before the authorities arrive! Unless…" She looked at Claudia, pouting. "Are you the authorities? Am I under arrest?" She slowly drew her sword, directing her attention to the blade, which she rolled back and forth before her eyes. "I sure hope not…"

Dorothy tensed, as her eyes flicked from Claudia to Sparky, both of whom looked back with apprehension. She moved her hand to Bess's hilt.

"Oh, put it back in your pants! The three of you!" Strontium stood tall, wooden fists planted on hips. In the ensuing silence, the tapping of her foot against the floorboards filled the room.

Felicia laughed again. "Yes, mother." She returned her blade to its scabbard. "Poor Cyrus is right, though. We can't dally here. I assume, Special Agent de Queiroz, you are not here to arrest me, and in fact have traveled here alone, either against Cody's orders, or simply without his knowledge. If so, welcome to our band of outlaws! I accept your aid, if so offered. If not, please let me make my case for continuing our quest, rather than taking your lover home to whatever version of domestic bliss and squabbling you two enjoy. May we discuss over dinner? My treat, of course."

Claudia stared at the animated doll in the room, who, like everyone else, had shifted attention to her. "Strontium?" She turned to Dorothy. "Is that Strontium?"

Dorothy held her hands out. "Yes. I still love you."

Claudia stared at Dorothy's outstretched palms for a few seconds, then threw her arms around her. "Do you promise?" she whispered in Dorothy's ear.

"Oh, please," said Felicia.

Both Sparky and Strontium turned on her and shouted, "Shut up!"

"I promise," said Dorothy. "With all my heart."

"Does this mean we can go home?" asked Claudia.

Dorothy released her and stood back. "No. For one thing, we are still fighting. You put a tracking device in my bag?"

"You put a sleep spell on me!"

"Ladies, please." Felicia gestured to the door. "We should take this elsewhere and leave this poor man and his poor customers in peace. My offer of dinner stands, and there is much we need to talk about."

"You can't possibly mean to suggest we can all simply stroll into a restaurant," said Dorothy.

"Actually, I meant to suggest we could order a pizza."

Dorothy looked out the second story window of Felicia's apartment. A slice of cheese pizza with a single bite taken from it sat on a paper plate in her hand. The five of them had slipped out of Alabaster's Magic Shack through a back door, and made their way across town via back alleys. Strontium wore a borrowed cloak whose hood safely concealed her head, but which did not hide her wooden feet, nor the clacking they made against the cobblestones. Dorothy feared they would draw attention, but a walking mannequin—though probably not subtle enough for a restaurant visit—did not qualify as sufficiently unusual in the post-Mayhem world to warrant suspicion.

During the twenty minutes it took to reach this destination on foot, and the hour since they arrived here, she refrained from pursuing any discussion with Claudia on the topic of the various laws they currently violated. They similarly avoided discussing the status of their relationship. Claudia's arrival provided the one complication finally able to persuade her she had gotten in over her head.

Instead, she probed Sparky for details on her whereabouts after vanishing in the forest. As suspected, a shunting spell had been used against her, transplanting her hundreds of miles from her companions. Lingering traces of the summon pixie spell Dorothy cast on her earlier allowed the pixie to track her, eventually arriving at Kansas City not long after Claudia came to town via the Transit Worm.

The shunt, a simple, microcosmic wormhole spell, required little training to learn, but a great deal of energy to cast, especially on a pixie. Whoever attacked them had done so with resources beyond Dorothy's.

Strontium sat still in a chair as Claudia drew a face on her wooden head with a set of colored markers. At each stroke, Sparky added a magical nudge to compensate for Claudia's lack of art training or aptitude, resulting in an ornate, cheerful caricature.

"Does this look anything like me?" asked the witch.

"I have no idea what you looked like," said Claudia.

Sparky tapped her chin. "I think it evokes your face more than literally representing it."

"In other words, no," said Strontium.

"We improved it!" said Sparky with a wide grin.

Felicia joined Dorothy at her window-gazing. "We should be safe enough here for the night. I doubt the NCSA knows about this hideout."

She took a bite from her own slice. "I must say, as much as your world lacked, pizza delivery is a miracle unto itself. My compliments to your civilization."

"I don't want to drag Claudia into this," said Dorothy.

"I don't believe I saw any dragging. This is free will in action."

"You weren't at all surprised she tracked us down, were you?"

Felicia shrugged. "I predicted it would take her at least two more days to catch up to us. If we hadn't been attacked, I probably would have been right."

"So," said Dorothy, "this was your plan all along?"

"Not exactly, but a variable I had already taken into account. There are places where her voice talent will come in handy, but I had other plans ready if we didn't have access to it."

Dorothy looked over to Claudia, putting the finishing touches on Strontium's new visage. "There's a variable you didn't take into account. Will we be able to travel with her in that form? Does she need to be in the presence of the Scale for the magic to work?"

"I don't know the answers to either of those questions," said Felicia. "We have to assume they are both yes."

Dorothy looked at Felicia, who had taken another bite of her pizza. "That's... interesting. I think in your shoes, I might decide both answers are no. All you need at this point is my assistance, right? Wouldn't it be easier to leave the doll behind? Convince me the magic will still work? Surely your own goal will be easier to achieve without the added liability."

Felicia took a moment to chew and swallow. "All true, but if we take that chance, and we're wrong, your friend could end up trapped in this form. We have to risk bringing her."

"I don't think you're hearing my question," said Dorothy. "Why are you admitting this? Why aren't you lying to me? Convincing me to leave her behind. Sacrificing my goal to increase your own odds of success."

Felicia frowned. "I swore I would see this through. Do you still not understand that?"

"I understand you all too well. You need her for something, don't you?"

"That's absurd. Why would I need a walking doll?"

Dorothy shook her head. "For whatever wheels spin within the wheels of this plan."

"Whether you believe this or not, the only value I place on your friend is the help she brings me from you, and I know the only way to guarantee that help is to honor my agreement and restore her true body. If you are afraid her new form makes her too great a risk, we can end this bargain here and now. Your mind is clear now, and your sister-witch has a sort of autonomy, if an imperfect one. If that satisfies you, we can both walk away. That's not my preference, as I still need the Scale, but if you continue to see deception in my every deed, perhaps you're not the safest partner for me anyway. You are free to return to your life. I would ask only that you compensate me for what I paid to get Strontium this far."

As Felicia said this, Strontium stood from her chair and looked around the room. Her face now bore the permanent image of an old woman with cartoonish features, smiling vapidly. "Hey, assassin, where's your toilet?"

"Do you need to relieve yourself?" asked Felicia.

"I wish! Just looking for a mirror."

Felicia pointed to a door, and Strontium strolled to it.

"Did you really pay for that with a bag of coins?" asked Dorothy. "How much do I owe you?"

"Eight thousand dollars. The coins in question were doubloons, part of my private collection. Easy to fence, difficult to trace. It astonishes me how much commerce you people do in cyberspace. Where is your sense of discretion?"

"I pay you eight thousand dollars, and we can all go home?"

"Yes," said Felicia. "Don't even pretend you can't afford that. I've seen your house. Pay me back, and on my honor, we are settled. My vow not to kill you and yours will remain in force."

Strontium gazed at herself in the bathroom mirror. A soft cackle emanated from within. How many times had Strontium looked into a mirror in the last five years with Dorothy's eyes, to see a face not her own? How many times had Dorothy looked in a mirror, seeing something ineffably different about the most familiar face in her memory? Did the sight of Strontium's false face, the wooden doll, feel liberating, or merely comical? Did Strontium feel whole yet, or did she share the unexpected pang of internal loneliness now taking Dorothy by surprise?

"No," said Dorothy. "Thank you, but we agreed to a real body, and I won't quit until she has that. I will hold up my end of the bargain to see that happen. To be clear, if you're still hiding something from—"

Strontium fell backward, pinwheeling her arms as she went down. She hit the bathroom floor with sufficient momentum to slide half a foot into the main room.

Felicia dropped her plate on the floor and ran to Strontium's side. She knelt beside the prone mannequin and lifted her shoulders to raise her to a sitting position. "Strontium?"

"I'm fine," said the witch. "Just a little out of sorts. This isn't like walking on real legs."

Felicia helped her to her feet. "Are you in any pain?"

Strontium shook her head. "Whoa! That feels looser." She moved her hands to the sides of her head to hold it steady. The last segment of her left pinky finger had lost its wooden covering, exposing a single metal pin, connected to a hinge at the joint.

"Let's get you into a seat, please," said Felicia, guiding her back to the table. "Pixie, please search the floor for bits of wood."

"Do I take orders from her?" Sparky asked Dorothy.

"Do it," said Dorothy. "Strontium? How do you feel?"

Strontium eased herself back into the chair. "I feel fine. Caught me off guard, is all."

Felicia produced a small tool from her belt and inserted in into Strontium's neck.

"What are you doing?" asked Dorothy.

"Tightening." Felicia pulled the tool out. "Is that better?"

Strontium let go of her head, and rolled it around. "Yes. Thank you."

"Is this what you need?" Sparky dropped a cone of wood on the table, less than an inch long, with a wide crack running from tip to base.

Felicia picked up the fragment, and slid it onto the exposed pin on Strontium's finger. "This will have to be glued back on. Sit still. I'll be right back." She stood. "Dorothy? A word, please?" Felicia walked to her kitchen, Dorothy in her wake.

"I guess that answers the question of how great a risk she poses," whispered Dorothy.

"Indeed it does. We will have to watch her at every moment. She feels no pain, so she will have no idea if she suffers any injuries, and it's reasonable to expect she will be accident prone." Felicia took a deep breath, and blew it out. "If you want out now, if you choose to preserve her in this state, and keep her safe at home, I will waive the eight thousand. I cannot ask either of you to go any farther than this."

Dorothy looked over her shoulder at Strontium, seated with her back to the kitchen. "I can't leave her like that."

Felicia nodded. "Then it's time for you to hear the details of the task ahead of us."

[11]

THE PLAN

Dorothy, Felicia, Strontium, and Claudia sat around a dining room table. Leftover pizza grew cold in a half-empty box on which Felicia had sketched a crude map of North America. An X marked their current location, with a dotted line leading from it to a location some indeterminate distance south of there. Another dotted line led northwest from that point, terminating in a circle. Sparky stood on the box, hands on hips, examining the lines.

"We seek two objects in order to employ the Scale of Hypatia," said Felicia. "One of them, obviously, is the Scale itself. There is every reason to believe the Scale perished along with most pre-Mayhem artifacts in 2004. Fortunately, it has come to my attention that a survivor of what you call the non-real world has seen the scale, and is willing to reveal its location for a price."

"The Scale grants wishes, right?" asked Dorothy. "Why does your contact need a price? Why not keep the Scale and wish for the money?"

"Wishing for wealth is a sucker's gambit," said Felicia. "Any child from my world will tell you that. It's the easiest road to misery and death. As it happens, there are two reasons he wants to bargain for the information instead of taking the Scale. First, he needs a magical talisman I happen to possess, and second… the Scale does not work for dragons."

"Your contact is a dragon?" Claudia made a note on a legal pad in front of her. "Reason number one why this is crazy."

"He's a disabled dragon, if that helps," said Felicia.

"Tell me you don't mean Ruprecht," said Sparky.

Strontium laughed. "The Wingless Worm? He's alive? Oh, this is too rich."

"Ruprecht?" said Claudia. "Help us out, magical people."

"Ruprecht the Tiny was my world's single most pathetic dragon," said Strontium. "Apart from his size, which wasn't much bigger than a cow, he lost his left wing in a flying accident. Not even a fight—he smashed it into a cliff. No fire-breathing, no magic, it's a wonder he survived as long as he did. Are you telling me after all the good people we lost to the Mayhem Wave, the Wingless Worm outlived them?"

"Yes, I am telling you that," said Felicia. "He and I have been corresponding for months."

"Corresponding about what?" asked Dorothy.

"It came to his attention last year that I possess a stone of regeneration. A very useful item for someone in my line of work, I should add. One cannot keep up one's professional reputation short a limb, as too many of my colleagues have learned over the years."

"He plans to grow his wing back," said Dorothy.

"Obviously," said Felicia.

"Will that work?" asked Claudia.

All four of the others said, "No," simultaneously.

Felicia laughed. "Look at us all agreeing on something. What a team we make!"

"A regeneration stone imprints on its user," said Dorothy to Claudia. "If the stone has been used even once, it will be worthless to anyone else. Even if it hasn't been used, if it's small enough for Felicia to carry, it won't be big enough to heal an injury as severe as a lost dragon wing."

"The latter, as it happens," said Felicia. "It's a fresh stone, but too small for his purposes. If he tries it out, he will feel it going to work on him, but it will be weeks before he discovers it isn't strong enough. Might even grow himself a miniature wing, but that's all."

"That's a very dangerous game you're playing," said Dorothy.

"He's playing a similarly dangerous game, though he doesn't know I'm on to him," said Felicia. "The location of the Scale is worthless without the means to activate it. Hypatia's clerics devised a means to harness the Scale's power, but without the spell, it's an inert chunk of dragon armor."

"He thinks you don't know that, or you don't have the spell?" asked Dorothy.

"Precisely. He is incorrect on both counts. Acquiring the spell is the next item on our agenda." Felicia tapped the end of the trail on her map. "This is the lair of the wizard Atrylyn. She died nearly ten years ago, and her home has fallen to ruins. I learned two years ago she had contact with the Scale before the Mayhem Wave, and used it to increase her powers before it was stolen from her. We need to breach her library, and find her journals. The spell will surely be in there."

"Won't someone have looted her home by now?" asked Dorothy. "It's been ten years."

"Possible, but doubtful," said Felicia. "For one thing, the ruins are overrun with thunder toads, not at all worth the risk for casual looters."

Claudia jotted that down. "Reason two: thunder toads."

"Atrylyn's presence in your world was not widely known. She returned in the counter-bomb wave, and kept her survival a secret. No one knows she was alive, let alone dead now with a library to raid."

"And yet, you know," said Dorothy.

Felicia shrugged. "I'm the one who killed her."

"Let me see if I understand all of this correctly," said Claudia. "First, we meet with a dragon, give him a useless rock, and he tells us where to find the Scale. Then we raid the house of a wizard you killed, fight our way past..." She consulted her legal pad. "*Thunder toads*, then tear apart her library looking for a book that has a spell in it that will make the Scale work. Then we're done?"

"Not quite," said Felicia. "We still have to activate the Scale to restore Strontium to her true form. Also, knowing the Scale's location may not be enough information if it has been safeguarded or has a protector. That may require further ingenuity, negotiation, or violence. Otherwise, yes, then we are done."

Claudia made another note on the pad. "Can we go back a couple steps? I'm still a little fuzzy on how you knew this Ruprecht was still alive, and how he found out about your stone."

Felicia smiled. "I may have leaked that information to get his attention. As for how I learned of him, my trade secrets are not part of this conversation. Believe me when I say my information is reliable. I have been doing this kind of work for a very long time."

"Uh huh." Claudia stood. "Well, that's a lot to think about, for sure. Dotty? Can we have a little chat in private, please?"

Dorothy looked at Strontium, who nodded. "Felicia? Is there somewhere Claudia and I can talk?"

"There's a deck outside my bedroom." She pointed. "Right through that door."

"Thank you." Dorothy stood and held out her hand. "Shall we?"

Claudia followed her to Felicia's bedroom, and shut the door behind them once they were inside. They continued out the sliding glass door in back, and closed that behind them as well. Below them, a tiny, fenced-in yard gave forth the scents of flowers and freshly mown grass into the warm air.

"Where is Ian?" asked Dorothy.

"I told him to go to the Codys' after school yesterday. Haven't heard from him since then, but I trust he made it there all right."

"Harrison knows you're here."

"He knows I went after you, but not where," said Claudia.

"He should have dropped a tracking device in your purse," said Dorothy.

"I don't think he's that bright." Claudia stared out over the city. The residential neighborhood included many such second floor decks, and the pleasant summer afternoon had encouraged many occupants to take advantage of them. "This is crazy, Dotty."

"I know, I know." Dorothy sighed. "Selfish, too. Don't forget to tell me how selfish it is. Felicia knew all the right buttons to push. Knew exactly what I wanted more than anything in the world. I let her push those buttons, because I wanted my best friend to have a life outside of my head, and I wanted to have a mind all my own, so you wouldn't have to share me with anyone else."

"You still love me?"

"More than ever. It was never her."

"So… You're cool with the tracking device?" asked Claudia.

"No," said Dorothy. "Do you forgive the sleep spell?"

"Nope."

"Then I guess we still have things to work on." Dorothy looked out on the city of strangers, and let a silence settle between them for a while before speaking again. "Thank you."

Claudia frowned. "For what?"

"For coming after me. I didn't think you would, and now I'm glad you did, and I wish I could have asked you to come with me in the first place."

"I'm never not going to come after you," said Claudia. "That's what 'I love you' means, all those times I say it."

Dorothy's throat tightened. Her mind returned to the ring waiting at home. Claudia's words sounded very much like a vow, and one she would happily return. She closed her eyes and nodded.

Claudia took her hand. "Dotty, we have to go home. Let's get Strontium back to the Council of Mages and see if they can do something for her."

"I want to do better by her than that," said Dorothy. "She saved my life. If there's a chance I can give hers back to her, I have to take it."

"Dotty, this is Felicia fucking Kestrel! It's great she got Strontium out of your head, but it's Felicia fucking Kestrel! You can't follow her into this craziness."

"There's something different about her."

Claudia took a step back. "About who? Felicia?"

"Yes," said Dorothy.

"Fucking Kestrel?"

"Yes! I can't explain it, but there's something going on here, deeper than an assassin luring a witch into some elaborate plot. She's… I don't know. She saved my life. There were these cursed wolves, and I killed one of them, and another one almost killed me, and she saved me."

"Because she needs you," said Claudia.

"You didn't see it," said Dorothy. "The way she reacted to killing the wolf. There was something emotional there."

"It's an act."

"Maybe. There are other things. She has made promises, and kept every one of them. Even when she thought I was trying to kill her by giving Bess to her, she didn't attack me."

Claudia's eyes went wide. "You gave her Bess?"

Dorothy drew the short sword and held her up. "I still have her. Don't worry. It was a mistake. I thought I was giving her another sword."

Do you need protection? asked Bess.

"No. Thank you, Bess." Dorothy returned Bess to her sheath.

"Dotty, please, listen to yourself."

"I have been listening to myself for three days. I have listened to myself try to provoke her, and not give her a chance, and at every turn she has been forthright."

"Do you trust her?" asked Claudia.

Dorothy bit her lip. "Yes. I know how that sounds, and I know what I would say to anyone who said these things to me. There's something going on here, and I truly don't believe it's an evil plot."

"She is an evil person."

"Is she?" asked Dorothy. "Maybe she is. Maybe evil is a thing some people just are. Or maybe it's a thing people do, and so far, she hasn't done anything evil since I joined her."

"Three days," said Claudia. "Stacked against a lifetime of murders."

Dorothy shook her head. "What if this is her first step on the road to redemption, and we push her away? She said herself she wants the Scale to heal, not to harm. You look at her and you see a monster, and I see that too, but there is pain there as well. Real pain. What if what she wants is to heal that pain? What if this is how the killing ends? Can we tell her no?"

"What if you're wrong?"

"Then Sparky kills her," said Dorothy. "Or Bess kills her. We have two failsafes, and she knows that, and she still wants to work with us. I say we make the leap. For Strontium's sake."

"Just for Strontium?"

"All right, damn it, for Felicia's sake, too. I know it's a gamble, but think of the payoff if I'm right."

Claudia narrowed her eyes. "I won't pretend not to hate her."

"I haven't been, and I don't expect you too, either."

Claudia wrapped her arms around Dorothy and held her tight. "Please don't be wrong about this," she whispered in her ear. Dorothy nodded in response.

Hand in hand, they walked back through the two doors. They found Felicia sitting next to Strontium, applying a small clamp to her pinky finger, a tube of wood glue on the table beside them. She looked up as they came into the room. "Well?"

Dorothy and Claudia looked at each other one more time. Claudia nodded, and Dorothy looked Felicia in the eye.

"We're in."

[12]

THE WINGLESS WORM

Felicia purchased four tickets on the Mississippi Basin Transit Worm under assumed names. Despite Dorothy's concerns, neither the conductor nor the other passengers gave Strontium a second glance. Her cover story, as a prototype wooden robot on the way to a demonstration, did not prove necessary. Covered in newly purchased clothes, including a feathered hat and sunglasses to conceal her felt-tip crafted eyes, she appeared no more unusual than the average elf or centaur passenger.

The four of them sat in two pairs of facing seats, with a table in between them. Claudia consumed a little less than half the surface with a game of solitaire.

"Our destination is at least a two-hour hike from the Worm station," said Felicia. "We should probably allow for three, in case our wooden friend needs the extra time to keep up."

"Is there any reason we can't all wait for you to do that on your own?" asked Claudia without eye contact, before turning over a group of three cards and playing the top one. "I mean, you're the one with the stone. Do you really need us all to tag along?"

Felicia frowned. "I would prefer backup. This is a dragon, after all. If that doesn't suit you, I can do this on my own."

"I don't want any of us to get separated," said Dorothy. "We can't use our phones to communicate. If something goes wrong, it would be hours before anyone would know."

"It was just a suggestion," said Claudia. "No need to get twitchy."

"Red five on the black six," said Strontium.

Claudia looked up. "You know solitaire?"

"Only from watching you play right now. It doesn't look that complicated."

"Well, now…" Claudia flipped all her cards face down and gathered them back into a deck. She shuffled. "Seeing as how you're such a quick study, how's about we make this more interesting? Wanna learn poker?"

"Ha! That one I know. You sure you want to play against someone with such a good poker face?" Strontium folded her fingers and rested her chin on them.

"You'll have to take those shades off."

Strontium removed the sunglasses, to stare Claudia down with her felt-tip marker eyes.

"That's more like it." Claudia finished shuffling, and offered the deck to Strontium to cut. She declined by tapping the deck, and Claudia dealt two cards to each person at the table.

Strontium lifted the corner of her cards long enough to peek at them, and set them back down.

"Two dollar, four dollar," said Claudia. "Bet's to you, Dotty."

Dorothy eyed Claudia with suspicion. "I don't have any chips."

"What do you have in here?" Claudia opened the top of Dorothy's bag, sitting between them.

"Hey!" said Sparky from within. "Knock much?"

"Sorry. You got anything in there we can use as poker chips?"

"I have no idea what that question means," said the pixie.

"Never mind, I got this." Claudia grabbed a box of breath mints, popped the top off and dumped approximately a dozen in front of each player. "Those are two-dollar chips, Dotty. You need to put one in to call, or fold."

"I know how to play, thank you." Dorothy lifted her cards, a ten and a queen, off-suit, and pushed one mint forward. "Call."

"Call," said Claudia. "You're the little blind, Strontium. Pretend you have half a mint in front of you."

"You'll all have to pretend that," said Strontium. "Fold."

"Option, bitch?" said Claudia.

Felicia picked up her cards, and took several seconds to examine them. She pushed one mint forward. "There's my blind." She pushed forward another. "And my raise."

Dorothy looked at her cards again.

"Are they better now?" asked Claudia.

"They're the same. Call."

"In," said Claudia. "Pot's right. Flop." She slid one card off the top of the deck and pushed it aside, then turned over three cards. Three of spades, jack of diamonds, seven of hearts. "Garbage. Your action, killer."

"Check," said Felicia.

"Check," said Dorothy.

Claudia pushed a mint forward. "Bet."

Felicia picked up her cards again. Her eyes and lips had gone dead, revealing nothing. "Call."

Dorothy pushed her cards to the center of the table.

"Two players, pot's right. Turn." Claudia burned another card off the top, then turned over the five of diamonds. "Possible straight on the board."

Strontium looked away. "Damnation."

"Somebody folded a four-six," said Claudia. "Tough break, witchy-doll. Your bet, slasher."

Felicia drummed her fingers on the table. Her lips thinned. "Check."

Claudia pushed two mints forward. "Bet."

Felicia sat back in her seat, picked up her cards again, and tapped them twice on the table. "Call." She added her mints to the pot.

"Two players. River." Claudia burned one more card, then turned over the three of diamonds. "Pair of threes, possible straight, possible flush. Psycho?"

"Bet," said Felicia without hesitation.

"Somebody has a three," said Claudia. "Won't be good enough, though. Raise."

"Re-raise," said Felicia.

"Ooh." Claudia looked at her cards. "Well, I know you don't have pocket threes, because I have this one." She turned over the three of clubs from her own hand. "Either you feel great about your kicker, or you caught that flush. My, my, my. Can you feel the tension, crowd?" She pushed two more mints out. "Cap."

"Call," said Felicia.

"Sucks to be you, bitch." Claudia turned over her other card, the seven of clubs, revealing a full house. "Flopped two pair. Caught my boat on the river."

"So did I." Felicia turned over her cards, a pair of jacks, both black. "Jacks full of threes. All those mints are mine."

Strontium thumped the table. "Damn! Nice slow play. You had me fooled."

Claudia sat back, and opened her arms in Strontium's direction. "Oh, thank you, my friend. That's what I was waiting for."

"What do you mean?" asked Dorothy.

"She had the nuts on the flop," said Claudia. "Best possible hand. Unbeatable, at least until the next card. You thought she had shit, right?"

"So?"

"She means, Dr. O'Neill, oh trusting partner and companion on this endeavor of substantial risk and dubious gain, I can still lie to you, and you can still believe me, despite every precaution you think you've taken." Felicia stood. "Charming object lesson, de Queiroz. If you'll excuse me, I need a drink."

The assassin scooped the pile of mints from the center of the table and dropped them in her pocket before taking her leave.

A passing breeze momentarily drew away some of the perspiration on Dorothy's forehead, and brought a modicum of relief from the heat. Hiking through the forest landscape that still defined much of post-Mayhem North America evoked memories of her first few months living in solitude, with various resources spaced by miles, and no means of transportation save by foot. Though she endured the exercise at the time in good spirits, she found now she did not miss it.

"Are we there yet?" Ahead of Dorothy, Claudia marched on with no outward indication of weariness, perhaps from genuine fitness, perhaps out of need not to show weakness to their leader.

"Soon," said Felicia.

Strontium, incapable of fatigue in her wooden form, matched Dorothy's pace by her side, with Sparky riding on her shoulder. So far, though not the speed liability Felicia had feared, she had stumbled twice, both times suffering no more than scratches to her palms.

"How are you holding up?" asked Dorothy.

"Same as every time you ask that," said Strontium. "Well enough."

Dorothy shook her head. "I'm sorry. You understand I can't help worrying about you, right? I feel like you were safer in my head."

"Do you miss me?" Strontium's drawn-on face made the sincerity of the question impossible to read.

"Maybe? A little? I don't know. I spent most of my life with only one consciousness in my mind. You'd think I'd be able to get used it again. It's... a strange feeling being all alone in here now."

"Hm," said Strontium. "Can't say I disagree. Mind you, I don't know how much of the weird is having a mind to myself, and how much is having a mind inside this contraption."

88

"Hopefully you won't have to wonder much longer," said Dorothy.

Felicia halted, and looked to her left, twitching her nose. "Hold up." She took several measured steps, sweeping the ground with her eyes, then stopped and crouched.

"Find something neat?" asked Claudia.

"Dragon scat. We're closer than I thought." She stood and squinted. "Tracks, too. They're at least two weeks old, but should be easy enough to follow. Come on." She set out in a new direction.

Another ten minutes of hiking later, the tracks took them to a ravine, where a tiny stream disappeared into a fissure in the bedrock the size of a small car. Dorothy drew four newly purchased headlamps from her bag and passed them around.

Felicia donned her light and peered into the crack. "You'll want to hide your pixie now."

Sparky hopped from Strontium's shoulder into Dorothy's open bag.

"Stay quiet and hidden, please," said Dorothy.

"I'll do my best," said the pixie. "If you need me, give a holler. We should have a code word or something."

"How about Sparky?" said Dorothy. "It has the virtue of being easy to remember."

"That should work. Did you know you have a tortoise skeleton in here? I'm not judging or anything, but, weird."

"I'm aware. Leave it alone."

"How's the climb look?" asked Claudia.

"Easy," said Felicia. "There are human-sized stairs and a rail. The stone is damp, so you'll want to watch your step."

Claudia frowned. "Why would a dragon need human-sized stairs?"

"Either he has human henchmen, which is not as unusual as you might think, or this was originally a human hideout and he made it his own." She looked at Dorothy. "You ready for this?"

Dorothy patted her side, confirming one more time she wielded a weapon probably capable of taking out a runty, flightless dragon should things go badly. "Let's do it."

Their descent proved manageable, if slow. Claudia and Dorothy spotted Strontium from behind and in front. Though not as steady as the others, she maintained her footing down the few dozen winding stairs carved from the cavern walls and floor.

Felicia touched down on the smooth floor and cupped her hands around her mouth. "Ruprecht?" Her call echoed back to them with slight delay, defining a relatively small chamber. She ran her headlamp beam along the back wall, revealing a single passage in the rear.

A voice returned, gravelly and bass. "You're early."

"Are you decent? Should we wait outside?"

A snort followed, which resolved itself into a laugh. "Never decent, but don't let that put you off."

Felicia laughed loudly in reply, and strode forward.

Beyond the first chamber, the rear opening led to a winding but short tunnel. As they rounded a turn, light beyond that of their own lamps illuminated the way. The tunnel ended in another chamber, itself ending in a hole several feet across, open to the elements. The trickling stream that had accompanied them on their journey ran to this opening and dropped out of sight beyond it. Apart from daylight, only additional rock looked back at them through it.

Ruprecht sat in the center of this room, a four-legged dragon somewhat larger than the cow-sized animal Strontium described. A fifth limb, the beast's remaining wing, now useless without its mate, twitched and spread as they entered. Ruprecht's head and face, apart from being unadorned with brass prosthetics, bore an unnerving resemblance to Basil Heatherington, the half-dragon who held Dorothy captive five years earlier. Bile rose in her throat at the unpleasant reminder.

"So many of you," said the dragon. "To bring me one stone? Which one of you is Felicia?"

"I am. My apologies for the confusion. These are my partners."

Ruprecht drew his lips back into a toothy smile that gave Dorothy chills. "I see. Well then, down to business. You have my stone, I have your information. Shall we exchange?"

"If you know the location of Hypatia's Scale, the stone is yours."

The dragon smacked his lips and shifted his weight, pulling his body around in a quarter turn. He flapped his wing once before folding it against his back. The action produced a slight breeze in the cave, stirring up odors of musk and decay. "Yes, yes. The Scale. I imagine you are eager to find it. You must travel to a ruined stronghold, a hundred and forty leagues hence, on a pair of river islands. Your journey from here will be upstream."

Felicia's face went dead as she took in this information. "A pair of islands?"

"Yes," said Ruprecht. "Joined by a footbridge. On the northern island lies what is left of the workshop of a great sorceress."

"Atrylyn," said Felicia.

Ruprecht laughed. "The late. In her library, you will find what you need."

"Felicia?" said Dorothy.

The assassin lifted her hand sharply to silence the question. "Forgive me, sir dragon, but I have been to the ruins of Atrylyn's keep, and the Scale is not there."

"The Scale? Oh, my, no. The Scale is not there. She once possessed the Scale, though she lost it in a duel."

"A duel?" said Dorothy. "With whom?"

Ruprecht laughed. "Does it matter? Another wizard, I suppose, though really, it could have been anyone with sufficient power to challenge her for it. I imagine there are many who would consider it the ultimate trophy if they knew it still existed. I'm sure there are even those who would hope to use it as Hypatia herself did, to rebuild her empire."

Dorothy frowned and looked at Felicia. "What does that mean?"

Felicia did not make eye contact. "I haven't the foggiest idea."

"Now, now, my dear," said Ruprecht. "Don't be rude. Your companion has questions. Can it be you haven't been entirely frank with her about your goals?"

Dorothy's heart pounded. She held her rage in check, and addressed the dragon. "Is the Scale a weapon?"

"A weapon?" Ruprecht affected shock with a clawed foot in front of his mouth. "A weapon? Would Hypatia the Gracious employ a weapon to cement her authority? Oh, my, no! The Scale is a tool of utmost generosity. Hypatia built her empire on gifts, not violence. She used the Scale to grant the hearts desires of those who came to her, in exchange for obedience. A plate of her own armor, torn from her very being for the benefit of others. She wielded it as a symbol of her willingness to sacrifice for the greater good. A better dragon than I, to be sure."

Dorothy allowed herself some measure of relief at these words. Though Ruprecht's story of the Scale's history grossly contradicted Felicia's, his description of its nature matched the assassin's claim.

"Enough!" shouted Felicia. "Why are you sending me to Atrylyn's keep if the Scale isn't there?"

Ruprecht pushed out his lower lip in a grotesque mockery of a pout. "Forgive my ramblings. Let's keep to business, yes? What you seek from the enchantress is in her library. Once deprived of the Scale, she found she could not abide the loss, and so she devoted her powers to locating its new hiding place, which she succeeded in doing. Alas, the Scale is a tricky thing. One cannot simply steal it. Instead, she visited the Scale, employing it in secret from time to time. She could not risk revealing she knew its location, so she wiped the information from her own memory, relying for every visit on a map she drew in her journal. Find that book, find that map, and you will find the Scale."

"This is not what we discussed!" said Felicia. "You claimed you had seen the Scale yourself!"

The dragon closed his eyes and turned his head to the side. The popping sound of cracked neck joints flooded the echo chamber. "Did I? I thought I only told you I knew its whereabouts. I promised to lead you to it, which oath I have now discharged. I believe you owe me one regeneration stone."

"If you know where the Scale is, why not tell us yourself?"

He harrumphed. "Little sport in that, I would think. Tell me, assassin, what has it cost you to get even this far? Have you killed anyone on this quest?"

"No," said Dorothy.

Felicia looked at Dorothy with wide eyes. "Dorothy…"

"I think you have," said the Dragon. "It shows in your bearing. Who was it? Some woeful bandit on the road? Self-defense, I wager. Surely you could rationalize that, at least before the fact, mm? An animal, perhaps? Some mindless beast? Would that even penetrate, I wonder."

Felicia stared down the dragon with steely eyes. "You know. Don't you? You know what they did."

"Certainly I know. Delicious irony. Very droll."

"Droll?" Felicia took a step forward. Her hands twitched. "Droll? This is amusing to you?"

"Not half so amusing as learning what you will do when I eat one of your friends." The dragon moved his gaze around the room, lingering on each woman for a second.

Claudia looked at Dorothy with practiced calm and silently mouthed, "Sparky."

Dorothy opened her bag.

"They're not my friends," said Felicia. "Your threats are wasted. They do however carry enough combined might to reduce you to a smear on this cavern wall. I suggest you reflect on that as we take our leave."

Felicia produced the regeneration stone from a pocket and tossed it. Black and smooth like a river stone, it landed with a soft clatter, bouncing against the cavern floor before coming to rest at Ruprecht's feet. The gesture elicited no reaction from the dragon. Felicia backed away from him. "Ladies, we are finished here."

Ruprecht sprang. As the four women did their best to scatter, he flipped his tail around, catching Strontium in the midsection. She clattered against the stone wall, landing near the entrance to the tunnel.

Dorothy shouted, "Sparky!" as she drew Bess.

The pixie shot upward and arced to their foe, in time to catch a sweeping blow from his only wing, swatting her to the floor. She bounced twice, throwing out a shower of orange sparks.

"No!" shouted Felicia. "Stop it! They will kill you!"

"I think not," said Ruprecht. "They haven't the balls. Anyway, that's more your bailiwick, isn't it? Have you no knives for me, murderer-for-hire?"

"Dorothy! Take the others to the tunnel, now!" Spring-loaded daggers leapt from Felicia's sleeves to her grip. "This is your last chance to let us leave in peace, worm. Don't squander it."

"Nonsense. All but one of you may leave in peace in a moment."

Dorothy glanced back at Strontium, still splayed on the cavern floor. With an instant to decide whether to follow Felicia's directive or take more assertive action, she nodded to Bess and charged the dragon.

As he did with Sparky, he slapped her with his wing in mid-leap. Unlike Sparky, Dorothy got in one good bite with the sword before tumbling to the ground, slicing a notch in the wing at least ten inches long.

"Ho! Well cut! I had you for the mouse of the group. Now I know better."

"Why are you doing this?" asked Felicia. "What do you have to gain?"

"Sheer entertainment, which is more than enough. Such a rare opportunity to see the magic. What an oddity you are. Which one should I devour? Do you have a favorite?" He looked around again, and fixed his eye on Claudia, the only one of Felicia's companions still standing. "This swarthy one seems your type."

"Fuck you!" shouted Claudia.

The enclosed space magnified the concussive effect of Claudia's voice power, and Dorothy's body rattled as the words passed over her several times in rapid succession, triggering a painful nausea.

Ruprecht shrieked. The target of Claudia's attack, he suffered the brunt of the sonic barrage. He fell onto his side, blood pouring from his ears, body wracked with spasms. His screams continued, interrupted only by wheezing as he sucked in more air.

"Dorothy!"

Felicia's cry registered in mute under the ringing in Dorothy's ears. She stood and nodded to the assassin in acknowledgement.

"We need to go, now! Get your pixie! I'll get the doll!"

Before Dorothy could process or respond to that plan, a flash of crimson light permeated the chamber, momentarily blinding her.

Ruprecht's screams halted.

As Dorothy's eyes adjusted to the trauma, she frantically surveyed her surroundings.

The dragon lay still, blood now streaming not only from his ears, but from snout and mouth as well, in greater quantity.

Strontium, now on her feet, faced the beast, forearms crossed in front of her face. Her right hand, and the stump where her left hand had been, put out tendrils of ochre smoke. She dropped to her knees. "I guess that answers whether I can do magic."

"What have you done?" screamed Felicia. "He was beaten! Helpless! We could have escaped!"

As the others stared at her, she fled down the tunnel alone.

[13]

ENIGMAS

Dorothy knelt at Strontium's side. "Can you walk?" Her voice competed with the lingering effects of Claudia's sound bomb in her head.

"I don't know. Give me a sec."

"Dotty?"

At the sound of Claudia's voice, spoken in a subdued tone, the ringing in Dorothy's ears faded to nothing. Claudia's power, the power to be heard, had been approved years ago as a treatment for aural trauma from acoustic shock, and she earned a small annual retainer from Chicago Memorial Hospital to remain on call for such injuries. In this case, cause and cure coincided. Dorothy had never experienced the effect personally, but she had seen the studies. Making a new connection, she directed her attention to their fallen foe.

Ruprecht exhibited no signs of healing, or indeed life.

"I'm all right," said Dorothy. "We need to move, now. Please check on Sparky."

"Is Felicia coming back?" asked Claudia.

"How should I know?" snapped Dorothy. "Can we focus on getting away from this cave first?"

Strontium attempted to push herself up, but the stump on her left wrist slid against the moist stone floor, toppling her anew. On her back, she held the ruined limb in front of her face. "Oh, hells! I lost a hand!"

Dorothy looked around the floor for fragments. "I'm sorry. I thought you knew. I don't see it anywhere, and I'm sorry again, but I don't think we should linger here searching for it."

Strontium held up the stump. "Look at it! It's not broke. It's burnt." The end of her forearm, blackened and cracked like a faded ember, put out a wisp of smoke.

"Don't touch it, it's still hot. You must have incinerated it with your spell. What was that?"

"Temporary blindness," said Strontium. "Or so I thought. Looks permanent from here."

"Why don't we take a break from the magic for a little while. Just until you have a better sense of your new body."

"No argument here."

"I have Sparky," said Claudia.

"I'm okay," croaked the pixie.

Dorothy lifted Strontium to her feet and put her undamaged arm around her shoulders to help bear her weight. "All right, people, let's clear out."

Their trek to the surface went much more sluggishly than their descent. Strontium's unsteadiness extended beyond her obvious injury. When they reached open ground, Dorothy propped the doll against a tree and tested leg and hip joints. Several had loosened in the melee, easily repairable with the screwdriver on Dorothy's multi-tool pocket knife.

"Hey, check this out," said Claudia.

Beside her, a full sheet of paper pinned to a tree with a dagger read, "Worm station." A sheath for the dagger lay at the foot of the tree.

"She'll probably want that knife back," said Strontium.

Claudia strapped the sheath to her belt. "Tough shit."

———

They arrived at the Worm station filthy and exhausted, to find Felicia sitting outside on a park bench. She wore a red and white sundress; a wide-brimmed hat with an oversized, artificial rose blossom; and sandals. The rapier in its scabbard on her back would have sharply clashed with this outfit in the world of Dorothy's youth. Here and now it wouldn't even stand out. On the ground beside her sat three paper shopping bags. "You look terrible. Where's my knife?"

"You mean my knife?" said Claudia.

"Touché." Felicia stood and handed Dorothy, Strontium and Claudia each a bag. "Change. Put your clothes in the bag and give the bag back to me."

Dorothy opened her gift. Inside she found a fresh, blue and white striped polo shirt, white shorts and checkered canvas loafers. "Where are we supposed to change?"

"I suppose that's a question of modesty, but I would recommend the ladies' room."

Dorothy found a family bathroom, and the three of them locked themselves inside. It took twenty minutes to disrobe and redress Strontium, whose torso and limbs had suffered hundreds of tiny fractures in the wake of her explosive spell, with rough edges that kept catching on the fabric of her long sleeves and ankle length capris.

Once changed, Dorothy buckled Bess to her hip. Though the short sword and scabbard went invisible, the belt itself stood out, the worn leather and clips clashing against her clean, white shorts.

Claudia donned a navy shirt dress, belted at the waist. She fished a captain's hat from her bag and modeled it in the mirror. "Yeah, I don't think so." It went back in the bag.

Newly attired and freshened as much as possible, they opened the door to the sight of a frowning mother towing two crying toddlers. Dorothy offered her best vapid giggle and shrugged as they hastily retreated. They returned to Felicia, still on the park bench.

"Where's your hat?" asked Felicia with a frown.

"I'm not wearing that."

Felicia stood. "You most certainly are. That skunk stripe in your hair might be the most identifiable feature in this group. Easy to pick out in a crowd, easy to pick out in security footage. I have tech for both of you that will interfere with facial recognition software, but there's nothing I can do about your hair."

Dorothy gazed on Claudia's white poliosis patch, a biological oddity she had come to find endearing. "She's right. I'm sorry. Cover it up."

Claudia glared back at her with narrowed eyes. She pulled the hat out of the bag and donned it, tucking stray hair underneath the sweatband. Once she finished straightening it, she stood at attention and snapped her rigid hand to the visor.

Felicia handed Dorothy and Claudia each an ear cuff. "Put these on. They generate a field that randomizes the points an AI would use to identify you. It's an electronic illusion. Your faces will still look like faces. Anyone who knows you will still recognize you on security footage, but they will have to look through it manually, which will slow them down."

Claudia eyed hers with suspicion. "Why didn't you give us these back in Kansas City?"

"I didn't have them then. If you don't trust it, don't wear it. I don't have the time or energy to sell subterfuge to you."

"I'm just saying. For someone as sneaky as you are, this seems like you're going pretty sloppy in the stealth department. It almost seems like you want to be caught."

Felicia laughed. "Is that how it seems? Maybe I'm adding risk to this operation for the sheer thrill of it. You enjoy a game of chance, don't you? Haven't you ever made a decision by flipping a coin?"

"I don't know that I would use a coin to choose between freedom and life in prison," said Dorothy.

"Well, that's you. Put the cuffs on, please."

Dorothy clipped hers to her right ear, where it buzzed faintly for half a second, then went quiet. She looked at Claudia, who shrugged and followed suit.

Felicia took the three paper bags. "I'm going to stow this in a locker. Then we need to catch a shuttle to the dock."

"There are a few things I think we need to discuss on the way," said Dorothy.

"Save it for the boat. We'll have a full day on the river with nothing to do but talk. Come on."

<hr>

The shuttle bus deposited them, and a dozen vacationers, near a spread of docks on the bank of the Red River, surrounded by activity from dozens of sailboats.

"Are we hiring a boat, or does one of these belong to you?" asked Dorothy.

"The latter. This way, please."

"Is this a good time to mention I can't swim?" asked Claudia.

"In the event of an emergency," said Strontium, "I can be used as a floatation device."

Claudia laughed. "Look at you, making airline jokes. Dotty never told me you were this cool."

"It must have slipped my mind," said Dorothy.

"Someone is going to want to keep Strontium steady on the dock," said Felicia. "It floats. I don't want you to lose your footing."

Dorothy took Strontium's hand. "Noted. Which boat is yours?"

"The one hiding in plain sight." Felicia pointed to the end of the nearest dock. Moored there, a fifteen-foot paddlewheel boat rocked gently. Its façade resembled a riverboat hotel, in miniature, with three faux stories painted in pink and white on the sidewalls. An ornate brass railing ran the whole way around the deck. Across the bow, in white cursive, read the name, "Joyhawk's Gambit."

"Please tell me you have a casino on that thing," said Claudia.

"Alas, no." Felicia led them to the boat. Closer to it, details became easier to make out. The gated rail enclosed a walkway along both sides and the bow, including a ladder to the roof, also railed in and equipped with furniture. "There are two cabins and a common room on board, all of which are a little cramped, I'm sorry to say. It's self-piloting, so we can all get a good night's sleep, which we will need before walking into a nest of thunder toads tomorrow."

"Two cabins?" said Strontium. "Hells. Does that mean I have to bunk with you?"

Felicia laughed. "Certainly not. One of the cabins is mine. You all get to share the other one."

"Dibs on the roof," said Sparky from inside Dorothy's bag.

"I may join you there," said Strontium. "Turns out I don't sleep anyway."

This brought Dorothy up short. "What? You didn't sleep last night at Felicia's apartment?"

The doll shook her head. "Spent the night in the kitchen. Didn't seem worth bothering you about."

"I suppose that leaves the other cabin for you two lovebirds," said Felicia. "See? This is turning into a romantic getaway. You're welcome."

Claudia opened the gate on the rail, hopped onto the deck, and went inside.

Dorothy helped Strontium step from the dock to the boat, then crossed over herself, watching the doll with care.

"I need to sit," said Strontium. "This floor is moving. Can a doll get seasick?"

"I'm sure not," said Dorothy.

"There are seats and a table in the common room," said Felicia. "Make yourself comfortable."

Strontium nodded. Gripping the rail with her remaining hand, she inched her way to the door and stepped inside.

"You still need me to keep my head down, boss?" said Sparky.

"Probably a good idea until we get away from all these eyes," said Dorothy.

"Gotcha." The pixie climbed over the side of Dorothy's bag and dropped to the deck, where she walked to the door. Like Claudia's white stripe, Sparky's signature orange flight streak provided too easy a marker for anyone looking for them this far from the copious pixie traffic of New Chicago.

Felicia drew a touchscreen remote control from some hiding place in her dress and entered something into it. "Trouble in paradise?"

"I don't know what you're talking about," said Dorothy.

"Sure you do." Felicia pulled the gate shut and pressed the center of her remote. Moorings detached themselves and retracted into the hull. The paddlewheel churned backward, drawing the boat away from the dock in an unhurried reverse. "Neither of you can hide your emotions. You'd both make terrible assassins."

"Thank you. That's the kindest thing I've ever heard," said Dorothy. "Don't worry about us. We're experiencing a disagreement. Nothing we can't work out."

"About me?"

"Obviously about you."

Felicia smiled. "Thank you for standing up for me, assuming you are."

"I wouldn't call it standing up, but you're welcome." Dorothy looked over her shoulder at the closed door, attempting to gauge its degree of sound-proofing. "If Strontium isn't sleeping, we may have a problem."

"How so?" said Felicia. "I would think a wooden brain is immune to the effects of sleep deprivation, no?"

"No," said Dorothy. "This isn't about neurotransmitters. It's about magic. Transformations can trigger all kinds of psychosomatic responses. Human minds tend to react to different states by clinging to their humanity. I have seen it happen to people who have been temporarily transformed into animals. Implanting a mind in an inanimate object is unfamiliar territory for me, but we have to assume it runs the same risk. There is a good chance Strontium may start experiencing symptoms of sleep deprivation simply because on some level she believes she should. We will need to keep a sharp eye on her."

"I see," said Felicia. "Yet another variable I did not anticipate. I am sorry about that."

"Those are starting to pile up. You should also be aware that what she did to that dragon was unintentional. She can wield magic in this body, but not in a way that will be predictable. If her judgment starts to slip the longer she stays awake, we may be looking at a very real danger."

Felicia sighed. "Understood. I'll do whatever I can to keep her from hurting herself or anyone else."

"Thank you." Dorothy scrutinized the assassin's face, now oddly subdued. "What aren't you telling me?"

Felicia turned her gaze to the river. The wheel came to a stop, and allowed the boat to drift for a few seconds before engaging in the opposite direction, propelling the boat in a new heading with a bit more vigor. "The same as anyone doesn't tell anyone: almost everything."

"You know what I mean."

"I already told you this isn't going to be your chance to get the know the real me, so cut the shit, O'Neill."

"I have no interest in getting to know the real you," said Dorothy. "The real you is a vile harpy who kills for money and sport. I despise the real you, and the only thing I appreciate about working with you is you have kept her so well concealed from me. So, when I ask what you aren't telling me, I don't mean you should open up and tell me your feelings. I mean you should come clean about what's really happening on this half-assed quest."

Felicia turned to face Dorothy, and for a moment, her eyes took on a softness at odds with her entire character trait inventory. "Well. That's a lot to process. Would you mind being more specific?"

"I'd be delighted. What happened in that cave?"

"Your girlfriend and sister-witch killed a dragon. Rather clumsily, I might add."

"Yes, they did," said Dorothy. "After which you fell apart over it. Why? What was he to you?"

"A means to an end. I have been nothing but transparent about my professional relationship with that worm, and I do not grieve his loss."

"All right, let's explore that for a bit. He wanted to eat one of us. Why?"

Felicia shrugged. "Because he was a dick?"

"I know a lot of dicks. None of them ever tried to kill and devour my loved ones."

"Basil did. He would have eaten you all, you know."

The image of the half-dragon newly assailed Dorothy, now replete with the remains of her then five-year-old adoptive sister Melody dangling from his jaws. "Oh, for God's sake! Don't change the subject! He said he wanted to see what it did to you. What did he mean by that? What did you mean when you said he knew what they did? Who are they, and what did they do?"

"Oh," said Felicia. "That. I won't be answering those questions. Is that all you have?"

"Fine. Keep that to yourself as long as it doesn't get us all killed. We have a bigger issue than that. Ruprecht's story contradicts what you already told us about the Scale. What was all that about ripping the Scale from her own body? You said she lost it in an attack. You also said her reign declined after that event, but Ruprecht said the Scale was the key to her power. What about Atrylyn losing it in a duel? Should I ask which one of you is wrong, or which one of you is lying?"

Felicia sighed. "That's much easier to answer. Neither and neither. I understand you have very little experience in this arena, so I can forgive your confusion. It's not uncommon for legends about real events to vary in the telling. The objective truth is probably somewhere between what I told you and what he told us. Hypatia ruled her empire for hundreds of years, and by all accounts did so with fairness and compassion, uncommon traits in a dragon, as I'm sure you know. Did you hear anything to contradict that? Did you hear anything to contradict the Scale is a tool for healing? He said himself it wasn't a weapon, which is exactly what I have promised you all along. When Atrylyn had the Scale, and how she lost it, are of no consequence to the mission. In either version of the story, her fortress is still our next stop."

"Really?" said Dorothy. "I would have thought with something this powerful, the devil would be in the details. I can't help but think the explanation you just gave me would be indistinguishable from what someone who knew nothing at all about the Scale would tell me. I also can't help but wonder if you have dragged us along on a fool's errand, driven by your desperation for whatever gain the Scale will bring you, and your desperate hope it will all work out if you keep pushing forward."

Felicia waited a beat before asking, "Are you finished?"

Dorothy shook her head. "What is this about? What does the Scale mean to you?"

"We are very close to getting you what you need, after which point my problems will be none of your concern," said Felicia. "We have about half an hour of daylight left. I'm going to retire, and I suggest you do the same."

Dorothy put her hand on Felicia's shoulder, bracing for a flinch that didn't come. "You wanted my help. Let me help you. Is what you're hiding from me really worse than what I already know about you? I'm still here, Felicia. Be straight with me."

Felicia looked down. She reached for Dorothy's hand, and laid her own on it. They stood there in silence for a few seconds. Then Felicia gently removed Dorothy's hand from her shoulder, strode away without making eye contact, and scaled the ladder to the roof, where she took a seat in a reclining chair and stared at the cloudless sky.

Dorothy looked back at the receding dock as the sailboats shrank away from her. As she invited their beauty to calm her current agitation, an inescapable truth struck her. Each gracefully cruising hull bore one or more souls fighting their own unique battles.

[14]

GAUNTLET

Perched on the edge of the NCSA building roof, Dorothy faced away from the street below, spread her arms, and leaned backward. Freefall did not trigger the expected discomfort or nausea. She found the sensation indistinguishable from floating on her back in a warm pool on a hot summer day. Wind trickled upward past her ears and tossed her hair in a pleasing manner.

Above her, hovering and yet descending with her, her ten-year-old adoptive step-sister Melody Cody looked down on her in curiosity. She beat her purple butterfly wings, sending a downdraft to compete with the wind rushing up from beneath her. "Dorrie? What are you doing?"

"I'm flying," said Dorothy. "I figured it out."

Melody giggled. "Silly, that's not flying. That's falling."

Dorothy woke with a start. Her surroundings greeted her with comfort but unfamiliarity, and it took a few seconds to resolve them into the tiny cabin aboard Felicia's riverboat. She rolled over in an otherwise empty bed, finding herself alone in the room. Sunlight provided partial illumination through a single porthole, but not in a way that gave clear indication of the time of day.

She rolled out of bed, still dressed in her polo and shorts, and ventured out, barefoot, to the similarly unoccupied combination galley/dining room/living room. After a short visit to the head (barely a closet, but sufficiently equipped with toilet and sink), she went out on deck. From the walkway, the noonday sun more clearly presented itself.

This far from the city, the view of the riverbank consisted only of desert landscape.

Voices came from above. Dorothy ascended the ladder to the roof, and found Claudia and Strontium lounging there in chairs. Sparky sat on a table next to a square glass filled with amber liquid and ice.

"Morning, sleepyhead," said Strontium.

"Good morning." Dorothy pointed to the glass. "Is that whiskey?"

"Cool your jets," said Claudia. "It's afternoon. I'm allowed."

"So much wrong with what you just said, but let's start with afternoon. Why didn't anyone wake me?"

"Didn't see the point. You looked so peaceful there. I figured I would leave you to your dreams."

Torn between whether to be touched and grateful for the gesture, annoyed by the presumption, or bitter about the dream Claudia had in fact left her to, Dorothy dropped the matter. "Where's Felicia?"

"Is that a joke?" said Strontium. "Do the math. She's in her cabin."

"Has anyone seen her yet today?"

"Yepper. She got up around dawn and did a hundred laps around the deck." Strontium illustrated this by twirling her finger several times. "That's not an estimate. One hundred laps on the nose. Then she went back inside. Hasn't come out since."

"Which is fine by me." Claudia took a sip of her drink.

"Will you put that down, please?" said Dorothy. "We have a big day ahead of us, and I don't want to spend any of it sobering you up."

Claudia, still holding the glass, gulped the contents before setting it back on the table.

"I suppose there was little hope in asking you to act like an adult for one day. Have you at least had something to eat, or are you now liquored up on an empty stomach?"

"I had a sandwich. I'm fine."

At the mention of food, a pang of hunger hit Dorothy in the gut, simultaneous with the awareness of how long she had now gone without eating. "That makes one of us, then."

A *boom* sounded in the distance, from somewhere upstream. A few moments later, a louder explosive noise followed, which trailed off to a low rumble.

Claudia sat up. "What the hell was that?"

Sparky's eyes went wide, and she pulled her knees to her chest. "That was a thunder toad. We must be getting close."

"That was a toad?" said Claudia. "Holy shit."

Felicia poked her head out the door and called up from below. "I assume you all heard that? Would everyone come downstairs, please?"

Dorothy helped Strontium down the ladder. The tiny fissures in the surface of the doll's finish had collected some grime since the day before, rendering them more visible, and more plentiful than Dorothy realized. They all made their way to the common room, where Felicia had laid two folded black outfits on the table.

"O'Neill and de Queiroz, you'll want to suit up for this. We will be at Atrylyn's islands in about two and a half hours. These jumpsuits will give you more mobility than what you're wearing, and pockets for the equipment we need to carry in."

"Equipment?" said Dorothy.

"Where's my jumpsuit?" asked Strontium.

"You're not coming," said Felicia. "Between your missing hand and your joints repeatedly coming loose, you'll be a liability. I'm sorry to be so blunt."

"Horse pucky! You can't leave me behind. That's a magician's library in there! This is the first part of your mad plan where you actually need me."

"O'Neill should be enough witch for what we're doing here today. Thank you for offering, but—"

Strontium pounded her charred stump on the table. "That little girl hasn't got a clue about what you'll find in there! I've been doing magic for twice her lifetime over! You're going to choose a wizard's apprentice over that?"

Dorothy put her hand on Strontium's handless wrist. "Sister, we're only worried about your safety. If anything happens to you—"

Strontium jerked her arm back. "Who's this 'we'? You think that killer gives a hot damn about my safety?" She pointed to Felicia with the stump. Her felt-tip face continued to smile childishly at everyone in the room.

Dorothy looked at Felicia, who gave her the slightest shake of her head. "Sister, I am asking you, as the person who cares about you more than anyone else in the world—"

"That would be Ian, not you. Let go of this, child. You can't stop me coming in there with you."

"All right," said Felicia. "Come then. I won't be held responsible for your fate in there."

"There's your true colors," said Strontium. "Worried, my ass."

"With that settled..." Felicia turned her attention to Sparky. "I trust you will offer less resistance to being left behind?"

"Yes, ma'am! No resistance at all!"

"Wait," said Dorothy. "We can't bring Sparky?"

"Thunder toads eat pixies," said Felicia.

Claudia broke the awkward silence following that statement. "There's something that eats pixies?"

"I really don't want to talk about this," said Sparky.

"Damn."

"What equipment are we taking with us?" Dorothy picked up her jumpsuit and looked it over.

"Rope, burglar's tools, things of that nature," said Felicia. "Apart from getting past the toads, which will not be fun, Atrylyn's library will have booby-traps that need to be disarmed."

"You do understand we have no experience with that?" asked Dorothy.

"Follow my lead, and you'll be fine. The traps aren't anything deadly or particularly dangerous, just discouraging. Spells of uncontrollable itching, piercing noises, severe diarrhea, and so on. Their intent is repulsion, not violence. Atrylyn was strongly averse to harming others, even those she considered mortal enemies."

"I bet that made her easy to murder," said Claudia.

Felicia gritted her teeth and looked away from her taunter. "Not as easy as you might think."

"That's enough," said Dorothy. "Focus on the mission, please."

"I'm not the one who needs to worry about losing focus." Claudia stood, collected her jumpsuit, retreated to her cabin and slammed the door.

"Christ on a stick."

The *Joyhawk's Gambit* coasted to a stop. The rotten wooden dock it came to rest against bowed under the weight of dozens of greenish-brown amphibians, each one the size of a bear cub. Beyond the dock, they covered the island, easily numbering in the hundreds. Tongues shot into the air a few at a time, in a perpetual feeding ballet. Somewhere among them, one croaked. The sound split the air and rumbled out.

"Jesus!" said Claudia. "How the fuck do we get past those?"

"Very carefully, as they say." Felicia handed Dorothy and Claudia each a pair of earplugs, then passed them a box of latex gloves. "Don't touch their skin, unless you want to spend the next two days hallucinating, and risk permanent brain damage. Don't agitate them if you can help it. A few thunder-croaks will be an inconvenience. If we trigger a cascade, these earplugs won't be worth a damn."

"Are you sure you want to do this?" Dorothy asked Strontium.

"I don't have ears and I don't have skin," said the witch-doll. "I'll be fine."

"What could possibly go wrong?" muttered Claudia.

"We won't be able to hear much until we get inside, so everyone keep an eye on everyone else as we cross, please. I don't want anyone to be left behind." Felicia fixed her own plugs in place.

Claudia faced away from her and said quietly, "I hate you."

Felicia stepped off the boat, planting her foot in the gap between two toads. "I know. And no, I can't hear you. You're that predictable."

"La-de-da." Claudia inserted her earplugs.

Dorothy drew a leather purse from her bag, and poured several small, polished crystals into her palm. She selected an amber one, riddled with flaws, and put the others away. Focusing on the dozen or so toads nearest to her, she whispered over the crystal, then tossed it into their midst. A visible wave rippled outward from it as it struck the ground, enveloping the animals. When it dissipated, they all slumped down, eyes closed, bodies still pulsing with breath.

Felicia offered a nod of approval for this tactic, and stepped gingerly through the pack of sleeping toads.

Even given the magical assist, traversing the land from riverbank to crumbling fortress proved tricky, but doable with patience. Every two minutes or so, a distant, random toad would produce the dreaded thunder. Despite her certainty of mental preparation, Dorothy jumped every time. The gaps between detonations allowed for her heart rate to return to normal, but no more respite than that.

Strontium, ahead of Dorothy and never out of her sight, tripped over a toad and landed face down on another. The toad under her responded to the affront with an explosive croak, issuing sufficient force to flip the doll in the air and drop her on another of its ilk. The next toad responded in similar fashion.

Felicia, on point, spun around and shouted, "Everyone freeze!"

Dorothy complied with the unnecessary command, desperately hoping a third croak would not come. Once certain the immediate noise danger had passed, she made her way to Strontium, and pulled her upright.

Strontium shook off the assistance. "I'm fine!"

The closer they got to the ruins, the fewer toads they encountered, until eventually they could walk freely. Felicia reached the wall first, and waited. Once the party had all gathered there, she removed her plugs.

"Are you all right?" she asked Strontium.

"Never better," said the witch-doll.

"That wasn't so bad," said Claudia. "Oh, wait. Shit. Did I just jinx everything?"

"Probably," said Felicia. "If anything goes badly now, we'll all know it was your fault."

"Can we not do this right now?" said Dorothy. "How close are we to the library?"

Felicia pointed to the narrow river separating the two islands. A footbridge extended from the fortress to a similar structure on the other side. "If we can get up to that walkway, I know how to jimmy the door from there."

"I can jump at least that high," said Dorothy.

"We can't get in through the hole in the wall?" said Claudia.

Felicia frowned. "What are you talking about?"

Claudia pointed behind her, in the opposite direction of the bridge. "You didn't see the pile of rubble crossing over? Pretty sure there's a hole behind it."

"Show me."

Claudia led the three of them down the wall and around an obtuse corner. A few yards beyond lay several chunks of broken stone. "That."

Felicia approached the discovery with obvious caution. One of the fragments clashed with the masonry both in color and texture, revealing itself on closer inspection to be metal, not stone. A broad wooden pole sat lodged in it, its end snapped off and badly splintered.

"That there's a troll hammer," said Strontium. "Either we got company, or we missed the party."

"Damn it," whispered Felicia.

A gap, tall and wide enough for two grown men to enter walking side by side, led to an open passage. Half the shattered rubble from the troll assault had fallen inward.

"Do we proceed?" asked Dorothy.

Felicia climbed over the rocks in reply.

Dorothy donned her headlamp and helped Strontium navigate the makeshift entrance. Inside, rather than the booby traps Felicia prepped them for, they found only broken furniture. A ram's horn lay split near the entrance, likely once an enchanted alarm whose wail would have made advancing—or even thinking—impossible, now spent. Some distance into their incursion, Dorothy stepped over several torn burlap bags, empty but still putting forth traces of a sour aroma she recognized from her lessons with Aplomado on defensive mixtures as a powder of perpetual itching. Some luckless troll had taken that bullet for them long ago.

Felicia crouched by an overturned table, poking at fragments of broken, green glass with a stick. "This was her laboratory. You wouldn't know it now. Come on." She stood, and walked through a smashed wooden door into a corridor. They followed her as she strolled down the hall with no clear sense of urgency or emotional response to the unexpected destruction. They passed two lethargic thunder toads, and gave them wide berths.

The library, identifiable as such only by the handful of tattered scrolls left behind by looters, lay in a similar state of devastation. Felicia plodded into the center of the room, stood still for a few seconds, then fell to her knees and hung her head in silence.

"Now what?" whispered Claudia.

"Do you know *Reveal Map*?" asked Strontium.

"No, but give me a minute." Dorothy held out her palm and willed her spellbook forth from its storage space in her own person. It shimmered into existence there, and she thumbed through it to find the incantation.

"I can do it if you need me to," said Strontium.

"Don't, please. I have it." Dorothy dissolved the book back into herself, then extended her arm and made a fist. She spoke a three-syllable chant in repetition until a sphere of pale blue light formed around her closed hand. Taking a deep breath, she counted to seven, then spread her fingers. The light pulsed outward, expanding to fill the room, then vanished. "Look for a glow, anywhere in the room. If the map is still here, even if she concealed it, we will see something."

"It won't be," said Felicia. "And even if you can find it—"

"Found it." Claudia pointed upward. The ceiling shone back at her in thin, illuminated trails and radiant landmarks.

"Damn, that's clever," said Strontium. "Can't steal a roof."

Dorothy formed opposing ells with her thumbs and forefinger, and looked through this frame at the map above her. A copy of the image detached itself from the ceiling and descended, shrinking to a few inches in length. She produced her book again, and opened it to a blank page near the back. The floating image landed on the paper and fixed itself there. She snapped the book shut and reabsorbed it. "We have it now, Felicia."

Felicia stood. "It doesn't matter! Look around you! Do you see a spellbook? Without Atrylyn's knowledge of how to operate the Scale, finding it won't give us anything but a piece of dragon hide."

"Maybe we can bring this to the Council of Mages," said Dorothy. "I know that's not what you want to hear, but—"

"They won't help me with this."

"No, they won't, but they might help me. You said you wanted to use the Scale for healing. If I tell them that—"

"They won't do it!" said Felicia. "Nothing you tell them will persuade them to do this for me!"

"Spellbooks leave a residue," said Strontium. "Depending what she had in it, I might be able to recover some by scraping the ether in this room. Been a long time since I did an ether-scrape, but I think I still have one in me."

"I don't know if that's such a good idea," said Dorothy. "We would only recover spell fragments at best, and there's a risk of damaging the walls. I don't want to be trapped in here if the scrape takes too long."

"Nonsense. Won't take more than a minute."

"Is this something you can do?" Claudia asked Dorothy.

"No, and I don't think you should try it either, Strontium. Let's take a moment, please, and consider our options."

"Child, I have this." Strontium raised her one good hand and her stump, then held them vertically aligned. Yellow light arced from her fingers to her stump. She swept this line in a slow circle around the room. Random sparks leapt from the walls, as did flakes of stone.

Dorothy summoned her spellbook to absorb these sparks, and whatever information they carried. The scrape drew more residual magic from the room than Dorothy expected, perhaps enough to reassemble the proper spell once she had a chance to inventory it. Unfortunately, it also created the exact hazard Dorothy feared, as a crack appeared in the far wall and ran up to the ceiling. "Sister, stop!"

Strontium ignored this directive. A piece of the wall the size of a golf ball snapped inward, pelting Claudia in the leg.

"Fuck! God damn it, Strontium!" Rubbing her injury, Claudia stepped backward, toward a thunder toad that had until then lain camouflaged in a dark corner.

"Claudia!" shouted Dorothy. "Look out!"

Too late, Claudia spun. Her foot caught on a crack in the floor, and she tumbled, planting her face directly onto the toad's back.

Dorothy pressed her hands against her ears, a fraction of a second before the thunder-croak. The shockwave pounded the room, tossed Claudia off the toad's back, and sent Strontium sprawling.

Though her quick thinking had saved Dorothy from the brunt of the sonic boom to preserve some of her hearing, the pain still staggered her. Claudia would heal them all as soon as she regained her composure enough to speak.

"Fuck!" Claudia shouted. "I got it in my mouth! I got it in my mouth! Dotty! Help me!"

Dorothy froze. Claudia's words did indeed heal her inner ears, but they represented a crisis she had no plan for.

As Claudia's eyes rolled into her head, the hallucinogenic toad-skin secretions taking hold, Felicia ran to her side.

Dorothy spared a glance back at Strontium, who had gotten back to her feet. The doll gave a feeble thumbs-up.

Claudia collapsed to the floor. Felicia pulled a hypodermic from a pocket on her jumpsuit, tossed aside the cap and jabbed the needle into Claudia's arm. "Stay with me, de Queiroz. Think about the happiest place you've ever been. Happy thoughts. Thoughts of comfort. What's your favorite food?"

Claudia shrieked.

"Shh! It's all right. I've got you." Felicia stroked Claudia's forehead and cheek, and her eyelids fluttered in response.

"This…" Claudia gulped. "My fault. Jinxed the mission."

"No," said Felicia. "No, honey, you did everything right. There was no jinx."

"Promise…?"

"Cross my heart." Felicia, tears running down her cheeks, kissed Claudia on the forehead.

Dorothy took a step back, uncertain whether to be more concerned about Claudia's hallucinations or Felicia's uncharacteristic behavior. This murderer, this soulless monster had shifted into full, compassionate nursing mode. Diabolic act? Personality transplant? Angelic possession?

"Hang on…" Dorothy drew Bess.

Do you need protection?

"Information." Dorothy held the blade out at arm's length, with the flat facing Felicia and Claudia. Their images, reflected in the polished iron, revealed a green aura around Felicia's body. "How could I have been so stupid?"

"Dorothy." Felicia wiped her eyes. "We need to get her back to the boat. The drug I gave her will help fight off the hallucinations, but the best treatment is comfort."

Dorothy walked to Claudia and knelt beside her. She took her face in her hands and kissed her gently on the lips, causing her twitching to partially subside.

"That will help," said Felicia. "Help me get her to her feet, please."

"There is an enchantment on you," said Dorothy, still looking at

Claudia. "I assume you have been under this spell since you first came to me. Am I correct?"

Felicia hesitated. "Yes."

"Are you under the control of a wizard? Please know if you lie to me about this, I will kill you, here and now."

"I swear to you, I am not."

Dorothy allowed herself a moment of belief before pressing forward. "I need to know the exact nature of this spell before we take one more step on this journey. Who cast it? When? Why? What effects are you experiencing?"

Felicia took a deep breath. "Please don't ask me that. Please. If you have any mercy whatsoever."

"Answer my questions or die."

Felicia choked off a sob. "I don't know the name of the wizard who cast the spell. I'm sorry."

"Keep talking."

"There is a new assassins' guild. I offered them my services, but my failure at Fenway has crippled my reputation. They needed assurances, so they hired a wizard to burden me with this obstacle. They need me to prove I can overcome it."

"What obstacle?" said Dorothy.

"Please. Dorothy. I am begging. Don't do this."

Dorothy turned to face Felicia, her face now a mess of tears and bloodshot eyes. "What. Obstacle."

Felicia hung her head, gripped with new sobs. After about ten seconds of sniffing, hyperventilating, and regaining what little composure she could, she raised her eyes.

"Empathy."

[15]

CONFERENCE

D orothy sat by Claudia's bedside for the better part of an hour, waiting for her to sleep. During that time, Claudia rambled incoherently, in a state somewhere below true consciousness. Felicia's counter-agent to the hallucinogen also acted as a sedative, providing her patient the necessary relaxation to fight off the toxin, but frustrating Dorothy terribly in preventing her from communicating with the woman she loved.

At last, Claudia's babbling settled into a soft snore. Dorothy leaned over to give her a kiss. Claudia's cold lips did not respond, but Dorothy lingered there anyway, in the hope some of the sentiment might yet find its way into Claudia's heart.

She made her way to the roof of the *Joyhawk's Gambit*, now paddling downstream. Strontium stood at the rail there, watching the river go by. She turned to look at Dorothy, providing an excellent view of the new damage she suffered in Atrylyn's library. Her head had split on hitting the floor, leaving an angry crack on the right side of her face. It ran through the drawn-on eye, and severed the smile into something less cheery. "How is she?"

"Sleeping. Finally." Dorothy looked toward Felicia, seated, facing away, clutching a mug of coffee in both hands. "We need to have a conference."

Sparky, sunbathing on a cloth napkin spread out on the table, sat up. "The four of us?"

"The five of us." Dorothy drew Bess.
Do you need protection?

113

"Counsel," said Dorothy. "You are as much a member of this expedition as any of us, and I want to hear whatever you have to say."

You honor me with your respect.

"You've earned it. Felicia? I need your attention, please."

Felicia looked up. "Yes?"

"First of all, I need to know if Claudia is going to be all right," said Dorothy. "Tell me she will be all right. Because so help me, if this scheme of yours costs Claudia her mind—"

"She will recover," said Felicia. "If she were at risk for brain damage we would have seen nosebleeds by now. She needs rest, but she will be all right."

Dorothy nodded. "I will take you at your word. We need to discuss the other matter."

"Is this where you tell me our partnership has come to an end? If so… I would like to part ways amicably, if at all possible. I will buy your passage back to New Chicago, and provide you with anything you ask of me to make amends, short of turning myself in."

"I'm afraid I don't have that luxury," said Dorothy. "Even if I did, the answer to your question would still be no. I intend to see this through, though probably not the way you intended."

Felicia took a deep breath. "All right. You have my attention."

"Good. First of all, I need full disclosure on one point of information. Do you plan to remove the enchantment of empathy with the Scale? Was that always your intent?"

"Yes," said Felicia.

"Thank you for your honesty," said Dorothy. "I'm sure you can appreciate why I can't allow that to happen."

"That's not up to you."

"Right now, everything is up to me, so let's not waste any of the time we have together dancing around that point."

Felicia shrugged. "Conceded."

"Thank you," said Dorothy. "Now, as I said, I can't allow that to happen. I'd like to talk about alternatives."

Felicia offered a bitter laugh at that. "Alternatives to being who I really am? I can't imagine you have anything to offer me on that count."

"That's not how I see it. From what I've seen, there is a version of you, the real you, with the potential to be so much more than you've let yourself believe you can be."

"You've seen nothing but the façade of this spell. Underneath it, I am the same person who twisted a knife in your shoulder to hear your sweet, sweet screams. Without it, I would do that again without hesitation."

Dorothy looked at Strontium. "Can an empathy enchantment create feelings of friendship?"

"Nope," said the witch.

"I'm not your friend," said Felicia.

"Really?" said Dorothy. "I'm not sure whether you heard yourself use the word 'amicably' just now, but it sounded pretty sincere to me. I think your new perspective has given you permission to consider new ideas, and form new connections."

Felicia looked away. "Friendship is a distraction. I have never needed it before, and I certainly don't welcome it now. This magic in my brain is not a new perspective. It is nothing but a weakness."

Dorothy shook her head. "No, it's a cure."

"Cure?" said Felicia. "I think you left out the s."

Dorothy sighed. "I understand why you think of this as a curse—"

"You understand nothing! You think this is a cure? Do you imagine this spell has given me my first taste of empathy? That I finally know what it's like to have a conscience? That's not how it works. The empathy was always there, and I have spent a lifetime learning how to suppress it. My mentors taught me how to view the enemy through the coldest of lenses. It's a skill, and it took me years of arduous work and sacrifice to master. When I took a contract, I could expertly dehumanize my target. It was a job, and I took great pleasure in doing it well."

Felicia paused there and looked away. "Yes, I learned to enjoy cruelty. Inflicting pain is its own art form, and when the job called for it, I delivered it like a master. This spell... It strips away my ability to choose. Now all I can think about is the families my victims left behind. The ambitions they left unfulfilled. The pain and fear they experienced at the moment of death. The profound injustice of it all. I can't brush it aside anymore."

"What you call mentors I call brainwashers," said Dorothy. "They took you in as a child and taught you to ignore your conscience. You don't have to do that anymore."

"I *want* to ignore my conscience!" said Felicia. "You think this spell has made me see the light? That I know what it means to be a good person now? What do you imagine happens next? Should I learn a new trade? Go to college like you? Put the past behind me and start a new life? Raise a family?"

"Any of those things, yes," said Dorothy. "Or more."

"A quaint fantasy," said Felicia. "Let me ask you a question, as someone who has chosen to care about the welfare of others her whole life. What do you think my forced empathy will teach me to feel?"

"Love, for starters. You can build relationships now. I've seen you make headway there already. We are social beings Felicia. We need companions. You can have that now."

Felicia smiled, and for the first time since joining her on this endeavor, Dorothy recognized the plastic smile she knew so well from being her victim. "Love. Of course you would say love. What a picture-perfect frame of reference you must enjoy. No, Dorothy, my dear, sweet, faux friend. It's not love I feel. All I have in me these days is remorse."

Dorothy looked down. "I'm sorry. So sorry, truly. I know this will be difficult to believe right now, but you will move past that. Everyone has regrets."

"Regrets? Who said anything about regret? I regret many things. Wasted opportunities, gambles that didn't play out, so many times I turned right when turning left would have been to my advantage. I know how to manage regret. What I feel now is remorse. Mind-numbing, soul-crushing remorse. The absolute certainty I have done the wrong thing, over and over and over for twenty years of my life, and no reparations, no gestures of goodwill no matter how grand will ever, ever set it right. Does everyone have that? Do you?"

Dorothy bit her lip and looked away. "No."

"Well then," said Felicia. "There we are. Please, please, spare me your sanctimonious platitudes. You can never understand my pain, and you can never appreciate my need to be rid of it. There is only one path that takes me there, so unless you are willing to help me find the Scale and undo this curse, we have nothing left to discuss."

"Except you don't really know if that will work," said Dorothy. "Do you?"

Felicia scowled and looked down.

"I'm right, aren't I?" said Dorothy. "Empathy spells aren't meant to be used like this. They are defensive magic intended for use on beasts to make them vulnerable and easy to kill or escape from. There is no precedent for what you are trying to do. You're just guessing it will end your pain. There is no guarantee lifting this spell will restore you to who you were before. You could end up worse in any number of ways."

"You've done your homework," said Felicia.

Dorothy held up her hand. The red leather spellbook materialized in it. "Homework is my forte."

Felicia nodded. "I'm willing to take my chances."

"That's a hell of a chance to take just to go back to being a murderer," said Dorothy.

"Can we kill her now?" asked Sparky.

I will dispatch her at your command, said Bess.

"No!" said Dorothy. "Stand down! Both of you!"

"Both?" said Felicia. "The sword wants me dead as well? How do you feel, Miss Strontium?"

"I've taken a bit of a shine to you, since you ask," said Strontium. "This version, anyway. Never met the evil you."

"Two to two," said Felicia. "Should we wake the tie-breaker downstairs, or do I get a vote?"

"We are not voting on whether to kill you!" said Dorothy. "No one is killing anyone!"

"Aw," said Sparky.

"Cling to your child's fantasy of redemption for me all you want," said Felicia. "I hope for your sake when the time comes to admit it's impossible, you don't feel what I feel now when you have no choice but to put me down."

"As much as I do want to redeem you, that's not actually why I still need you alive," said Dorothy. "We are still on a mission to find that scale. I can't leave Strontium in this state. We have to see this through to the end."

"Don't you worry about me, sister," said Strontium. "Buy me a new hand when we get back to Chicago. I'll be fine in this body however long I'm stuck in it."

"No, you won't," said Dorothy. "You've already gone two days without sleep, and now Claudia is suffering the consequences."

"That's not on me."

"I'm sorry, but it is. I hoped the loss of sleep wouldn't affect you, but your judgment is clearly impaired. Between your difficulty wielding magic and your sleep deprivation, you are rapidly becoming a liability."

"Fiddle-faddle!" said Strontium. "I'm fine!"

"You're not fine," said Dorothy, "and I think you know it. You want to put on a brave face so we don't worry about you, but it's more than the danger you represent in this state. If you continue missing sleep, you will go mad. I don't enjoy being blunt about this, but it's true. I'm the one who led you into this disaster, and I cannot stand by and watch you slowly lose your mind over my bad choice. Felicia, I cannot honor our original agreement to help you use the Scale for your own purposes, but I still need to find the Scale. I would like to discuss any other terms you would accept to finish this quest with me."

Felicia stood. "Save your breath. I will finish this quest with you, if such a thing is still possible, with no need for compensation."

"That sounds a little too easy," said Strontium. "Why?"

"Because I care what happens to you. There's no point in concealing that anymore."

Dorothy bit her cheeks.

"Don't you dare smile at that, Dorothy O'Neill. It's not real concern. It's compulsory. I truly hope one day to tell you all to go to hell, and mean it. Until then…" Felicia bowed. "I remain at your mercy." Without waiting for a response, she slid down the ladder to the walkway, went inside and slammed the door.

[16]

COMPROMISE

Dorothy woke in darkness to the sound of whimpering. Claudia had yet to regain a coherent state of mind, and whatever false images served as her dreams provided many opportunities for cries of distress. As much as she wanted to be there when Claudia woke, Dorothy needed some air on this restless night.

Outside, this close to morning, the sliver of waxing moon lay hidden below the horizon, providing no illumination. Dorothy turned on the floodlamps to survey the landscape. The riverbank stared back at her, fixed in place. She leaned over the rail. Water drifted past the hull, stern to bow. She walked back to the paddlewheel, newly aware of the absence of its churning, and found it stationary.

"What are you doing up?"

Dorothy jumped at the sound of Felicia's voice. She turned to find the former assassin leaning against the rail, plucking petals from a rose and dropping them in the river. "I could ask you the same. Why aren't we moving?"

"I dropped anchor around midnight," said Felicia. "Claudia will need another day to recover from the toad venom. We shouldn't move her, and I didn't think it wise for us to spend a day moored at the docks like sitting ducks waiting for someone to come arrest us."

"Oh." Dorothy looked out over the river trickling by. "I needed a break from watching the woman I love suffer in her sleep. Is it okay that I stepped out? Does she need to be monitored?"

"No, there's nothing you can do for her at this point. She wouldn't know whether you're there or not."

"What about you?"

"Getting ready for my morning run. You're standing in my road, by the way." Felicia tossed the naked rose stem into the water.

"Will you two keep it down?" came Strontium's voice from above. "Some of us are pretending to sleep."

"I will leave you both in peace, then." Dorothy entered the common room and took a seat at the dining table. Wishing for a book to pass the time, she remembered she had one and opened her hand. The small, red leather-bound tome materialized there. She flipped to the back and found the map image she had scanned from Atrylyn's ceiling. Every detail appeared on the page in stark black, as though scratched there with a dip pen and India ink. The enchantress had clearly labeled her own keep with the word "sanctum." Dorothy followed the trail of the river from there with her finger until it put forth a tiny, white spark as she reached their own location.

Outside the porthole, Felicia ran by, the padding of her footfalls so soft as to be inaudible. Dorothy closed her eyes, and concentrated on her equilibrium. Aplomado had taught her methods of magically enhancing her own senses, including her sense of balance. As Felicia completed her circuit around the walkway, the boat shifted under her weight, side to side, to and fro, describing an elliptical rocking, likely less than a degree in each direction.

Returning her attention to the map, near the top, she located the words "Legatum Hypatiae." Hypatia's Legacy? Surely a reference to the Scale. Unfortunately, distances on the image appeared to be out of proportion, evoking a general set of instructions rather than a true map. Latin phrases littered the drawing, associated with arrows, some of which contradicted others. Above their objective (assuming she correctly interpreted it), three toes, like a bird's foot, pointed downward.

The rocking ceased. A few seconds later, the door opened. Felicia crossed the room, took a dishtowel from the perfunctory kitchen counter and wiped her brow with it before sitting down opposite Dorothy.

"How's your Latin?" asked Dorothy.

"Excellent. Wizards tend to write in Mock Latin, however, which can be more challenging."

"Great. This is going to take some decoding."

"You know," said Felicia, "we still have the problem of the missing spellbook."

"I am aware," said Dorothy. "I still think we should engage the help of the Council of Mages. If you help me find the Scale, I will take it from there."

"I don't fancy being arrested at the end of this quest."

"Then I will give you a wide head start before calling Aplomado. The only one who gets arrested will be me."

"Agreed," said Felicia.

Dorothy paused. "Unless you want to reconsider turning yourself in. Given your current state, we might be able to get you a pardon, or a suspended sentence or something."

Felicia shook her head. "You aren't going to give this up, are you?"

"I don't think so, no."

"That isn't what I want. I would rather spend the rest of my life in prison without this spell in my head than live free with the pain."

"Then... then maybe you should turn yourself in for that reason," said Dorothy. "There are many ways to lift an enchantment. You don't need the Scale. Ask the council to wipe the spell in exchange for a plea bargain, and go to jail."

"This conversation is not taking a very Felicia-friendly direction."

"You said you'd rather be in prison with the enchantment removed. I am offering you that."

"As a last resort!" said Felicia. "We're hardly there, yet."

"Do you have a better idea?" asked Dorothy. "Do you think you can find another wizard to do this for you?"

"Don't you think I would have tried that first? None of the independent wizards will risk crossing the assassins' guild." Felicia leaned back in her chair. "You know, yesterday, when you thought I was in top form, you despised me. Today, now that you know I have been neutered, you have made me your personal project. I must say, I don't care for this."

Dorothy looked away. "I didn't despise you yesterday."

"No? The real me is a vile harpy? That doesn't sound familiar?" Felicia pouted and said in a childish voice, "Words hurt, Dorothy."

"Mock all you want. I still believe we can find a solution to this problem."

"Oh." Felicia cracked her knuckles. "There is a solution. It's elegant, and simple, and it will get me everything I want. All I have to do is push past the empathy to make it happen. The guild gave me ten contracts. People of no consequence, men, women, and children, arbitrarily chosen for this assignment. Once all ten are dead by my hand, they will remove the curse."

Dorothy's heart accelerated. "Are any of them... have you...?"

"Not yet, no."

"Maybe that should tell you something. Instead of going after those ten people, you came to me. Isn't it possible you want my help more than you want to shake off this spell?"

"I knew what those kills would do to me," said Felicia. "No, thank you. I am not that desperate yet, though I haven't ruled it out."

"Rule it out, please." Dorothy looked at the map again. "What if… what if we compromise? What if I help you use the Scale to lift the enchantment, and you swear to me you will retire from killing?"

Felicia laughed and shook her head. "That's…" Her smile faded. "That's oddly tempting."

"It will stop the pain," said Dorothy.

"What would be become of me after that?" asked Felicia. "No conscience, yet forbidden to employ the only skill I have ever known? Part of me wants to accept your bargain, but I think it's the false part of me, the empathy that doesn't belong. Once that is gone, would you trust the rest of me to honor our agreement?"

"Swear it by a guild contract. You said there is no stronger bond. Is that true?"

"True enough. The guild takes rather severe measures to preserve the integrity of the code. I don't dare back out. That would be a first, swearing on an assassins' guild contract *not* to kill anyone, but the code would still apply."

"All right, then," said Dorothy. "Yes, I will trust you."

"Maybe." Felicia's face went slack. "Maybe. Once the curse is lifted, I won't be this person anymore. You do understand that? I will be the person who cheerfully stabbed you, the vile harpy. If you dream of this ending in a friendship of any sort, you need to snuff that right now."

"You can't know that. Maybe some part of this person will stick around. Maybe with killing no longer an option, you will be free from having to suppress your conscience." Dorothy looked away. "Or maybe you will live your life in frustration at being bound to a promise you hate. Maybe this person will truly die. I will miss this person, believe it or not, but if I can end your pain, and if there will be no more killing, I have to consider it."

"I won't commit to this," said Felicia. "It does tempt me, but I need to give this a great deal of thought."

"I won't commit to it either. As much as I want to help you, I don't know the risk of unleashing the killer is justified. I'm sure we will have at least a few days before anyone needs to decide anything. Let's both take our time on this."

"Agreed."

They sat in silence for a while, allowing this new aspect of their alliance to sink in. When Felicia stood to leave, Dorothy asked, "Does the guild know you are trying to lift the enchantment on your own? If so, what will they do about it?"

"Those are both good questions," said Felicia. "I honestly don't know the answers to either, but if I had to guess…"

"Yes?" asked Dorothy.

"I would guess they do, and they would wreck our hoverbikes and sic cursed wolves on us, or tell a dragon to eat us." Felicia retreated to her cabin, and quietly shut the door.

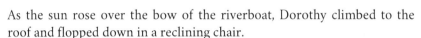

As the sun rose over the bow of the riverboat, Dorothy climbed to the roof and flopped down in a reclining chair.

"Rough night?" asked Sparky from her spot on the table.

"That's cute. Yes, it's been a bit of a struggle. Claudia is simultaneously asleep and delirious, which has been exhausting to watch. I may have cut a deal with Felicia that will haunt me forever, and we are probably being dogged by the assassins' guild. How is life on the roof?"

"Pretty quiet," said Strontium.

"Back up," said Sparky. "Assassins' guild? Are you at all worried about them making you dead?"

"I'm not sure," said Dorothy. "Between my Isthmian blade and my spitfire pixie, I feel pretty cocky, to be honest. Felicia might not be so lucky."

"So?" said Sparky.

Dorothy sighed. "Don't be like that."

"Like what? Need I remind you why you brought me along?" The pixie drew her finger along her neck and made a ripping noise.

"That was before I understood what was really happening," said Dorothy. "She's not a killer anymore."

"Don't let that weepy face fool you," said Strontium. "That's a killer. She might be in a slump now, but I bet she'll find her violence. Take care you don't fall for her hard luck story. I hate to say it because I do like her, but I'm with the firefly on this. Maybe it's time we throw her overboard and finish up without her."

Dorothy sat up. "I can't believe you two. If Felicia hadn't come to me, you would still be a disembodied mind. We have a real chance of getting your true body back thanks to her."

"That wasn't for my benefit, and you know it. She played you to get what she wants, and what she wants is to be evil again."

"What she wants is for her pain to end. You have no idea what she is going through right now. None of us do. Horrible people brainwashed her when she was just a little girl, and they made her do terrible things. Would you be able to live with knowing what she knows about herself?"

"She wants the cruelty back," said Sparky. "Doesn't that make her a bad guy right there?"

"I don't know!" said Dorothy. "I don't know what the right thing is. She asked for my help, and she offered her help, and she is suffering. That's all I can think about right now."

Sparky put up her hands. "Hey, boss-lady, it's your call."

Dorothy stood. "I'm sorry I got you both mixed up in this. I need to do some thinking."

"Sister..." said Strontium.

"No. Not now. Excuse me, please." Dorothy returned to her cabin. She watched Claudia squirm for a few minutes, then climbed into bed, took Claudia in her arms, and fell asleep.

DECISION RULES

For the second morning in a row, Dorothy awoke alone in her cabin. Though the location did not disorient her this time, the solitude did, and it took her a moment to realign her expectations with her observations. She found Claudia in the common room, in a pink bathrobe, bags under her eyes, half-heartedly pushing some untouched scrambled eggs around a plate with a fork.

"You're awake," said Dorothy.

Claudia nodded.

"How are you feeling?"

"Not so great," said Claudia. "Better than yesterday. I'm still seeing trails, so please don't move around a lot. Oh, and helicopters. I still hear helicopters."

Dorothy advanced to the table in slow, smooth movements, and took a seat. "I'm glad to have you back. You had me worried."

"Thanks."

"Have I said yet how sorry I am I dragged you into this?"

"I don't remember," said Claudia.

"Well, I am sorry I dragged you into this. Your brain is very important to me, and I am extremely glad to see it still works."

"I'll probably forget again, so keep saying that."

Dorothy smiled. Her mind flashed forward, to sitting across a breakfast table from Claudia well into their golden years. Overlaid against that, the image of caring for an invalid Claudia, unable to think or communicate, haunted her. They had dodged that bullet today, but would they always? Perhaps not, but in that moment, Dorothy understood that if she needed to stay by Claudia's side and care for her that way, she would do so without regret. For better or worse. She shook her head to dispel the woolgathering. "Has anyone brought you up to speed?"

Claudia nodded, then shook her head, then winced and put her fork down. "Sorry. Give me a second."

"Don't push yourself."

"It's okay. I can feel it getting better. Just… damn." Claudia took a tentative bite of egg. Her features relaxed as she chewed and swallowed. "Felicia made me breakfast."

"Did she tell you things have changed?" asked Dorothy.

Claudia nodded, this time more sluggishly, with no evident disorientation. "Something, something, curse. She said you would explain it better."

"Felicia is under an enchantment of empathy," said Dorothy. "She has been this whole time, but I only figured it out yesterday."

Claudia lifted her eyelids past their half-mast. "Empathy? Shit. Did you do that to her? No, wait, you said you didn't know. Sorry."

"It's all right. You're still not yourself. The assassins' guild hired a wizard to do it. That part is a long story. The important thing is that for the first time since she was a child, for the first time since the assassins got ahold of her and ruined her, she cares about what happens to other people. That's why she has been behaving differently from expectations."

"Wow." Claudia stared at her eggs, freshly prepared by the woman she stabbed through the heart five years earlier. "So, what, she's like a good guy now?"

"That's what we are trying to figure out," said Dorothy. "I find compelling evidence to support that. The others are less persuaded. For the time being, it would be helpful if you would refrain from calling her bitch or psycho to her face. Can you do that?"

"Maybe." Claudia sat up. "Did she kiss me?"

"Yes."

"Jesus." Claudia sat in silence for a few seconds. "If she's good now, why didn't she say that up front?"

Dorothy sighed. "That's the troubling part. She wants to use the Scale of Hypatia to lift the enchantment. She considers it a curse, because it causes her so much pain to know how many people she hurt in the past."

Claudia laughed. "Tough shit on her. Sounds like justice to me." Her smile faded. "We're not letting her do that, right? Lift the spell?"

"That's the other thing we are trying to figure out."

"Dotty! For fuck's sake!"

126

Dorothy held up her hands. "I know, I know. Believe me, I've been over all of this already. We're not talking about letting her go after that. She would still end up in prison, probably for life. The others have all told me we should throw her overboard now and be done with her. I assume you'll tell me the same thing."

"I don't know if I would go that far. She did make me some eggs."

"And treated you for toad-induced delirium."

"That, too," said Claudia. "Dotty, if she's good now, let her stay good. You were the one who wondered whether evil is a thing people do, or a thing people are, right? Well, here's your answer. Somebody changed Felicia's evil setting to off. We should leave it there."

"That's not what happened," said Dorothy. "The spell only changed one aspect of her personality, which is the need to consider other people's suffering. Other things about her are starting to change because of that. What if the spell gave her the opportunity to start over? She has been an assassin since she was twelve years old. Maybe younger. She has never known a life that didn't include violence."

"Most of which she caused."

"I know! All right? I know that. She has done terrible things. Maybe she did them because she never had the chances other people had. The chances we had." Dorothy reached across the table and took Claudia's hand. "The chance for a real future. There's a lot here to think about."

Claudia's hand went slack. "If you're wrong, how many people die?"

Dorothy pulled back. "I don't know."

"Yeah. I don't think there's as much to think about as you do." Claudia went back to work on her eggs.

Dorothy stood on the bow of the *Joyhawk's Gambit*, watching the city approach from several miles out. By now, word of Ruprecht's death would have spread among certain elements of the local population. Once they landed, she and her partners would have little time to get out of town before they came under unwanted scrutiny. She ran her finger along the brass rail of this beautiful and absurd boat, her home for three days now. Like so many valuable things on this journey, they would have to abandon it.

"You'll want to change before we dock," said Felicia from behind her.

Dorothy looked down at her own black jumpsuit, which she had not removed since their foray into Atrylyn's fortress two days earlier, and at

Felicia in her sundress and hat, somehow strikingly fresh despite the lack of a shower on the boat. "I will, thank you."

"I talked to Claudia. She's not at one hundred percent yet, but she should be okay to get to the Worm station. Please keep an eye on her."

"You don't have to tell me that," said Dorothy.

Felicia bit her lip. "Right. Sorry. Listen, I have done a lot of thinking about your offer. It's not my first choice, but I am willing to consider it, under a few conditions."

"Felicia…"

"No, hear me out. I'm not talking about freedom. If we do this, and I am still not committing to it, I agree that prison is the safest option for everyone. That said, I want to talk about how that would work. I won't surrender if I know I'm going to end up in a maximum-security facility without a window. I think it's reasonable for me to ask for a few comforts. I want to talk to Cody about going back to work for the NCSA. He already offered me my job back, so I think he will take the meeting. I was trying to kill him at the time, so it might have been a ruse, but at least it won't be a new idea for him, I can work from my cell as an analyst. There's a lot of good I can do, even from behind bars."

"I really don't want to have this conversation right now."

"I'm not asking you to make a decision," said Felicia. "I'm giving you some ideas to consider while we both think it over. If you decide you don't like them, I am open to counter-proposals. Either one of us can walk away from this negotiation at any time."

"Then I am walking away."

The color drained out of Felicia's cheeks. "What?"

"It won't work. I have been weighing this since yesterday, and it's a bad idea."

"We don't need to decide this today."

Dorothy shook her head. "I'm sorry, Felicia. I truly am. We can still discuss alternatives, but I will not string you along with the hope of that happening. We don't even know if we will be able to make the Scale work when we find it. I'm still sifting through what Strontium was able to pick up with the ether scrape. Hopefully it will make more sense when we have the Scale right in front of us, but we can't know that until we get there."

"So you won't even consider trying?" Felicia narrowed her eyes. "That's you making excuses. You can do better than that."

Dorothy sighed. "Fine. It's not about that. The risk of lifting the enchantment is too great. We can't know what will happen to you, and we can't trust it won't make you violent again."

"You already have my promise," said Felicia. "No more killing."

"You can make promises about what you will do, but not about what you will feel. I don't want you turn back into a monster. I want you to consider therapy instead. Let's work on healing your pain instead of taking away your empathy."

"Therapy? You think if I talk about this, it will make me all better? What are the standard exercises for repentant murderers to help them stop feeling bad about what they have done? There, there, Felicia? Stop beating yourself up? Or, wait, do you mean medication? I'm already under a personality-altering curse, and now you want me on personality-altering drugs?"

"That's not my field," said Dorothy. "You probably wouldn't have to take anything involuntarily."

"It's possible, though. Instead of a minimum-security prison, I could end up committed to a psych ward."

"Honestly, I have no way of knowing how to treat what you are going through. Even so, I don't think lifting the spell is the answer or safe."

"You can't treat what I'm going through! You think your mundane world doctors can correct magically created emotional problems? That's not a viable alternative! It's a plan to make you feel better about yourself! Bah!" Felicia pounded her fist on the railing. It returned a bass note as the shock reverberated around the deck. She looked upriver, away from Dorothy, away from their destination. "It was sincere."

"What was?"

"Amicably. I meant that."

Dorothy frowned. "Are you trying to manipulate me?"

"I don't know. Is there a difference between manipulation and communication? How does one tell them apart?" Felicia looked down at the water. "I have never had a friendship before. It should not surprise me I lack the skills for it."

The word tugged at Dorothy's heart. "I don't know what to say."

"It's much better if you don't say anything at all right now. It's my fault, really. I never should have let myself take this partnership seriously. You're a very kind person. You have surrounded yourself with kind people. Even expecting that, it caught me off guard. I shouldn't have let it get to me, but I am... compromised. This curse... I have lived with it for four months now. My perspective has become slippery. The things I want, the things I fear, they keep shifting underneath me, and there is no way for me to know how much of that is an illusion brought on by the curse, and how much is natural growth from seeing the world through new eyes."

Felicia paused there, turned around and leaned back on the rail. She looked at Dorothy with wary eyes. "When I set out on this quest, all I wanted was to end the pain. I wanted to stop caring about the lives I have ended. I wanted their faces to stop haunting me. I still want that, I suppose, but I think I would keep the pain at this point if it meant I could know the truth about who I am. The assassins took me in as an orphan when I was eight years old. They're probably the ones who made me an orphan in the first place. I've never heard the story of what happened to my parents. I don't even remember them now. I don't remember much at all before that. Until this year, that didn't bother me. It does now."

"I'm so sorry," said Dorothy.

"Stop that. I don't give a damn about your sympathy. I'm not asking you to comfort me. I'm asking you to help me. You want me in therapy? Done. On one condition. Send the real me to that psych ward, not this pastiche. Don't treat the depression. Treat me for... I don't even know what the diagnosis would be. Help me overcome a lifetime of conditioning. Help learn to be the person you think I need this curse to be."

Dorothy swallowed the lump in her throat. "I can't do that."

"Why not? You said yourself you think there is a version of me worth saving. Why won't you help me find her?"

"Because if you lift this curse, you might not want to be that person anymore. Therapy can't help a person change if they don't want to change."

"I want to change!" said Felicia.

"Yes!" said Dorothy. "You want that now! Can you promise me you will still want that without the spell?"

"That's what the psych ward is for! Lock me up! If I still want to change, then I become your patient. If I stop wanting to change, I become your prisoner. You have nothing to lose!"

"I have everything to lose!" Tears nagged at the corners of Dorothy's eyes. "I don't want to lose *you*."

Felicia nodded, with no change in facial expression. "You know, I've always been able to take betrayal in stride. That's part of my profession. Just business. I had no idea it could feel personal."

"Felicia..."

"Shut up." Felicia pushed off from the rail and opened the door. "We dock in fifteen minutes. Change your damn clothes."

Felicia held the door, and Dorothy held her tongue.

[18]

CLUES

They rode the Worm in silence. Claudia took the opportunity to get another hour of much needed sleep. Strontium pretended to do the same. Felicia had acquired a hat and veil at one of the clothiers in the station to add to the doll's ensemble, hoping to render her cracked and cartoonish face less unnerving. That cost them what little time they would have had to retrieve their own clothes from the locker where she stowed them earlier. They boarded the train still in their boating garb.

Dorothy used this lull to review the spell fragments she had gathered from Strontium's ether scrape. References to the Scale appeared sporadically throughout. She got as far as piecing together a reference to an offering, but not clearly enough to attach significance to it. Setting that aside for the moment, she flipped to the back of her book to study the map again. As Felicia had not spoken to her since their unfortunate conflict on the boat, she found herself at a dead end with respect to unpacking the Mock Latin clues sprinkled throughout.

Felicia sat with her arms folded across her chest, and the brim of her hat pulled down over her eyes. Like Strontium, she pretended to rest, but even less convincingly.

Dorothy, without alternatives, and in need of moving forward in whatever arrangement, partnership, or relationship she and Felicia would ever hope to find, plunked her book down on the table in front of her. "Felicia?"

No response.

"I know you don't want to talk, and I'm fine with that," said Dorothy. "All I need is for you spend some time with this map. You may do that without speaking to me if you prefer."

"Give it to me," said Felicia from under her hat.

"It's right in front of you," said Dorothy.

Felicia tipped up her brim. Even through her narrowed eyelids, bloodshot veins made themselves known. She slid the book closer to herself, and leaned in, concealing the side of her face from Dorothy with her hand. "Legatum Hypatiae means Hypatia's Legacy. The Scale is right here at the top of the map."

"Yes," said Dorothy. "I gleaned that much. What I don't understand are the directions for how to get there. Do you have any idea what significance the bird talons have?"

"What talons?"

Dorothy willed herself to relax. "The three talons at the top of the page. The middle one appears pointed to the Scale. I thought that might symbolize something. Be some sort of clue."

Felicia continued to examine the book with no sign of activity.

"Felicia?"

"Hold on."

Dorothy waited.

"Oh," said Felicia. "That's perfect."

"What is it?" asked Dorothy.

"It's the world's worst joke, and it's all on me." Felicia leaned back, took off her hat, and rubbed her face. "The Scale is in the one place I can never go. The lion's den, so to speak. I am both honor-bound and emotionally compelled to lead you to it. I suppose it was always meant to end this way. Better to accept it."

"You know where the Scale is?"

"The city, if not the precise location. I imagine once we get there, we will have all manner of resources to track it down. Or, rather, you will."

"Speaking in riddles is a very non-real affectation," said Dorothy. "Could we please make this plainer for the riddle-impaired?"

Felicia slid the book to Dorothy. "Those are not talons." She thumped three different phrases written in Atrylyn's gibberish. "Connect those dots. They make up a short but complete story about a hapless fisherman."

"I don't understand."

"Your talons are lakes."

Dorothy looked at the map again, with a different paradigm. What she took to be talons now resolved themselves to bodies of water, crude depictions, more evocative of their stations than their shapes. Two thick dashes to the right of this triplet image now joined them in her view as connected via an invisible river. The center lake, here shown as vertical, reached down to touch the words Legatum Hypatiae, not as a giant bird pointing to an object, but as a lake whose shore hosted a city. Her city.

"That's Lake Michigan," said Dorothy.

She and Felicia faced each other wearing very different expressions, and said together, "The Scale is in New Chicago."

Dorothy looked over a stone wall down the Missouri River. She and her companions took a short break as they travelled by foot to Felicia's apartment safehouse in Kansas City, staying off the main roads to avoid too many eyes. The city, once a metropolis of hundreds of thousands, housed less than a tenth of that in the post-Mayhem world. Apart from the river port, most construction continued at a good distance from the bank, and as such they encountered little traffic. Forest growth, not fully cleared here, and the occasional dwelling, largely concealed their movement.

The wall rose at least twenty feet from the flowing waters at this point. By next spring, it might barely contain them, depending on rainfall and snow melt, both now far more difficult to predict than they had been before the worlds merged.

The prospect of an afternoon of rest, a home-cooked meal, a shower, and fresh clothes from Felicia's considerable wardrobe beckoned Dorothy. Constant monitoring of both Claudia, not yet fully recovered from her hallucinations, and Strontium, damaged now beyond any simple tightening of joints, made the hike to that goal a profound challenge. Felicia, though still generally non-verbal, contributed to the care of their diminished companions, more than once catching them as they stumbled.

Dorothy approached Felicia, who had taken a seat a few yards away from the rest of the group. "You don't have to come with us."

"I was thinking the same thing," said Felicia.

"Claudia and I can turn ourselves in as soon as we arrive. With the NCSA and the Council of Mages working on this problem, we can find the Scale on our own. The council should be able to reverse engineer it." Dorothy sat down beside Felicia, who did not move. "There's no need to put you at risk of capture. I will take full responsibility for letting you go."

"When we get back to the hideout I can come up with some evidence I coerced you," said Felicia. "You can say it was you that escaped from me, not the other way around."

"That's kind of you to offer, but I think we should handle this without any additional deception."

Felicia shrugged. "Old habits."

Dorothy laughed softly. "Can we...? I don't know how to ask this."

"Stay friends?" said Felicia. "I don't know if that's what either of us should aspire to at this point."

"Well, yes, that, since you seem willing to at least contemplate it. Thank you for that, by the way. I meant something more... professional."

"I don't take your meaning."

Dorothy looked back at her charges. Claudia and Strontium sat still, with equally empty looks on their faces. "I don't want you to think you can't ever come back. When we part ways, I don't want you to think of anything as final. I can't offer you what you want, but that doesn't mean you won't ever want something I can offer you, if that makes sense."

Felicia picked up a pebble and tossed it at a sapling, some ten yards off. It struck the inch-wide trunk hard enough to shake its leaves. "All I want is the one thing you will never give me. It was probably a mistake for me to want anything in the first place. If I ever decide I want something else... I will remember this conversation."

"That's all I ask." Dorothy stood, and extended her hand. "Let's get moving."

As Felicia stared at the offered hand, her face went rigid.

Dorothy flinched, upset she had somehow pushed this already awkward dialog too far by a simple gesture of assistance. She flinched harder as Felicia went for her sword.

"Draw," said the assassin.

Dorothy took a step backward, images of Felicia's shredded corpse lying before her. Could Felicia be despondent enough to commit suicide by enchanted short sword? "Felicia! No!"

"Draw!" Felicia leapt to her feet, rapier at the ready.

Bess tugged Dorothy's hand to her hilt. It landed there with a sting, and Dorothy's resistance to Bess's directives disintegrated. She drew the sword and spun in a half circle, turning her back on Felicia and raising the flat to shield her face. Felicia's reflection from behind her glowed bright emerald in Bess's blade, her sword also raised in attack position.

A throwing knife collided with Bess, putting out the ring of steel on steel as it fell to Dorothy's feet.

You need protection.

"Oh my God!" Dorothy looked around at the collection of scattered houses, trees, and contours in the land that could serve as blinds, sparing a glance at Claudia and Strontium, both now standing and looking around. She threw her free hand in Claudia's direction. "Armor!"

Claudia's shirt dress flashed silver blue, then expanded with a series of metallic clicks. The skirt rolled down to cover her exposed legs, and short sleeves extended in ever smaller segments to cover arms, wrists and fingers. A cage snapped down from her captain's hat, shielding face and neck. As the final segments snapped into place, Claudia drew the dagger, stolen from Felicia, from her belt.

"Sparky!" shouted Dorothy to her bag, closed on the ground nearby.

An orange streak sprang from the bag, terminating in the pixie, who hovered in front of Dorothy. "Hostiles?"

"Yes."

"How many?"

"Unknown," said Dorothy.

"Kill them?" asked Sparky.

"Incapacitate them."

"On it!" Sparky flew away. A few seconds later a cry of pain and astonishment came from the forest, followed by a scream of agony. The pixie returned, a spot of blood newly decorating her forehead. "One kneecap, at your service."

"Ruthless," said Felicia. "I'm glad I behaved."

"Count on it," said Sparky.

A focused gust of wind ripped the pixie from Dorothy's view. Sparky squealed as she sailed directly toward a tube held by a man half-concealed by a tree. It sucked her in with a slurping sound. He screwed a cap onto the end, clipped the tube to his belt, and ran.

Dorothy sprang into the air, employing the controlled leap that Aplomado counted among his go-to combat moves. Either overestimating the distance she needed to travel or underestimating the amplifying effect that holding Bess would produce, she shot over the head of her target and clipped her arm on a tree branch. She tumbled to the ground, and executed a tuck and roll that brought her upright and facing her quarry from the other side. Ignoring the throbbing in her arm, she pointed Bess at her opponent. "Drop the tube! Now!"

He drew a sword.

Dorothy's heart rate accelerated as she braced for Bess's next maneuver. This man would be her first human kill. She understood this moment would come when she first strapped the sword on days earlier, and dreaded its inevitability. That she would slay this man to save her close friend helped her intellectualize it, but not welcome it.

The man advanced.

Bess did nothing.

Sweat poured down Dorothy's forehead in the August heat. She dared not break visual contact with her opponent to wipe it away, and it flowed into her eyes. Blinking magnified the sting. "Bess? I need you here."

No, you do not.

For a moment, Dorothy took this to mean her time to rise had arrived, and her rite of passage lay in this act of violence.

Then Felicia caught up to him.

Her first stroke caught him in the back, deep enough to get his attention but not to remove him from the field. He spun to counter attack, and swung broadly enough for Felicia to dodge his blade with no apparent effort. As she rose from her duck, she sliced him across the abdomen. He dropped his sword to clutch his wound.

Felicia pounced, employing the rapier's defining function: piercing. Her sword entered his torso above his belly, right below the sternum. Halfway in, it stopped, perhaps snagged on a rib. She screamed, like an injured rabbit, and threw her weight into the thrust, sending the blade in to the hilt. The point emerged from his back, tearing cloth and heralding a spout of blood.

Dorothy ran to her side, the pain in her arm fading to numbness.

Felicia planted her bare foot on the man's chest, and yanked. It took two pulls for the sword to come free. He toppled to the forest floor, gasping as bubbles formed in the blood rushing from his injury. Felicia stood panting for a moment. Then, with a berserker cry, she chopped at his neck.

Dorothy fell to her knees at the sight of this carnage. "Felicia! Stop!"

The assassin ignored her friend's pleas, hacking away at soft tissue and bone with her magically reinforced blade, over and over, awash in the spray of blood. At last the man's head rolled to the side under the river of gore flowing from his open neck.

Felicia stood over him, body shivering, her red and white sundress now saturated in crimson, her sword darkened and slick. She looked up at Dorothy with dead eyes, clear trails forming through the spatters on her face. Wordlessly, she chopped once more, this time through the strap that held the tube to her victim's belt, and fled into the forest.

With no time to analyze her choices, Dorothy grabbed the container and bolted back to the river.

Claudia stood over one assailant on the ground, telltale spots of blood on his ears. Two more men advanced on Strontium. She spread her feet apart, looked up at the sky, and shouted the opening words to an incantation.

"Strontium! Stop! I'm coming!"

Dorothy's warning came too late or from too far away. Strontium's wooden legs exploded from underneath her, sending splinters of shrapnel in all directions. Many of them lodged in the flesh of her targets, who cried out in pain, then went silent. More deflected off Claudia's armor dress.

A small antigrav flier emerged from behind the river wall. Boxy, marked with dirt, wear, and evidence of minor mishaps, it bore little resemblance to the sleek, manta-ray-shaped craft employed by the NCSA. A forward-mounted dome covered a single-pilot cockpit occupied by a bearded man in a crash helmet that obscured most of his face.

A harpoon shot out from the flier's underbelly, spearing Strontium in the back as she struggled to crawl away with her one good arm. The cable behind the harpoon went taut, and lifted her off the ground. It reeled in rapidly, and she disappeared into an open hatch before the flier's engines kicked in. It tore upward and away in a wide arc, leaving a sonic boom in its wake.

Dorothy opened the tube and shook it.

Sparky fluttered out, weaving in an irregular spiral. "Whoa…"

Dorothy pointed upward. "Follow that! Go!"

Sparky managed a feeble salute, zigged back and forth a few times, then streaked away. Both pixie and aircraft vanished out to specks against the evening sun.

Dorothy ran to Claudia's side. "Are you hurt?"

Claudia removed the helmet and shook her head. "I'm okay, thanks to you." She threw her arms around Dorothy and leaned on her. "I need a minute to catch my breath. The helicopters are back."

Dorothy kissed her, and gently lowered her to the ground to sit. She looked at Claudia's foe, curled up and whimpering on the ground, ears bleeding, a dozen visible splinters of wood sticking out of his left side, arm and hip. Behind her, two more men lay still, their eyes open and blank, hundreds of wooden projectiles buried in their flesh.

Claudia pointed to the one she fought. "I don't think he's doing so well."

Dorothy looked to the sky, where two of her friends flew away to parts unknown, and to the forest, where another friend, perhaps, fled from her only support system, in a pain she could not imagine. She knelt at the side of her only living captive of the fray that cost her most of her companions.

"He's about to be doing a lot worse."

[PART 3]
WYVERN

INTERROGATION

Dorothy inspected the assortment of wounds on her hostage. The splinter impalements, though alarming to look at, showed little sign of bleeding. Most protruded from exposed flesh, while several more shards of wood lay scattered nearby, perhaps deflected by his clothing. Claudia had taken the brunt of the doll-shrapnel assault, protected by her armor, probably saving his life. He would need the services of a surgeon, but could probably expect a simple procedure. Many simple procedures.

His ears had put out less blood than she expected. Dorothy flashed back to images of the wounded dragon, but the close quarters and acoustics of the cave had maximized damage from Claudia's sonic shock there. Here in the open, and fortunately for him, much of Claudia's attack passed around him and dissipated.

"I want to ask him some questions," said Dorothy. "It's probably best if he can hear them."

"Hey fuckhead," said Claudia. "The witch lady wants to chat. Get it together. And by it, I mean your eardrums."

Claudia's words did their work. "What are you doing to me?" Panic edged into the man's voice.

"Healing you," said Dorothy. "This is not the part where you become frightened. That part comes later."

"I can hear you! Did you just bewitch me?"

"No, my girlfriend be-scienced you with her telekinesis particles to repair the damage to your tympanic membranes and regenerate your cochlear

141

hairs. The buzzing and ringing in your ears should subside quickly if it hasn't already. As I said, the bewitching comes later." Dorothy looked down Bess's blade at her miserable captive. "Or sooner, I suppose. I just lost two friends, and you personally seem to have threatened someone who means more to me than anyone in the world. I don't take kindly to any of that."

"Are you gonna kill me?"

"Probably not. That isn't my style. But, well…" She held Bess high and sighed with gusto. "Enchanted sword. She quite literally has a mind of her own."

I do not slay the helpless, said Bess.

Dorothy frowned at the blade. "Shh! I know that."

"Oh, shit," said Claudia. "She's talking to the sword again. That never ends well."

"What? What does that mean?"

"Meh. I've already said too much." Claudia looked away.

"Wait a minute," said the man. "Are… are you the good cop?"

Claudia pointed to herself with wide eyes. "Me? Fuck no. Want me to pop your eardrums again? I wonder how many times I can do that before they won't grow back."

"Don't! Please! I don't know anything!"

Dorothy and Claudia looked at each other with raised eyebrows.

"What are you going to do to me?" asked their captive through tears.

Dorothy sheathed Bess. "Call you an ambulance."

He continued to sob. "Wh-what?"

"Call you an ambulance. You have injuries we can't treat here, and you need to see a doctor. From what little field medicine I know, you don't appear to be in any immediate danger, but I don't want to risk moving you. We will do what we can to make you comfortable, then we will leave and call for an ambulance. How close is the nearest road?"

"I…" The crying stopped. He looked around, attempted to sit up, and cried out in pain when one of his newly implanted quills brushed the ground.

"Please lie down," said Dorothy. "This is why we didn't want to move you. You came through the forest. How far to the nearest road?"

He eased himself down to a lying position on his side, all splinters pointing up, sucking air through his teeth and wincing. "Half a mile, maybe. You're not going to torture me?"

Claudia laughed. "Torture you? Of course not! Torture is completely ineffective. That's like, Intelligence Gathering 101."

"She's a spy," said Dorothy. "You can take that to the bank."

"Then… What was all that… with the sword?"

Dorothy drew Bess again. "Petty bullying? Blowing off steam? That was cruel. Sorry, I have had a terrible day." She pointed the sword to the remains of the other two assailants. "If those men were your friends, you're having a difficult day, too. I offer my condolences."

"I don't understand," he said.

He is not alone in that, said Bess.

"You're not our enemy," said Claudia. "You were, ten minutes ago. Now you're a pathetic bastard who can't do anything but lie there and hurt."

"I thought you were going to ask me questions."

"I was," said Dorothy. "Then you said you didn't know anything. This interview is over. All that's left is to get to you a hospital, and back to your family, if you have one."

"We can't stick around for that, though," said Claudia.

"Yes, I'm sorry about that, too," said Dorothy. "I hate to leave you here alone, but we don't really have a choice."

"They weren't my friends," he said.

"Oh," said Dorothy. "Well, I remain sorry for whatever loss they represented to you. Did you know them well?"

"No. I met them today. Don't even remember their names. This was supposed to be a quick job. Easy money. No one was supposed to get hurt."

Dorothy scowled. "None of *you* were supposed to get hurt. Someone threw a knife at me, and someone else drew a sword on me."

"I know. The whole thing went to shit so fast." He winced. "Pardon my language."

Claudia covered her smile with a hand and turned her head.

"No, it's all right," said Dorothy. "You've been through a lot."

"Thanks," he said. "It wasn't supposed to go down like this. Any of it. We were hired to do a simple snatch-job."

Claudia whirled on him. "Is that a crack about our vaginas?"

His eyes went wide. "No! Kidnapping! A kidnapping job!"

Dorothy put her hand on Claudia's shoulder. "Would you be so kind as to refrain from your usual antics, please?"

"He fed me a straight line!" said Claudia. "I can't help it! It's like a reflex!"

Dorothy turned back to the subject of her interrogation. "Kidnapping, you say?"

"Kidnap two girls," he said. "What could go wrong?"

"Setting aside none of us have been girls for quite a few years, which two of us were you supposed to kidnap?"

"She didn't say. Just told us to find two gi— um, ladies, and get 'em to the flier. Then we get here and there's three of you, and that creepy doll-thing. I said we should abort, everyone else said take'm all. Let her sort you out."

"Let who sort us out?" asked Dorothy.

"I don't know!" he said. "Wizard-lady! The one who hired us! Like I said, I don't know anything!"

"Yes, that's too bad. It's all right. You can't tell us what you don't know."

"Are you sure you can't wait with me until the ambulance gets here? I feel a little woozy. What if I pass out?"

Dorothy sat down next to him and put her hand on his forehead. "Hmm." She leaned down and touched his brow with her lips, allowing them to linger there for a few seconds. "You don't feel like you have a fever. You've hardly lost any blood. If you are feeling faint, it may be the stress." She followed this with a soft stroke to the side of his face. "Try to relax."

He confirmed her speculation about not losing blood, as a great deal of it rushed to his cheeks.

"Did you meet wizard-lady in person?" asked Claudia.

"No," he said. "I heard the others talk about her."

"What did they say?" asked Dorothy.

"Not much. What she wanted us to do, how much she was going to pay us."

"They didn't say why she wanted us kidnapped, or where she wanted you to take us?"

He shook his head. "Our job was to get you to the flier."

"We're going in circles now," said Claudia.

Dorothy stood. "I agree. We need to get moving, and find a safe way to call for that ambulance."

"Wait," said the man. "You're leaving?"

Claudia ignored the question. "Is it time to call in the NCSA?"

A voice came from the edge of the forest. "I would prefer if you could hold off on that for now." Felicia stood there in nothing but her underwear and the rapier scabbard. She had wiped the blood from her face, but her hair remained matted with it. "You have a man back here with a shattered patella who needs medical attention. It sounds like he knows more than what you got from this one."

"Did you torture him?" asked Claudia.

"What? Certainly not! Information gathered from torture is horribly unreliable. I would have thought you knew that. The only reason I ever used it was because I enjoyed it so much."

Dorothy looked back at her captive, who had gone pale. "You'll be fine. Apparently, we are not leaving you alone after all."

"We need to get back to my safehouse quickly," said Felicia. "I know where your sister-witch is."

Dorothy walked to Felicia, held out her hand, then held back, unsure of the best gesture of comfort. "Are you okay?" she whispered.

Felicia frowned. "No. Obviously. Can we move forward, please? These people are not from the assassins' guild. It was never the guild on our tail."

"I think I deduced that from talking to our friend, here," said Dorothy.

"Then who took her?" asked Claudia.

"Rosebud," said Felicia.

"Rosebud? Like the sled?"

"Like the wizardess." Felicia put her hand on Dorothy's shoulder. "They were never after me, Dorothy. They were after you."

[20]

CATHARSIS

For the first time since setting out from New Chicago four days earlier, Dorothy and her companions finally drew some stares. Though the sight of a walking mannequin had fazed no one, a woman in nothing but underwear and sword somehow crossed the curiosity threshold. Dorothy and Claudia kept Felicia between them as they made their way to Felicia's apartment, but did not sufficiently conceal her.

Felicia drew a key from her bra, and let them inside. She dropped a knapsack filled with knives she had carried all the way from the Worm station. Her current condition now exposed to her companions, she had given up wearing them for show. "There's juice and beer in the refrigerator. Wine rack in the dining room. If you need something harder, the liquor cabinet is above the dishwasher."

"All I want right now is a glass of water," said Dorothy.

"Plenty of that in the sink," said Felicia. "Please make yourselves comfortable. I hope no one is surprised I would like to take a shower before we discuss our next move."

"Do whatever you need to do to take care of yourself," said Dorothy. "We can wait."

"I won't be long." Felicia unbuckled the rapier scabbard and hung it from a hook near her apartment door, then disappeared into the bathroom.

Felicia had refused to discuss details on the street, and Dorothy did not begrudge her the time alone after their encounter in the forest.

Rosebud's identity, and reasons for hunting Dorothy, would keep for a few more minutes.

Claudia helped herself to a bottle of beer from the refrigerator, and dug through two drawers before finding the bottle opener. She flopped down in a sofa, took a swig, and set the bottle down on an end table without a coaster.

Dorothy unbuckled her sword belt, and laid it on the coffee table. Freed from the spell of concealment, Bess shimmered into view there. Dorothy found a glass, loaded it with ice, and filled it from the tap. The flavor had a distinctly different mineral bouquet than New Chicago water, but soothed her parched throat better than anything she could recall. She took a seat in a living room chair opposite Claudia, who did not make conversation or eye contact.

On Dorothy's arrival in New Chicago as a weary traveler, Claudia had offered her friendship, the only resident there to do so right away. She also played a pivotal role in having Dorothy's adopted father Harrison arrested as she and her nine-year-old adopted brother watched in horror. That contradiction had shaken Dorothy badly, making any real connection with Claudia challenging at first, if not impossible.

It took years for Dorothy to learn Claudia's geniality that day represented a crush on Dorothy she did not know how to manage. Harrison's unrelated arrest further complicated the situation. Throughout their adolescences and young adulthoods, that smoldering crush ignited to a secret love that drove a broader wedge between them in Claudia's certainty it could never be returned.

The more aloof Claudia became, for reasons Dorothy could not understand, the more Dorothy pined for her approval. Ironically, Harrison, with every reason to hold a grudge, became one of Claudia's closest friends during that time, making Dorothy's inability to connect with her sting all the more.

Then, as the two of them finally found an opportunity and willingness to attempt a friendship, Dorothy discovered Claudia's true feelings by accident. Able to analyze a decade of Claudia's behavior at last, Dorothy found room in her heart for a previously unconsidered idea: she could, and did, return those feelings.

Dorothy studied Claudia's face from across the room. Though her features lacked the mathematical perfection of a magazine cover model, Dorothy found her strikingly beautiful, visually and sexually, the only woman who had ever stirred that reaction in her, before or since. As she allowed herself to extrapolate their life together out to old age, Dorothy involuntarily sighed.

Claudia reacted to this, apparently aware of Dorothy's attention for the first time. "What?"

"Nothing," said Dorothy.

Claudia's face went slack. "Oh." She looked away again.

Dorothy's regret over dragging Claudia into this insane enterprise resurfaced. Claudia had tracked her down to rescue her from the villain Felicia, and in return for her devotion, she had suffered injury and indignity. That her patience had carried her this far spoke highly of her, but even someone as strong as she had limits. Dorothy would have a lot of work ahead of her making this up to her, even though Claudia would not expect that of her.

As she contemplated possible gifts that could make any dent in the debt of gratitude she now owed, she remembered the gift she had already purchased, at no small cost, now squirreled away in a dresser drawer hundreds of miles from there. Claudia's willingness to follow her halfway across the country reflected her own commitment to follow Claudia into whatever travails awaited her. They would weather this exhaustion-driven conflict, and when they returned home, Dorothy would find the right aplomb with which to offer Claudia the ring, and find the perfect moment in which to do so.

Dorothy's life and the lives of her loved ones did not lend themselves to perfect moments. The ring, while beautiful in all the ways Claudia would love, did not, itself, constitute what Dorothy truly wanted to give her. Their elegant restaurant experience awaited them whenever they wanted it. The moment, the truly perfect moment, would either never arrive, or had arrived now.

"I'm sorry," said Dorothy. A preamble, and necessary first move. Her heart raced as she plotted her next words, improv not being among her greatest skills.

Claudia looked at her with numb eyes. "About what?"

"Everything."

Claudia's eyes narrowed. "Be specific."

Heat rose in Dorothy's cheeks as Claudia deviated from her imagined script so early. "I'm sorry I lied to you about waiting a day before deciding. I should have been upfront with you."

"And?"

Dorothy's heart sank as the moment hinted at creeping away from her. "I'm sorry about the sleep spell."

"We're getting there."

Dorothy frowned. "I'm... sorry I risked hurting you to help

Strontium." She looked for some sign of nearing whatever slight deserved additional apology, so she could get back on track.

"Too broad."

"What?"

"Too wide," said Claudia. "Be specific."

"I don't know what you want me to say," said Dorothy.

"Say you're sorry for actually hurting me, not just risking it."

A lump formed in Dorothy's throat. She had already apologized for that. Claudia's claim in her semi-delusional state she would not remember the apology had played out to be true. "I'm sorry you got hurt. With the toad."

"That's pretty good."

"Was that what you were looking for? Are we all right now?"

"We're okay," said Claudia. "I'm not sorry about the tracking device, though."

Dorothy's heart, already clipping along, picked up speed. "Can we change the subject?"

"I'm just saying. You all would have been fucked in that dragon cave if I hadn't come along. You're lucky I found you."

Dorothy took the opening. "I am very lucky you found me. Luckier than anyone I know."

"Damn straight."

"We are both very lucky we found each other. The kind of luck people only get once in their lives." Her heart pounded as she moved forward.

"Found each other?" said Claudia. "What the fuck? That was all me!"

Dorothy winced. "Claudia…"

"No! Fuck that! You roofied me to get the hell out of Dodge! I busted my ass to find you! Don't give me this 'each other' shit!"

"Claudia!"

"What?"

Dorothy stood. "God damn it! I am trying to ask you to marry me! Would you shut up and cooperate for once in your fucking life?"

Claudia's jaw dropped.

Dorothy's eyes bugged, and she slapped her hands over her mouth.

"You said fuck," said Claudia.

Dorothy nodded, tears forming in the corners of her eyes.

"That's not really something you say."

Dorothy shook her head.

Claudia sat still for a few seconds before breaking the silence. "This is the most romantic thing you've ever done. I don't even know…"

Dorothy threw herself onto the sofa, grabbed Claudia's face and kissed her. After some time, she came up for air. "Will you fucking marry me?"

"Fuck, yes!"

Dorothy burst into laughter, tears streaming down her cheeks. She pulled Claudia into her arms.

Behind them, from the bathroom, came a barking sound in fits and starts, rising over the white noise of running water. It passed. After a pause, it resumed.

"Shit," said Claudia. "That's a terrible cough. Is she okay?"

Dorothy pulled back and closed her eyes. "That's not a cough." She kissed Claudia one more time, and stood. Crossing to the bathroom door, she listened intently for any signs of improvement. Hearing none, she tapped gently on the door. "Felicia?" No answer. Dorothy rested her hand on the knob and counted silently to three before breaching Felicia's boundaries. It turned in her hand, not locked.

Steam poured out of the room in quantity and condensed on Dorothy's face. Felicia had turned on the light, but not the exhaust fan. Her bra and underpants lay draped over the wastebasket on the floor, a half-hearted attempt at disposal. Dorothy turned on the fan, and the room cleared out.

Felicia sat naked in the far end of her bathtub, curled in a ball, her sobs interrupted only by coughing fits. The hottest water pelted her from a showerhead set to power spray. A red trail trickled from her body, gradually mixing with the rest of the bathwater on its way to the drain.

Dorothy shut off the water.

Felicia did not move, even to look up at Dorothy's appearance in the room.

Dorothy kicked off her boating shoes, and stepped into the tub basin. She sat, and took Felicia into her arms. Her shorts wicked up the water and blood running beneath her.

Felicia curled into a tighter ball, and pressed her face into Dorothy's shoulder, where her weeping increased in intensity. Her black curls, now soaking wet and still bloody, rested against Dorothy's cheek.

Dorothy held her, and waited it out.

WINGS

F elicia sat at her kitchen table, nursing the iced coffee Dorothy had brewed for her while she slept. Though Dorothy and Claudia had changed into fresh clothes, Felicia still wore a white bathrobe and a towel around her head. Her morning shower had apparently provided more refreshment and less punishment than the scalding she had given herself the previous evening.

In the wake of Felicia's breakdown, neither Dorothy nor Claudia pursued their many questions. With Strontium and Sparky both missing, and a day lost, they no longer had that luxury. Dorothy placed a dish of cut fruit and buttered toast at Felicia's spot at the table. "We have a rescue to plan. Are you up to this?"

Felicia nodded, and put a strawberry in her mouth. She closed her eyes as she chewed. "I'm fine. We don't have much time. I'd like to be out of this building by noon. The Kansas City police aren't bastions of efficiency, but they are surely looking for whoever left that mess by the river yesterday, and the two survivors have probably given them semi-reliable descriptions of us from their hospital beds."

Hearing Felicia shift so seamlessly from absolute vulnerability to calmly discussing an exit strategy gave Dorothy chills. As much as she wished otherwise, she found it all too easy to picture the Felicia who twisted a knife in her shoulder with a smile of delight at her pain. She swallowed, and pressed on. "All right. Tell us about Rosebud."

"Rosebud is to Tim as Dorothy is to Aplomado." Felicia let that statement rest as she took another sip of her coffee.

Dorothy sat up. Tim, the wizard who engineered her abduction and that of more than thirty other woman and children for the purpose of human sacrifice, had died at her hand, decapitated by his own attack spell as Dorothy reflected it back to him. Though Strontium had been in control of her body at that moment, the image of Tim's headless body still held a prominent place in Dorothy's memory. "Tim had an apprentice?"

Felicia nodded. "Yes. A non-real indigenous human. Tim took her in as an apprentice wizard, and possibly as a lover, though that's not as clear."

"Ew," said Claudia.

"Indeed," said Felicia. "They struck whatever partnership they shared about three years before you and Strontium decapitated him."

"He did that to himself," said Dorothy.

"Toe-may-toe, toe-mah-toe," said Felicia. "Either way, he is deceased, and she likely holds you responsible."

"Wonderful. Does she want me dead?"

"You would have to ask her, which you will be able to do in about four hours. If I had to guess, she probably wants to kill you herself, after lambasting you with tales of how unworthy you are, and how grand a wizard the world lost when you took down her mentor."

"How powerful is she?" asked Dorothy.

"More than you, less than Strontium," said Felicia. "Keep in mind, this is a wizard who knows at least two ways to neutralize a pixie."

Dorothy's heart sank. "I sent Sparky right to her."

"I said neutralize, not kill. Fey are vulnerable to many kinds of magical attack, but killing them requires more power than any human wizard could muster. Containing them however is relatively simple. If Sparky hasn't returned, she is likely being held prisoner. How close will we need to be for you to detect her?"

"Half a mile," said Dorothy. "The spell for containing a pixie is a variation of the spell for summoning one. I know how to break that if I can get close enough to see her."

"I'm counting on that. We will need her when we rescue Strontium."

"You don't think Rosebud will kill Strontium?"

"She may not even know that is Strontium," said Felicia.

"The man I questioned said they expected to find two women," said Dorothy. "He said the doll was a surprise."

"Two women?" said Felicia. "Now, that's interesting. The gentleman I interviewed said nothing about that. He said they were trying to capture us all."

"They were, but only after they got here and saw how many of us

152

there were. Our guy said they were sent to kidnap two women. He was very specific."

"That means two things. One, Rosebud is aware you and I are working together, probably as a result of our encounter with the wolves, and two, she does not know Strontium separated from you, or that de Queiroz joined us."

Claudia raised her hand. "I'm sorry. I know this isn't the right time for this question, but are we seriously talking about a wizard named Rosebud? I'm picturing a five-year-old girl in a tutu."

Dorothy put her hand on Claudia's knee. "Get past that, please. A great deal goes into the selection of a wizard's name. It's an extremely personal decision, based on factors no outsider would understand. Pretend she has a more frightening name, if it helps you focus."

"Fine. I'm calling her Fang."

"Excellent choice." Dorothy directed her attention to Felicia. "She sent a band of brigands to kidnap you and me, and instead they returned with a broken, talking doll. What is her next move?"

"Her next move is to wait for us," said Felicia. "If she has your pixie, and if she deduces the doll is your friend, she will believe we are coming for them. And she is correct."

"Then it's time to call in the NCSA and the Council of Mages."

"Negative. Now we know a dark mage is involved, it changes the landscape considerably. The council might be able to shut down this wizard, but they will also assume control of our quest for the Scale. Strontium's best hope for returning to a human body will get tied up in red tape for who knows how long. Meanwhile, Strontium goes mad from sleep deprivation. You've seen this system from the inside. You know I'm right. For now, we are still on our own."

Dorothy closed her eyes. "All right. I assume you have a plan of attack?"

Felicia shrugged. "More or less. We are walking into a trap, without a doubt, but with resources she doesn't know about. De Queiroz, for one, can help us incapacitate any henchmen she may have waiting for us. Strontium can still cast spells in unexpected and highly destructive ways."

"If Strontium casts any more spells there won't be a Strontium," said Claudia.

"I agree," said Dorothy. "Let's take that off the table for now."

"That won't be up to us," said Felicia. "Strontium is a loose cannon now. Our best hope is she manages to salvage enough of her body to contain her consciousness. With or without our approval, she will try something. Let's hope we get there before she tries too much."

Dorothy winced. "Understood."

Felicia pointed to a window. "Ah, excellent. Our ride approaches." She stood. "We will talk more after we board. I need to change. Please be ready to depart in fifteen minutes."

Dorothy looked in the direction of Felicia's gaze. Outside, still a mile or two out, an enormous object with broad, flapping wings, approached by air. Dorothy jumped from her chair and ran to the window for a better view, still unable to make out details. "I am not riding another giant bat. Call that off right now."

Felicia laid her hand on Dorothy's shoulder, and Dorothy turned to her. "I would never do that to you. This is something much friendlier. Trust me."

Dorothy studied Felicia's eyes, somehow both soft and businesslike. "I do."

Felicia failed to conceal the beginnings of a smile, and turned away. "Good. Good. If you'll excuse me, I need to suit up." She retreated to her bedroom and shut the door.

Dorothy and Claudia spent the next few minutes double-checking what little they had on them. In Claudia's case, that amounted to the clothing she had borrowed. Dorothy inspected the contents of her bag, noting the fossilized tortoise skeleton had survived every episode of this adventure. Aplomado would be suitably proud of the care she took with her mysterious charge.

Felicia emerged from her bedroom clad in full assassin gear, the same outfit she wore at Fenway while planning to execute Dorothy and so many others, including Dorothy's five-year-old sister and fifteen other small children. All black, and covered in knives. Her girlish face looked out from beneath a beaked hood. "Follow me."

Dorothy set aside her revulsion at the sight of that outfit, forcing herself to perceive Felicia as the person she had come to know over the past week, not the monster who wore those blades. She followed Felicia to the kitchen.

Felicia opened the cabinet under the kitchen sink, removed a trash can, and slid aside a panel revealing a safe with a dial combination lock. It took her a few seconds to open. "Bag, please."

Dorothy opened her shoulder bag, bracing for whatever rare weapon Felicia wanted to stow in it.

Felicia dropped four bands of cash in Dorothy's bag, and walked away from the open, empty safe with a fifth band in her hand.

Dorothy looked at the bills. "What is this?"

"Money," said Felicia.

"Yes. I… Obviously it's money. What is it for?"

"You buy things with it."

Dorothy closed her bag, and followed Felicia to her front door. "I don't understand. Why are we bringing this along? Are we planning to bribe her?"

Felicia strapped on the rapier scabbard and a quiver of arrows, then grabbed a bow. "No. That's for you. Once we leave this apartment, I won't be able to come back to it, so I can't leave it here."

Dorothy's face went cold as the implications of this gift set in. "I can't take this."

"I don't need it," said Felicia.

"I can't… not knowing where it came from."

"Then donate it to a hospital or something. This is not up for debate. Come on."

Felicia led them to the roof of her apartment building. A craft perched there, the size of a small jet, and the approximate shape of an eagle. It flapped broad, feathered wings.

"What the fuck is that?" asked Claudia.

"It's our ride." Felicia jogged to the ornithopter, arriving at the cockpit door as it opened from within. She handed someone inside the band of bills she carried, and signaled for Dorothy and Claudia to join her.

They ducked as they ran, despite the flapping wings having at least two feet of clearance over their heads. Dorothy climbed inside, and took the seat behind Felicia, who had already strapped herself in next to the pilot. He turned to look at her, eyes invisible behind dark goggles, and she said, "I'm Dorothy."

"He doesn't care," said Felicia. "Buckle up."

Dorothy and Claudia fastened their seatbelts. The flapping motion increased dramatically, and the ornithopter lifted into the air. Dorothy's experience with air travel included both jumbo jets and smaller prop planes from before Mayhem, as well as riding in antigrav technology fliers as an adult. The ornithopter generated less noise than the former, more than the latter. Its wings beat furiously for a full two minutes before the pilot cut back on the power and locked them into gliding position. The noise dropped to silence.

"Where are we going?" asked Claudia.

"Taum Sauk Mountain," said Felicia. "Rosebud's lair is at the summit. The ornithopter will be able to approach silently. My first choice would be to parachute down, but I'm guessing this isn't the best day for your first skydiving lesson."

"Good guess."

"Once we land, what do we do?" asked Dorothy.

"Disable the help, more than likely," said Felicia. "If the people who tried to capture us are any indicator, she's using bargain basement security. The three of us should be able to get past them with minimal damage to them. If not, leave the killing to me."

"I can't do that," said Dorothy.

"This is not a debate. If you want to keep me from killing our foes, then do whatever it takes to make that unnecessary. Am I understood?"

Dorothy frowned. "I don't like it."

"Well," said Felicia, "now I know what you don't like. Once we get inside, we find Sparky and Strontium."

"That will be easy," said Dorothy.

"I assumed so. At that point, one of two things will happen. Either Rosebud tries to take us down, in which case your job will be to lay down magical defenses while I go in for the kill, or she will make a show of taunting you. The second is far more likely."

"What happens then?"

"You interrupt her, as rudely and arrogantly as you can, and challenge her to a magical duel."

"I thought you said Fang was more powerful than Dotty," said Claudia.

Felicia grinned. "More powerful yes, but nowhere near as bright. As the challenged party, she has the right of first strike. It will be something clumsy and ineffective, to give you a false sense of superiority."

Claudia laughed. "A slow play? You two have a lot in common."

"Are you sure about this?" asked Dorothy.

"Sure enough. When it's your turn, while she braces for an attack from you, use your shot to free Sparky. Once she is outnumbered, she will be easy to defeat. At that point, assuming she doesn't flee outright, we imprison her and call in the NCSA after we are gone."

"She won't see that coming?"

Felicia shook her head. "It's a violation of duel protocol. She will never suspect you of stooping to something that unspeakable."

"Seriously?" said Claudia. "That's what you're banking on? That she'll expect Dotty to play by the rules?"

"I wouldn't expect you to understand," said Felicia.

"All right. I will do all of that, with one stipulation," said Dorothy. "If we can't find Sparky, or you are wrong about any other part of this, we fall back and call in the council and the NCSA. I know that's not an ideal solution, but I won't risk this situation getting worse because we refused to ask for help."

"Dorothy…" said Felicia.

"If you need to time to escape, I will buy that for you," said Dorothy. "If that's your concern. I won't let them take you."

Felicia opened her mouth to speak, then looked down. "I know you won't."

"Then it's settled."

Felicia nodded, and turned forward to look out the windshield.

Claudia looked at Dorothy, and held up both hands with fingers crossed.

Dorothy smiled, then looked out the window at the landscape below cruising by without a sound, desperately hoping her trust in Felicia's judgment—and Felicia's integrity—would not undo them all.

[22]

ROSEBUD

The ornithopter circled the top of the mountain as Felicia drew a bead on Rosebud's home. Though largely camouflaged, and with no telltale roads leading to her door, her dwelling proved easy enough to find by proximity to the flier parked a few dozen yards from it. Rather than attempt a vertical descent, the pilot chose to glide down to a landing, activating the flapping wings to brake a few seconds before he touched down.

Felicia took point, leaping from the cockpit door and charging the house, arrow nocked. Dorothy and Claudia followed close behind, the latter again clad in armor magically converted from her clothing.

They encountered no resistance, or personnel of any sort as they crossed the terrain between their landed craft and the door of Rosebud's dwelling. The house itself, a modest building more reminiscent of a cabin than a fortress, showed no signs of activity inside or out. A single light shone from a second-floor window. The front door sat ajar.

Felicia paused at the open entrance. "This isn't right."

"Are they gone?" asked Claudia.

"I don't know." Felicia glanced back at the flier. "This place is only accessible by air. I don't see any depressions in the soil from another craft. Unless they set out on foot, someone should still be here."

"This isn't at all what you predicted," said Dorothy.

"Are we ready to call the NCSA?" asked Claudia.

"No! Not yet. Come on." Felicia pushed the door open with her foot. It swung inward with a slight creak. Sunlight illuminated the interior, exposing a foyer, with stairs leading up and a hallway leading farther in. The three of them entered with caution.

"Welcome," came a voice from above.

Felicia trained her arrow on the source of the voice, a bald man with a scraggly orange beard in a plaid flannel shirt. He looked down on them from the second-floor landing with little interest. "Come on up. No point dragging this out."

"Where is Rosebud?" Felicia did not lower her bow.

"Where do you think?" said the man. "Up here. She's waiting for you. All three of you. Come on."

"We are here for our companions," said Dorothy. "A pixie and a broken doll. Are they here? Are they unharmed?"

The man laughed at this. "I'd hardly say unharmed, but they were like that when they got here. Come on up and have a look."

Felicia folded her bow, attached it to a mount on her quiver, and replaced the arrow in its clip there. She then drew the rapier. "Stay close to me. Do not attack unless I order it or I die."

"Felicia," said Dorothy quietly. "None of this is what you said. Whatever trap she's laid for us, it's not the one you prepped us for. Let me call for backup, please."

"Trap?" said the man. "What would be the point of a trap? You're here for your pets, so come get them. No one's trapping anyone."

"Rosebud will let us take them without a conflict?" asked Dorothy.

"Far as I know. All she wants is a chat. Seeing as you killed those three boys she sent for you, seems to me you're the ones looking for a conflict."

Dorothy's heart picked up its pace. "Two of those kills were accidents. Strontium, the doll, did not mean to do that to them."

He snorted. "Two of them were. Not so the third, eh, assassin?"

"I did what I did in defense of my companion." Felicia stood her ground with the sword, but her voice had lost some of its boldness.

"That's your story. Sounded to me like an assassin doing her assassin things, but what do I know? You coming up or not?"

"Yes," said Dorothy.

The man stood back from the rail as Felicia led the other two up the stairs. Candles in sconces lit the hallway on the second floor. A single open door spilled more light outward. Their greeter walked them to this room.

Rosebud sat alone on an antique sofa, drinking from a steaming teacup. She wore the simple robe of a wizard, charcoal blue with wide sleeves and a hood resting off her head. The only light in the room came from a set of crystal candlesticks set on various surfaces, and a single log blazing in a half-sized brick hearth. Her pasty complexion stood out against her black hair in the shadows from the flickering lights. This, combined with the wide-framed spectacles she wore, rendered her face difficult to read.

Propped up in a cushioned armchair, the remnants of Strontium's wooden frame lay motionless. Her cartoon eyes, now more scratches than ink, stared blankly at nothing. Sparky, bereft of her wings, sat on an end table clutching her knees and rocking forward and back. She did not look up to greet her rescuers.

Rosebud set her teacup in a saucer on a coffee table in front of her. The porcelain *clink* it made as it contacted filled the room. She did not smile as she spoke in a sandpaper voice. "Ah, good. You're here."

Dorothy crouched by Strontium's side, inspecting her for any signs of activity. "Strontium? We're here. Can you hear me?"

The doll did not respond.

"Hey, pixie," said Claudia. "You still with us?"

Sparky showed no signs of awareness that anyone addressed her.

"What have you done to my friends?" asked Dorothy, trembling.

"Not a thing," said Rosebud. "They did that to themselves. Do have a seat, please. We have some things to discuss before I send you on your way."

Felicia pointed the sword at Rosebud. "We'll stand."

"We're not leaving without them," said Dorothy.

"Yes, yes," said Rosebud. "You can all leave together. Before you fret, your witch in the wood still lives. She's too damaged to move anymore, or speak, but her spark burns as brightly in that form as it did the day she disintegrated my lord's head."

"I did that," said Dorothy. "If you're looking to blame someone, blame me."

"Yes! Yes, you did! She did as well. Your merger is well known to me, little faux witch. I have had years to deduce the particulars of your blended state, watching you from afar. Your actions are hers, and hers yours. At least that was so until of late. Interesting choice to put her in a doll. Why not ask the Scale to generate her a body and transfer her directly from your mind then and there? What was all this temporary vessel nonsense?"

Dorothy gulped. She looked at Felicia, who took a step backward with wide eyes. "Felicia? What is she saying?"

"Don't listen to her," said the assassin.

Rosebud laughed. "Some alliance. I suppose you thought you were forming a real bond there. No? Ah, well. No, no, the doll was quite unnecessary. You'd have had the same result without it." She grinned. "Almost the same, I should say. In all the ways it would have mattered to you, at least."

"Felicia?" Dorothy's voice cracked on the word.

"The elf said it would never work without separating you first," said Felicia.

"The elf!" said Rosebud. "Look at her deflecting responsibility to an elf!"

"Don't listen to this villain," said Felicia. "She wants us to turn on each other."

Rosebud laughed again. "Oh, my, no. I don't want that. What I want is much worse."

Dorothy stood straighter. "I challenge you to a magical duel!" Too late, she remembered that plan hinged on using her turn to free Sparky, now a moot point. Having clumsily stumbled into the challenge, she braced herself for a genuine magical battle.

Felicia shook her head.

Rosebud cackled so loudly it threw her into a coughing fit.

Dorothy waited out the laughter, juggling her fear, confusion and embarrassment.

"Ha! A duel! Oh, my." Rosebud lifted her glasses and wiped a tear from her eye. "Oh, I can only imagine what trickery you rehearsed to go with that line. Well spoken, faux witch! I admire your brass. No, no, we won't be dueling today. There is no need for a duel when there is no insult. I offer you your friends to take with you. No conditions, no offense."

"Then what was the point of any of this?" said Dorothy. "Why take them at all? Why did you attack us in the first place?"

"To kill you, obviously," said Rosebud. "I spent years planning my vengeance for Tim. Pushed many pieces into place, waiting for the right opportunity. Then your very nemesis approached you with an offer of partnership and lured you away from the city and its protections. Had I known it would be that easy, I would have sent an untrustworthy snake to your door much sooner to draw you out."

"You cursed those wolves," said Dorothy. "The shunt spell on Sparky. That was you."

"Yes, yes. I also plotted with Ruprecht to betray you when I learned of your meeting with him. The poor devil."

"You tried to kill us twice, yet you now say we are free to take our friends and go? Why?"

"Because I finally understand the true nature of your quest," said Rosebud. "Ruprecht provided me with some information that put me on the scent. Your broken doll of a sister-witch confirmed my suspicions while she still possessed the ability to speak. I know now there is nothing I can do to your companions, nothing I can do to you, that would cause you more pain than the plan you already have for yourselves."

Dorothy looked at Felicia. "What does she mean?"

Felicia took a step toward Rosebud, extending her sword. "I do not know, and I do not care. If she is willing to let us depart with our friends, let us do so without delay."

"Our friends?" said Rosebud. "Our? Friends? As if you would ever be one of them! As if they would take you in, after what you have done, knowing who you are!"

"Fine," said Felicia. "Dr. O'Neill, if she is willing to let us depart with *your* friends, we should do so."

"I agree." Dorothy lifted Strontium. The doll's surface still warmed her skin, giving her a nugget of hope the witch still lived. "Claudia, please put Sparky in my bag."

"The Scale will never give you what you want," said Rosebud.

The blood drained from Dorothy's head. As she grappled with the faint feeling, she set Strontium back in her seat, and drew Bess.

Do you need protection?

"Answers." Dorothy advanced on Rosebud in her sofa, flipping the coffee table out of her way. She did not flinch as it crashed to the floor, inverted, shattering the teacup under it. "Tell me what you know about the Scale." She touched Rosebud's throat with the tip of the short sword.

"I know the same thing everyone you trust has told you from the start. The Scale is a fool's hope. You think it will give you what you want, but it won't. Do you suppose Hypatia ruled so many for so long by indulging them? Is that your image of how a monarchy works? Growing up in your idealistic republic I wouldn't expect you to comprehend the reality of absolute rule. Yes, she used it to grant wishes. Why did she do that, do you think? From the goodness of her heart? Her subjects loved their dragon queen, to be sure, but make no mistake about her relationship to them. She answered to no one. Millions embraced her dominion over them, but in the end, it was still dominion. Any sense of agency she ever gave them was pure illusion, and they brought that on themselves, every one of them." Rosebud leaned forward, pressing a dimple into her neck with Bess's tip. "The Scale may give you what you ask for, but it will never give you what you want."

"What does that mean?" shouted Dorothy. "I'm so done with riddles! What does the Scale do?"

"It gives you what you ask for," said the wizardess. "And it does it in the worst possible way. That's all I will tell you."

"Then I will kill you."

"Dotty!" said Claudia.

"Stay out of this!" said Dorothy.

"Oh, wait, yes," said Rosebud. "There is one more thing I will tell you."

"What?"

"That you're so close. You figured out Atrylyn's map, yes? You worked out where the Scale is?"

"That's none of your concern," said Dorothy.

Rosebud cackled. "Oh, keep your secrets. I don't care where it is, as long as you find it. If I knew, I'd tell you myself. Save you the fuss and bother of the hunt. You have the map, and I expect between you and your entourage you have the brains to decode it. Tell me, did it happen to mention you'll want to bring torches?"

Dorothy scowled. "What's that supposed to mean?"

"I can't imagine," said Rosebud. "The ramblings of a madwoman, most likely. I'm sure you'll manage with what you already know."

"You're trying to trick us."

"What would be the purpose in that, I wonder. You've so fabulously tricked yourselves, already. I could never compete."

Dorothy lowered the sword. In her other hand, she drew her spellbook from its ethereal hiding place. Pages flipped, moving by her will, until coming to rest on the appropriate passage. Dorothy read it aloud, its language still alien to her, but its meaning clear enough.

A halo of dust formed around Rosebud's head. It glowed in dull aquamarine, issuing a wispy hum in several tones, shifting through melancholy chords.

"This is a waste of your energy," said Rosebud.

"What are you doing?" asked Claudia.

Dorothy continued to chant. The ring of dust settled on Rosebud's head, contracted, and flowed down her face.

The wizardess did not blink, nor did her smile diminish. "It's a repellant," she explained to Claudia. "Your leader wants me not to follow her. She probably thinks I want the Scale for myself. That this is all a ruse to deceive you into taking me to it. This curse will keep me from pursuing you. It will indeed impel me to shun you, and reject all information about you. Once you leave my dwelling, it will protect you from any interference from me, or any exploitation of you on my part. In short, it will guarantee what I have already promised you. I can't say I blame her for not trusting me, but all she's doing right now is spending valuable magical energy to make herself feel as safe as she already happens to be."

"Shut up." Dorothy snapped her book closed. "We are through here."

"Best of luck to you both," said Rosebud. "I so wish I could come with you, and watch the moment when your hopes are crushed forever, and the pain of your failure consumes you."

"You'll have to imagine it." Dorothy sheathed Bess and turned on her heels.

Claudia held up Dorothy's bag. "I have Sparky."

Dorothy grabbed Strontium's remnant in her arm. She marched out the door and down the stairs without looking back.

[23]

THE SCALE OF HYPATIA

The pilot ignored Dorothy as she climbed into the ornithopter and set Strontium down gently in the narrow cargo area behind the back seats. She folded the doll's right arm—its only remaining limb—across its chest, in an attempt to simulate a comfortable position.

Felicia reached the craft a few seconds behind Dorothy. "You're taking us to the city of New Chicago. Set us down outside the city limits, as close as you can get to the Worm station."

The pilot nodded, and started up the wings.

As Felicia climbed into the co-pilot seat, Dorothy grabbed her shoulder. "Uh-uh. You're back here with me this trip."

Felicia slumped her shoulders and complied.

Claudia brought up the rear. She handed Dorothy's bag to her with care, then looked at Felicia sitting behind the pilot and frowned.

"I need you up front." Dorothy handed the bag back to her. "See what you can do to rouse Sparky. Faded wings mean depression, but she's practically catatonic. Whatever Rosebud told her about the Scale must have been much worse than what she told us. I need to know as much about that as possible before we get there."

"You still wanna go through with this?" asked Claudia.

Dorothy looked back at Strontium. "I don't see we have a choice now."

Claudia nodded, and secured herself in the forward seat.

With everyone aboard, the pilot pulled the cockpit door shut and ramped up the beating wings. The ornithopter rose into the sky.

It took several minutes for the pounding of the wings to subside. Dorothy allowed Felicia that much time before saying anything. If the assassin chose to use that pause to rehearse some complex fabrication, so be it. The ornithopter reached gliding altitude, and the noise cut out. Dorothy took a deep breath.

"I didn't lie to you," said Felicia. "Not once."

Dorothy reorganized her thoughts before speaking. "I never said you did."

"You were about to. I thought I would cut to the chase. I haven't lied to you since I first came to you a week ago with this proposal."

"Since you drugged me and tied me up, you mean."

"I said I haven't lied," said Felicia. "I didn't say I haven't done anything wrong or unkind. Not that it matters, but I didn't enjoy that. I would have much preferred meeting you somewhere for coffee. My treat. I didn't dare risk that, and you know it."

"I would prefer we not change the subject," said Dorothy. "You say you haven't lied to me. Say I choose to accept that at face value. Where does that put us? Rosebud said some very troubling things. Things that contradict what I've heard from you. The curious thing about that is you didn't accuse her of lying. All you told me was not to listen to her."

"She was trying to manipulate us."

Dorothy raised an eyebrow at that. "Or communicate with us. Who can tell the difference? What do you suppose her taunt about torches meant?"

"The Scale is underground," said Felicia. "Given we know it's in New Chicago, and we know Atrylyn was able to access it, the most likely hiding place is the Worm tunnels. There's an unused annex near the New Chicago station. A service tunnel. It's meant to take trains in for maintenance, but the connector to the main line is completely buried. Excavating it would have been too costly, so the city sealed it off and forgot about it. The access passage is behind a locked door next to the unisex bathroom in the main boarding area. That leads directly to the annex tunnel. The tube is three miles long, with two branches leading to walls of bedrock. Officially, no one has been inside that section of the tunnels in at least ten years. If we're looking for the Scale underground, that's where we need to start."

Dorothy listened to all of this with pursed lips. "Mm hm. Interesting how you seem to know this in such detail."

"I was Harrison Cody's assistant for two years. You don't think I spent that time tapping NCSA resources for every useful piece of information I could find?"

166

"I didn't say it was suspicious, just interesting. I came to the same conclusion as you, though nowhere near that precisely."

Felicia shrugged. "Precision is what I do."

"Yet everything you've told me about the one thing we are trying to find has been vague or flat out wrong," said Dorothy. "A bit inconsistent, that. Wouldn't you say? What should I make of it?"

"I told you," said Felicia. "Stories about legendary artifacts vary."

"You also told me the Scale can only be used for healing. That isn't true, is it?"

Felicia hesitated. "I don't know. I thought it was true. I only ever meant to use it to lift this curse. The legends are consistent in describing the Scale as something that cannot be used as a weapon."

"It will bring us more pain than anything Rosebud can do to us?" said Dorothy. "That sounds weapon-like to me."

Felicia crossed her arms and looked out the window. "I am sorry. Honestly. I don't know what she meant by that. I hope it isn't true." She turned to face Dorothy. "I swore an oath to you on an assassins' guild contract. I told you there exists no stronger bond, and that was true. Member of the guild or not, if I break that oath they will hunt me down and torture me to death for invoking it. If you choose not to trust me, there is nothing I can do about that. I neither need nor deserve your trust. You are correct to withhold it. On the other hand, you may certainly rely on my self-interest. I swore to you I would see this task through to the end. The consequences to me of breaking that promise exceed by far anything I would hope to gain from betraying you. Believe for now I am telling you the truth, because I don't dare do otherwise."

Dorothy scanned Felicia's eyes, hunting for signs of dishonesty. "Felicia... I want to trust you."

"Don't."

"Don't trust you?"

Felicia looked away. "Don't want that."

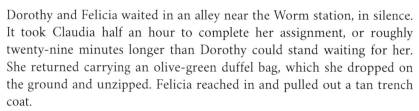

Dorothy and Felicia waited in an alley near the Worm station, in silence. It took Claudia half an hour to complete her assignment, or roughly twenty-nine minutes longer than Dorothy could stand waiting for her. She returned carrying an olive-green duffel bag, which she dropped on the ground and unzipped. Felicia reached in and pulled out a tan trench coat.

"They didn't have black?"

"They did, but when I asked the nice girl in ladieswear what the best knife-hiding color is, she suggested beige. Should I take it back?"

"Both of you, knock it off." Dorothy placed Strontium in the duffel and zipped it closed. "Once we enter the Worm station we will probably have five minutes before someone recognizes us. High-tech ear cuffs or not, Claudia, your face is the most well-known in the whole city. It's one thing to spend ten minutes in a clothier, quite another to walk through thousands of people waiting for their trains."

"I can help with that." Felicia removed her hooded tunic. Underneath, she wore a black t-shirt under an elaborate network of sheaths matching the ones on her belt, legs and boots, all occupied with shiny blades. She tossed the tunic to Claudia. "Cover up that hair."

Claudia pulled on the garment, and tugged the hood over her head. It sat more snugly on her frame than on Felicia's ballet dancer physique. "Wonderful."

They made their way through ticketing, having purchased their fares in advance with different assumed names than on their trip south several days earlier. That trick might not work a third time, but then, they wouldn't need it to.

The door waited for them exactly where Felicia described, latched with a simple padlock.

"Never a Cody around when you need one," said Felicia.

"Oh, please. I'm a Cody." Dorothy drew a pair of scissors in a cloth cover from her bag. She whispered an incantation that caused the lock to glow bright orange and then used the scissors to cut through it like taffy. It fell to the floor, and lay smoking as it cooled. They entered.

Once inside, Felicia let the trench coat slide off her shoulders and left it on the floor. Claudia peeled off the hooded tunic and tossed it back to her.

The three of them donned their headlamps and took their first steps on a three-mile trek through the dark. The light beams provided little information about their surroundings. Facing the tunnel walls treated them to the uniform view of a smooth surface never intended as a vista, and facing forward allowed the inky background to utterly consume their light. It made for slow going, with each traveler reluctant to push forward too quickly.

"Are we there yet?" asked Claudia after less than five minutes of this experience.

"No," said Dorothy.

"How about now?"

"Seriously, if we get there in less than an hour it will be a miracle. Please don't let that hour be a constant barrage of that joke."

"Okay, sorry." She paused. "How about now?"

"Stop it," said Felicia.

Dorothy opened her bag and peered inside. Sparky lay on her side, curled in a ball, eyes closed. Unsure as to whether pixies experienced true sleep, she chose not to disturb her passenger, and made a mental note to ask Aplomado for lessons in fey biology.

"If we are not able to transport the Scale, and if you can't figure out how to make it work, we should call in the council," said Felicia. "We will have nothing left to lose at that point."

"That's the plan," said Dorothy. "I'll do my best, but I know my limitations. Will thirty minutes be enough of a head start for you?"

"I won't need a head start."

Dorothy looked at Felicia, inadvertently shining her headlamp in her eyes. She looked away as Felicia threw up her arm. "Yes, you will. Once I call them, they could be here in fifteen minutes. The NCSA could be here in five. You'll need time to get to the surface."

"I won't need a head start because I'm not running. If you call the council, or the NCSA, or anyone else, I will be here waiting when they arrive."

"I don't understand."

"Yes, you do," said Felicia. "You just don't want to. I'm not running. No matter what happens at the end of this tunnel, the next step for me is surrender. There's nowhere else for me to go from here. I won't kill those ten people to return to the guild, and I can't go home alone to let this pain slowly grind me down to nothing. As much as I hate your therapy idea, it's the only option available to me that includes a shred of hope. I think I have come to terms with that. I'll turn myself over to the NCSA, and hope for the best. You'll put in a good word for me, I hope?"

"I... Yes, I will happily put in a good word for you," said Dorothy. "Are you sure this is what you want?"

"It is absolutely not what I want, but there is a chance it is what I need. I know this isn't really me talking. This is the curse. I'm not even sure if there is a me anymore. No matter what the cause, I have discovered in my time working with you I want to be a better person. I know I started this entire adventure with the specific goal of being a worse person again, but that's not what I want anymore. I've seen what you have, and it's better than any life I can buy. I want to be the kind of person who other people respect instead of fear. I want to be... liked."

"I like you," said Dorothy.

"Do you?" asked Felicia. "Are you sure you know what you are committing to with that declaration? It seems so simple to you, I'm sure. You like so many people. I've never had that pleasure, or that advantage, and I don't comprehend how one goes about liking someone in a personal way."

"Don't overcomplicate it. Your line is, 'I like you, too.' Give that a try."

Felicia responded with a silence Dorothy could not read, especially in her reluctance to blind Felicia with her headlamp again.

"Felicia? I can't—"

"I like you, too," said the woman who once hoped to watch Dorothy's death, and more recently prevented it multiple times.

Dorothy smiled. "An excellent first step. I know you don't think this is the real you, and I don't know how to answer that, other than to say the real you is whoever you decide she is, curse or no curse. Who you have decided to be these last few days is someone I am happy to call my friend."

Felicia did not respond right away. Rather than press that point, Dorothy allowed the silence. Felicia had much to contemplate, and Dorothy would provide her a support system as she moved into a new and terrifying phase of her life.

"Please let me use the Scale."

In the dark tunnel, Dorothy closed her eyes. "Please don't do this to yourself."

"I will surrender first," said Felicia. "Wait for the NCSA to get here. Put me in shackles. Magically paralyze me. Do whatever it takes to satisfy you I won't pose a risk. Let me swear to you on anything you will believe I will go to prison peacefully. Just please, please, give me the chance to learn who I really am."

"I can't do that," said Dorothy.

"I know you think that. My life as an assassin is over. Even if it turns out who I really am is that monster you despise, I will be powerless to do anything about it. I will be in prison, which is what that person deserves."

"I don't want to despise you. If that's who you are without the spell, I don't want to know it. Please let that person go. You are better off without her, and if she comes back, I will miss you so much."

It took Felicia a few seconds to respond to that. "If our positions were reversed, I wouldn't want to lose you either."

"Does that mean you forgive me?" asked Dorothy.

"Maybe. I don't know what it feels like to forgive someone." Without warning, Felicia hugged her, resting her head on Dorothy's collarbone.

"Jesus," said Claudia.

"Button it, de Queiroz," said Felicia. "I'm having a moment."

170

Dorothy laughed. "So you are." She hugged Felicia back, then pulled away. "Come on. Let's get this done. I promise when you turn yourself in I will be there for you." As she plotted out the details of how she would best achieve this, she planted her foot on something hard that cracked beneath her weight.

"Ow." Dorothy reached down and picked up something cool and flexible. She shined her headlamp on a watch with a metal band and a cracked crystal.

"What is that?" asked Claudia.

Dorothy looked more closely. "A Rolex."

"For reals? They still make those?"

"No," said Felicia. "That's worth thousands as a collectable. Tens of thousands if you hadn't broken it."

"Someone lost it in this tunnel?" Dorothy played the beam of her headlamp across the floor ahead of her. Several objects returned shiny reflections.

"Holy shit!" said Claudia. "Check this out!"

Dorothy turned her light in that direction, revealing a golden chalice in Claudia's hands and a playful grin on her face.

Felicia produced the unmistakable sound of a rapier being drawn.

"What's going on?" Dorothy laid her hand on Bess's hilt.

"We're in a cave, surrounded by treasure," said Felicia. "Do the math."

Dorothy gulped. "Dragon hoard."

"Dragon hoard," said Felicia.

"Okay," said Claudia. "We killed one dragon already, right?"

"That was without a doubt the easiest dragon to kill that ever lived," said Felicia. "Picture a beast twice that size. Now picture one twice as big as that. What you have in your head now is still well below average. A typical dragon could swallow us all at once without chewing or reduce us to ash in half a minute."

"Do you think this is what Rosebud meant?" asked Dorothy. "That we would find the Scale but be eaten in the process?"

"That lacks the subtlety of a wizard's taunt," said Felicia. "Though, even if she did mean something else, there could still be a dragon. Some other worm who found the Scale and added it to his mountain of booty. He might not even know its significance, just that it has value. That's often enough."

Dorothy drew Bess. "How are you at slaying dragons?"

I have slain two dragons, and failed to slay four others.

"I don't like those odds. If there were a dragon here, would you be able to tell?"

Aye, as would you. Dragons rarely employ stealth. They do not need it.

"What is she telling you?" asked Felicia.

"She says if there were a dragon here we would know it. What should we do?"

"Press forward, blades naked," said the assassin.

"That sounds seriously dirty," said Claudia.

"Quietly, please."

They followed Felicia's directives, silently advancing through the equally soundless tunnel. Artifacts of value appeared sporadically and in patches as they progressed. Eventually they grew so plentiful Dorothy needed to brush them aside to wade through them. Then dense enough she had to walk atop them.

Ahead of them, their torch beams exposed a wall signifying the end of the tunnel. In front of it, at least eight feet tall, on an altar in a grand niche, stood a golden column. It supported—and served as fulcrum for—a beam nearly as wide as the height of the base. A golden tray, large enough to comfortably hold an adult, hung from each end of this bar, suspended on trios of iron chains. An indicator needle at the tip of the column, pointing upward into a ring of gold with notches marking regular intervals, completed the unmistakable image of this device's function. They beheld an oversized pan balance.

Felicia fell to her knees and dropped her sword.

"The Scale of Hypatia," whispered Dorothy.

"Fuck," said Claudia.

Felicia turned around, stark confusion and fear in her eyes, evident even in the glare of her headlamp. "I don't understand."

"Tales of legendary objects may vary," said Dorothy. "Or so I am told."

"How can you mock me right now?" asked Felicia.

"It's not mockery." Dorothy shook her head. "Maybe it is. I don't know. Forgive me for feeling punchy after what we have been through to get here." She sheathed Bess, and climbed over the pile of loot to inspect the Scale more closely.

"Do you not understand what this means?" asked Felicia.

Dorothy opened her palm and willed her spellbook into it. "That's what I'm going to try to figure out. I don't see how this changes anything. Whether the Scale is a piece of dragon armor or a weighing tool shouldn't matter, should it? This is just another element of the legend that has been garbled in the retelling." Exceeding Dorothy's most generous hopes, the text fragments Strontium had obtained scraping the ether in Atrylyn's library cohered in the presence of the Scale. Though still incomplete, what did come through read more as instructions than an incantation.

Felicia climbed over the hoard, stumbling more than once. She reached Dorothy and slapped the book out of her hand. When it broke contact, it evaporated. The tendril of red smoke rushed back into Dorothy's body to be reabsorbed.

"How can you be a student of magic and not understand its rich history of irony?" cried Felicia. "You don't see how this changes anything? It changes everything! A dragon scale is a shield! It signifies protection! Such an object, enchanted, would aid those who used it, for their betterment or their health. That is why I thought the Scale could only be used to heal." She pointed to the Scale. "Look at that! What does it symbolize?"

"Balance?" said Dorothy.

"You fool! The balance scale is one of the oldest, deepest symbols on both our worlds! Where have you seen it? What does it mean?"

Dorothy's jaw dropped. "Justice. Oh, my God."

"Wait, isn't that a good thing?" said Claudia. "We like justice, don't we?"

"Oh, no," said Dorothy. "Oh, God."

Claudia shook her head. "What's wrong? I don't see the problem here."

"Arbitration," said Dorothy.

Felicia offered a bitter smile. "Now you see."

"Arbitration?" said Claudia. "What does that mean?"

"It means that justice is an absolute," said Dorothy. "The problem is it's never the same absolute from person to person. This is why we have so many judges. Justice is an ideal. The only way to apply it without bending to the whims of a despot is to have many, many people to argue the specifics. But Hypatia was a monarch. Benevolent, so they say, but if any of the stories we heard this week have even a kernel of truth to them, her rule was absolute. No checks, no… balance. One arbiter for all law, for all time." Dorothy hung her head. "This tool doesn't give people what they want or what they need." She looked at the duffel containing the battered shell of her dear friend. "It gives them what they deserve."

"There's your catch," said Felicia to Claudia. "Do any of us know what we truly deserve? Your friends would say I deserve death. Your lover says I deserve a chance at a new life. They can't both be right. You don't dare use this without knowing what you deserve."

"Then how do we figure that out?" asked Claudia.

A booming contralto came from behind them. "Oh, that part is easy."

Dorothy spun around. She lost her footing in the treasure and took a moment to regain her balance. When she looked up, her lamp shined into a pair of bright pink eyes that shined back at her.

The owner of those eyes spat a dozen fireballs at the tunnel walls. Some found their marks, igniting torches ensconced there. They illuminated the resident dragon, sitting on its haunches in a tube designed to accommodate a train car with plenty of margin for a magnetic cushion and maintenance equipment, filling half its width and most of its height. Pearly white scales covered the beast's surface, glistening iridescently as it moved, their paleness the result of a dragonish albinism confirmed by rose-colored irises.

Before this week, Dorothy had only ever met one dragon-kind, the half dragon Basil Heatherington. His form mimicked that of a human, or rather of an angel, were angel wings leathery and bat-like. They sprang from his back, distinct from his arms. Not so on the wyvern. Forelegs and wings coexisted, one and the same. In these close quarters, Dorothy had no sense of their span. She had no doubt, however, of being in reach of those claws.

"I tell you what you deserve," said Hypatia.

[24]

THE WISH AND THE CATCH

Dorothy went down on one knee and lowered her head. "Your majesty."

"Imperial majesty, if you must stand on ceremony," said the wyvern. "I don't require it of you. You may stand."

Dorothy rose, arms extended to keep her balance in the glittery detritus. The torches blazed brightly enough to reveal the scope of Hypatia's collection. Gold predominated. Though no longer as rare as it had been pre-Mayhem, it made up for its monetary depreciation by virtue of its shininess, a favorite quality among dragons. Ostentatious jewels abounded, as well as items of obvious technology. Anything of value to mortals warranted attention and acquisition.

"Queen Hypatia?" said Felicia.

"Again, Empress, though not for quite some time now. You may address me as Lurker Hypatia now, or Subterranean Hypatia, if you feel the need for a title. Madam Hypatia will serve." She spoke in a vaguely Mediterranean accent, not Greek, not Italian. Something non-real, presumably.

"Forgive us, Madam Hypatia," said Felicia. "We meant no trespass here. We believed you long dead."

"You're the one with the courage, I take it," said Hypatia. "Your friend with the green sack looks fit to soil herself."

Dorothy spared a glance at Claudia, frozen in place and trembling. "It's all right."

Claudia looked at Dorothy, and some degree of relaxation slipped into her posture.

"No, wait." Hypatia lowered her head, tiny scales along her neck ringing as they slid past each other. She brought her snout within two feet of Dorothy's face. "The one with the courage is you." She looked back toward Felicia. "You're the one with... something else. Oh, this will be intriguing."

"Madam Hypatia," said Dorothy. "If I may, my name is Dorothy. These are my companions Claudia and Felicia. We have come here in search of your scale, believing it can help my friend. Claudia? Would you open the bag, please?"

Claudia unzipped the duffel bag at her feet, and Hypatia's head went for it like a snake. Claudia cried out and fell backward, her bottom landing in the coin pile.

Hypatia ignored her, and sniffed the broken mannequin. "She is in terrible disrepair."

"She is a witch, trapped in that form after losing her mortal body. I hoped the Scale could restore her to what she was."

"Oh, it can. It can." Hypatia brought her gaze back to Dorothy. "That's what I made it for. Crises such as these. You were wise to come to me."

Dorothy looked at Felicia. "I came on advice from a friend."

"It was excellent advice. Now then, shall we begin?"

Dorothy's heart pounded. This magnanimous being offered her services, her magic, to accomplish the impossible, with utmost courtesy and understanding. Strontium's life could be regranted to her in moments.

Or it could all go horribly wrong. Rosebud's words ringing in her ears, Felicia's admonition foremost in her heart, Dorothy spoke. "I have... an apprehension I must broach first."

Hypatia pulled back her head, and asked with no change of facial expression, "What disquiets you?"

"I have some knowledge of magic, Madam Hypatia, and of wish-granting. Before we proceed, may I ask, what is the catch?"

"I don't take your meaning."

"Does this wish also carry a penalty? If so, may I know its nature? I want to make an informed decision."

"Ah," said Hypatia. "You speak of the sacrifice."

Dorothy's heart sank at the word. "Sacrifice?"

The dragon frowned, an action that took proportionately longer than a human, given the size of her brows. "Yes. Do you not know the workings of the Scale?"

176

"We were expecting…" Dorothy looked at Felicia again. "Something else."

"It is no matter. I can school you easily enough." Hypatia reached forward with her right foreleg, now clearly longer than it appeared tucked beneath her. Dorothy and Felicia lurched out of its way in different directions. The wyvern tapped the golden dish on the left with her claw, producing a ring and rattling of chains. "You place your wish in this tray." She pinged the tray on the right. "And your sacrifice in this one. If they balance, or if your sacrifice outweighs your wish, it is granted. If not, the wish in all its variations is forever denied."

Dorothy took a moment to absorb this. "I thought… I was afraid you would judge me. Only grant my wish if you found it just."

"Indeed I will! This is my measure of justice. For what could be more just than renouncing something you value as much as what you hope to gain?"

"I need to sacrifice something?" Dorothy looked around her. They had brought nothing with them but the clothes they wore. She opened her bag, immediately finding both her sleeping pixie and a great deal of cash. "Is money an acceptable sacrifice?"

"Do you value this money as much as your friend's life? Be honest with yourself. Lying to me will serve no purpose if the Scale rules the sacrifice inadequate."

Dorothy looked at the stacks of large bills, Felicia's compensation for the work of ending lives. "No, I do not value it as much as her life."

"Something else, then," said the dragon.

A box of mints. Half a roll of toilet paper. A pocket knife. A plastic-encased tortoise skeleton. All of these objects stared back at her, some of reasonable utility, but none with the value of a human life.

"I see you carry an Isthmian Blade," said Hypatia. "Perhaps you value that?"

Dorothy looked down at her belt, where Bess waited invisibly, though apparently visible to some. "I do value her. She is my friend, and I will not sacrifice one for the other. I am sorry, Madam Hypatia. I will have to find something to sacrifice and return at a later time."

Hypatia shook her head. "Alas, you are here now. One visit, one sacrifice, one wish. Depart, and our business here ends."

"One visit?" Dorothy looked to Felicia for any kind of support, but she had only a mournful head shake to offer. The wealth of things Felicia did not know or had gotten completely wrong about the Scale had now doomed Strontium to live out her days as a motionless block of wood. "Why can't we return?" Dorothy asked Hypatia. "Isn't the Scale your creation? Don't you make the rules? Can't I appeal to your understanding of our circumstance?"

"Alas," said the dragon. "I did make the rules, but they are fixed now. The Scale will only operate as I designed it to. There is no override, as it were. Please understand, the constraints were necessary. If I allowed for multiple visits, the potential for abuse would have been boundless. For my gifts to have merit, my supplicants needed to be sincere in their preparation. The limitations compelled any who came before me to ensure in advance their pleas would be meaningful. I am sorry for your disappointment, but the process cannot be altered. Whatever you intend to sacrifice must be something you brought with you today."

Dorothy held back tears. To have come this far, only to be turned away for insufficient briefing on the rules, pushed her to the breaking point. "Please," she choked. "I brought nothing else."

"Not so. The sacrifice may be abstract."

A tear broke through and ran down Dorothy's cheek. Her throat tightened. "Abstract?"

"Some quality you possess," said Hypatia. "Intelligence. Athletic ability. Sexual prowess. Acumen. There are many examples. Hundreds of supplicants have come to me to give up some intrinsic component of their very selves to achieve their wishes."

Dorothy looked to Claudia for guidance, and found only fear in her eyes. What part of Dorothy, after all, would her love counsel her to lose forever? She turned to Felicia, and found something even more troubling in her gaze. Wide-eyed astonishment. What aspect of this discovery could shock her friend more than it shocked her? She shook her head, desperate to clear it of confusion.

"Come now, Dorothy," said Hypatia. "Surely you value some facet of your being as much as you value this witch."

At the word "witch," images from the past five years flooded Dorothy's consciousness. Strontium and Ian taking her in as she and five-year-old Melody sought refuge from monsters who wanted to kill them. Strontium consumed by flames as she sacrificed herself to save Dorothy and the children when those monsters caught up with them. Finding a book impossibly inscribed to her, written in languages she did not know, but read fluently. Decoding the various spells they described, and discovering an aptitude for casting them she could not have imagined possessing. Using magic to protect her family and friends. Then discovering Strontium's mind trapped in her own, offering her silent guidance as Dorothy grew into a witch in her own right. Beginning an apprenticeship with Aplomado in the ways of sorcery, mere weeks after setting aside her life's ambition to become a professor of mathematics. Five years spent finding within herself a love of the mystical that overtook everything else true about herself.

She burst into tears.

"Dotty?" Claudia waded through the trinkets to take Dorothy in her arms.

"I'm all right," Dorothy whispered into Claudia's ear. "I can do this." She cleared her throat, wiped the tears from her face, and inhaled deeply. "I will sacrifice magic."

"Dotty!"

"No, it's all right. I lived without it for twenty years. I can live without it again. I love it, but without it I will still have you." She looked at Felicia. "All of you. This is worth doing. I have made my choice."

Hypatia's lips curled back in a smile somewhere between soothing and terrifying. "Then place your wish and sacrifice."

Dorothy picked up Strontium's broken form. "We're almost home, sister. See you soon." She kissed the top of the scratched, cracked, lifeless head, and placed the doll in the left tray. With the added weight, it lowered, pulling the indicator needle all the way to the left. Then she looked at the right tray. "How do I...?"

"For an abstract sacrifice, a declaration suffices."

Dorothy nodded. "All right. I wish for my witch-sister to be restored to her living body, in good health and fitness, and of sound mind. In return, I sacrifice my magical knowledge and abilities."

They waited.

The needle trembled, and shifted rightward as the bar tipped in the direction of Dorothy's offering. Her teeth chattered in anticipation of her sister's return, and anxiety at the feeling of having her life's purpose, newly discovered, ripped from her forever.

Little more than halfway to vertical, the needle stalled out.

The chattering in Dorothy's teeth increased as she stared at the indicator, willing it to complete its journey. It did not.

"I don't understand. What's happening?"

Hypatia shook her head. "It is done."

"But... but she's not back."

"Observe the Scale. You provided insufficient sacrifice."

It took several seconds for the grief contained in that statement to travel from Dorothy's ears to her heart. "No," she whispered. She ran to Strontium, still inert in the tray, surface still warm, now forever trapped in a motionless, expressionless doll. "No! Do it again! Strontium!"

Claudia put her hand on Dorothy's shoulder. "Dotty..."

"No!" She flinched away from the comfort. "No!" She whirled on the dragon. "This isn't right! This isn't justice! You can't leave her like this!" The words came out in spasms, between sobs.

"I am so sorry," said Hypatia. "You valued your friend's life more than you valued your witchcraft. There is honor in that. Please take some comfort from knowing it."

"No! This isn't right!" Dorothy pulled Strontium from the tray and held the lifeless doll to her breast. Witch and wood collapsed in a heap and slid several feet through the accumulated treasure, where Dorothy wept uncontrollably.

"There, there." The wyvern turned her eye on Claudia. "What of you, frightened one? Did you bring me a wish as well?"

Claudia ignored her taunt, choosing instead to clamber down to Dorothy and hold her as she sobbed.

"That leaves you, I suppose," said Hypatia to Felicia. "I can tell you have a wish. Did you bring a suitable sacrifice?"

Dorothy waited for Felicia to say no, for Felicia to come to her support in this lowest of moments, for the three of them to leave together and make the best of the calamity their choices had brought them to.

And she waited.

Felicia walked to Dorothy, gems and coin crunching under her feet. She looked down upon her only friend, the only human bond she had made in a lifetime of violence and cruelty. A tear fell from her eye, lost in the river washing over Dorothy's face.

"Felicia?"

The assassin strode away with purpose, and climbed into the left tray of the Scale.

Dorothy sat up, face soaked, throat raw. "Felicia! No!"

"I'm sorry," said Felicia. "Please know you were a good friend."

"What is your wish?" asked Hypatia.

Felicia looked up, steel in her eyes, tears on her cheeks. "I wish for the enchantment of empathy to be lifted from me. I wish to end my pain. I wish to learn who I truly am, and what I can be."

Dorothy stood, and immediately fell. "Stop her!"

Claudia made a move for the Scale, intercepted with terrifying speed by the dragon, who shot her foreleg into the treasure to form a barricade.

"What have you brought to sacrifice?" said the dragon. "What do you have with you that you value as much as being free of this enchantment?"

Felicia met Dorothy's eyes.

"Felicia..." whispered Dorothy. "No."

The assassin looked at the dragon. "Dorothy O'Neill's trust."

The needle ascended to the top of the gold ring, wavered there for a moment, then continued beyond the balance point by a clear margin. Felicia rode her tray upward, watching the other descend. When she passed the tipping point, her eyes went wide.

The assassin sprang.

She hit the hoard pile, and surfed it for several yards, scooping up Dorothy's bag in the same motion, before launching herself into a sprint. Hypatia rolled her body out of the way, allowing her to pass, and separating her from her former companions. As Felicia reached the edge of the torch-lit segment of the tunnel, she stopped and drew her sword. She turned, meeting Dorothy's eyes. At this distance, in this light, the glance conveyed little information. Dorothy desperately hunted for respect there. Or affection.

Felicia raised her rapier in salute.

Then she fled.

"What have you done?" shouted Dorothy.

"I granted her wish," said Hypatia. "That one understood the nature of sacrifice. How touching she valued your trust so much. Were you close?"

"Yes, God damn it! Now she's lost the one thing that stopped her from being a monster! A killer! She had a chance at a real life, and you ripped that away from her! If she goes back to being who she was, all she will ever know is solitude and violence!" Dorothy looked at Strontium, and tears sprang forth anew. "You ruined two lives today! Forever! What kind of benevolent monarch would do that to people begging for her help?"

"Benevolent?" Hypatia grinned. "Who could possibly have called me that?"

[25]

EMPRESS

Over Dorothy's head, the earth containing the Worm tunnel rumbled. No doubt a train had departed New Chicago in a neighboring tube.

She clutched Strontium's silent form close, and glared at the enormous dragon, sitting less than ten feet from her. "I hope you're not planning to kill us. Trust me when I say that won't end well for you."

Hypatia snorted. Smoke puffed from her nostrils, and she pulled her lips back in a playful smile. "I will take you at your word. Fear not. I have no intent to harm you." She shifted her massive frame in the tunnel, opening a clear passage back the way they had come in. "You are quite free to leave, though I hope you will choose to stay a while longer."

Dorothy pushed away the adrenaline rush triggered by this statement, refusing to trust the second chance it might imply. "Why would I do that?"

Claudia put her hand on Dorothy's shoulder. "Dotty, we need to go. Sparky was in that bag. We need to get her back from killer bitch."

"She didn't want the pixie," said Dorothy. "She wanted the money. That bag is probably already abandoned if Felicia knows what's good for her. If Sparky wakes up, that treacherous snake is dead."

"I thought you were close," said Hypatia. "That's not a kind thing to call a friend."

Dorothy drew Bess and pointed her at Hypatia's snout. "That's not your concern! You've done enough today to destroy that relationship. Don't you dare lecture me on how to feel about it! I have no way of knowing if anything she felt for me means a damn to her anymore. Even if it does, she's as likely to brush it aside as an impediment to her work, which is killing people. My dear friend may be my mortal enemy now, and I have no way of knowing!" She extended her sword arm farther in Hypatia's direction, less than a yard away from the wyvern's flaring nostrils. "So don't you dare tell me about kindness and friendship!"

I do not recommend combat under these conditions, said Bess.

"Noted," whispered Dorothy

The dragon moved in closer, perhaps in response to Dorothy's posturing, but with no change of expression. This near, the heat of her breath oppressed Dorothy, who stood her ground. "I meant no offense."

"Shut up," said Dorothy. "Why are you asking me to stay?"

"A proposal," said Hypatia. "I like the cut of your jib. Believe me when I say I am sorry for your loss today, but there may yet be something for you to gain from our meeting."

"Dotty..."

"No." Dorothy did not look at Claudia. "I want to hear this. I want to hear what a dragon who doomed my two friends to lifetimes of misery thinks she still has to offer me. Can I assume this is not a second chance at life for Strontium?"

"Alas, no," said Hypatia. "As I said, once a wish is denied, all its variations are forever denied as well. No one will ever be able to use my Scale to restore your friend. I am sorry."

"Save it. If not that, what do you imagine I could want from you, other than distance?"

Hypatia paused. Overhead, the ceiling tunnel rumbled again. Unusual for two trains to depart in such rapid sequence. Perhaps a newly arriving train explained one of the vibrations. "Very well. Directly, I have an empire to rebuild. For that, I need allies. You are a human of uncommon courage and intellect. I suspect you also wield some influence in your city. Do I read that correctly?"

"I am well-connected, if that's what you mean. How could you know that?"

Hypatia pulled her head back and rested her chin on her forepaws. "Wyvernly intuition, to be honest. You would be surprised how far that will stretch, given sufficient ambition."

Dorothy lowered her sword, but did not release it. She turned to face Claudia, whose calm demeanor in the face of this monster surely bespoke her trust in Dorothy's protection. Dorothy had suffered enough loss today of those in her trust. She took Claudia's hand, and passed

Strontium into her arm. Then she leaned in and kissed her, resisting the dread it would be their last.

"What are you doing?" said Claudia.

"I am staying," said Dorothy. "You are going. This dragon has shattered a piece of me I didn't know I had until this week, and if she feels she can make amends for that, I need to hear her out. But you don't. Please take Strontium to Aplomado, turn yourself in to Harrison, and explain everything. I need you safe. I just lost two people I cared dearly about. Please protect the one person I care about above all others. Will you do that for me?"

"Dotty... I can't leave you here alone."

Dorothy looked at Hypatia. "I'm not alone. I believe her promise not to harm me."

"Point of information," said the dragon. "I never promised that."

Dorothy pointed Bess at Hypatia's eye. "Promise it now!"

Hypatia laughed, a deep, bellowing sound that rattled the coins beneath them. "Oh, I have chosen well, indeed. All right, little witch, I promise I will not harm you, nor allow harm to come to you as we discuss the terms of your employment. If you refuse my proposal, I promise you free passage from this tunnel."

"And a full day's head start."

"Ha! And, as you say, a full day's head start." Hypatia directed her attention to Claudia. "Your friend is safe. You may depart in confidence of that."

"She's not my friend," said Claudia. "She's my fiancée."

Dorothy kissed Claudia again. "I love you." She offered her the sword.

"I... love you, too. What are you doing?"

"A highly trained assassin, with apparently no sense of loyalty, is right down this tunnel. Bess will protect you."

Shall I slay the turncoat? asked Bess.

"No!" said Dorothy. "Not unless you have to kill her to protect Claudia."

"Did she just ask you if I should kill Felicia?" said Claudia. "Because I'm down for that. I did it once before."

"No! Both of you! We are not killing her today!"

"Dotty, I know what it meant to you to save her, but the assassin who stole your bag is not the buddy we've traveled with all week. I liked her, too, but that person is already dead."

"You don't know that! I can't trust her anymore, but that doesn't mean I stopped caring about her!" Dorothy looked down. "Maybe I hate her. I don't know." Another rumble sounded overhead. Surely not a third train so soon. Three miles away from the main hub of the Worm station that noise could be any form of human activity. Construction, perhaps. Dorothy shook her head. "Please, for me, for today, don't kill her. Maybe I will feel differently tomorrow, but for today, I'm not ready to end it like that."

Claudia took Bess by the hilt. Her posture relaxed slightly at the moment of contact, and she held the blade up to her eyes. "I know. Don't freak out, Bess. This is Dotty we're talking about. We both gotta trust her." She paused. "Atta girl." Claudia gave Dorothy one final nod, then set off down the tunnel at a trot, broken doll tucked under her arm, sword at the ready.

"All right," said Dorothy to the dragon. "What's your proposal?"

Hypatia lifted her head, and turned, tracking Claudia's exit. "That was brave, allowing her to escape."

"Don't change the subject. You have something to say to me, say it."

The dragon turned back to her. "You're angry."

"You're goddamn right I'm angry!" said Dorothy. "I risked everything to help those two people, and now they're lost to me because of some damn dragon game! You'd better have something amazing in mind to make up for this."

"Chief advisor to the Empress," said Hypatia.

Dorothy crossed her arms. "I'm listening."

"I have a mind to rebuild my empire. That will require some support."

"Why now? Don't tell me you've been waiting to find the right partner."

"Nothing of the sort," said Hypatia. "This is no sudden impulse. When our worlds merged, I did not know what to make of my new circumstance. Exile is one thing. Solitude quite another. So few of my kind survived. So few of any kind. My Scale followed me into this new world, but without anyone to share it, what joy could it bring me? I languished in a mountain cave, barely motivated to hunt for sustenance. Then, after more than a year of this existence, the most wonderful thing happened."

"The people came back," said Dorothy. "Is that what you mean?"

"Oh! Yes!" said the Dragon. "Not in their former numbers, but so many more than the paltry few scratching out their civilization from nothing. The meager city over our heads sprang to a metropolis in a matter of months! I sensed this would become the seat of the kingdoms to rise. Using my sorcery to cloak my presence from curious eyes, I found my way to this chamber, to hibernate until the city grew to a proper country."

Dorothy looked around her at the amassed wealth in the tunnel. "Did you bring all this with you?"

"Ah," said Hypatia. "No, just the Scale. The rest was... a tax, I suppose is the simplest explanation. Travelers found themselves relieved of some portion of their coin as they passed near my enchanted lair. It draws gold surreptitiously. I will admit I was surprised at the magnitude of my haul when I woke after ten years of slumber. The city had grown beyond my most hopeful estimates, providing me with more than enough capital for my needs."

"Gold is much more common than it was before the Mayhem Wave," said Dorothy. "Whatever you hoped to buy with this, you should know it's not as much money as it looks like."

"No matter. My power does not lie in riches. The world is ripe now, and my opportunity has arrived to regain what was taken from me so many centuries ago."

"Taken from you?" said Dorothy. "Felicia said you foiled the coup attempt. Was that another thing she got wrong?"

"Foiled? Oh, my. Yes, I suppose she missed the mark on that. What did she tell you of my reign?"

"Mostly things that other people contradicted. She told me you ruled an entire continent for hundreds of years. Peace, prosperity, et cetera. She called you a benevolent monarch. Some other dragons tried to overthrow you, and in the battle, you lost a scale of your armor. Obviously, that part was completely off." Dorothy spread her arms in the direction of the giant pan balance behind them. "Behold the Scale of Hypatia, last remnant of the White Wyvern!"

"That seems to have been garbled somewhat in the translation."

"You think?" said Dorothy. "Apparently everything she told me was nonsense. She said the Scale was imbued with your magic, and the source of your power. When you lost it, your empire crumbled."

"That part is true enough," said Hypatia. "There was indeed a coup, not quite as unsuccessful as you were led to believe. My Scale was taken from me, though obviously not as your friend depicted. I fled my usurpers and went into exile. How ghastly the legends describe the Scale as a part of my body!"

"In more than one variation, apparently," said Dorothy. "Ruprecht, another dragon of Felicia's acquaintance, said you tore a scale from your body as a symbolic sacrifice, and used its power in acts of generosity to reward your subjects. That was obviously wrong, too. Rosebud..."

Hypatia tilted her enormous head with raised brows. "Rosebud?"

Dorothy looked at the Scale. The value of its gold frame alone would have staggered the economy of whatever nation possessed it, before the Mayhem Wave rendered gold both common and of somewhat lessened usefulness in its properties. "Rosebud. The wizardess. She told me you used the Scale to cement your rule. That you granted wishes as a means of controlling the people."

"Well now," said the dragon. "It seems at least one of your sources got the gist of my story right after all. The Scale is indeed imbued with my magic, as they all claimed. It is my primary tool, and prized possession. Your Rosebud was right to tell you my empire was built on the strength of this one object. Do you understand why?"

"It has been a very long week," said Dorothy. "If this is another riddle—"

"No riddle. I am sorry for your weariness. Sincerely. I simply want to know if you have divined the Scale's secret, now that you have fallen... into its influence."

"It grants wishes. That doesn't seem like a secret."

"It doesn't do anything of the sort."

Dorothy took a moment to let that sink in. "It granted Felicia's wish."

"Yes," said Hypatia. "At the cost of something far dearer to her. Do you think she feels satisfied with that outcome?"

Dorothy's throat tightened. "I wouldn't know. Perhaps she is sad, in her own way, and will cry all the way to the bank after her next contract. She could well be delighted. My trust probably doesn't mean a thing to her anymore."

"Ah. You do not understand after all." The dragon lifted her head and gazed upon the balance. "The Scale would never have allowed your friend's sacrifice if did not mean anything. It detects false offerings. That is why it did not work for you. You said yourself you lived for years without magic, and could do so again. Giving it up would not have caused you sufficient hardship, and so your sacrifice was rejected. The Scale accepted Felicia's sacrifice, proof enough it was real. You imagine her need for your trust would not outlive the compelled empathy she endured, but the Scale would never fall for such a transparent evasion. It would have detected the contradiction, and the wish would have failed. I assure you, Felicia's sacrifice was real, and she surely regrets it already. This is the Scale's most certain guarantee, and the key to my power."

Dorothy looked away from the dragon, down the blackness of the unlit tunnel. If Hypatia spoke the truth, somewhere down there, an assassin, free now to decide whether to care about the well-being of others or to treat them as dehumanized targets, desperately pined for the trust of an enemy. She had traded one pain for another, unwittingly ruining her chances of returning to her old profession, if that even remained her goal. She said herself she wanted to change. Could that be true? "Why would my trust still matter to her? Before the empathy spell, she was the most cold-hearted person I have ever known."

"Who can say? Minds and hearts are far too complex and erratic for proper understanding. Still, the fact remains, that person gave up something that continues to matter a great deal to her, even in her cold-hearted persona. It's a pity she fled so swiftly. Had she stayed, you could have seen the other half of the Scale's influence, and how I wielded it to rule a continent."

"The other half?" Dorothy turned back to the dragon. "What is this thing good for other than crushing dreams? Is that how you manipulated the masses into believing in your charity? By not giving anyone what they actually wanted?"

Hypatia grinned. "Do go on."

Dorothy's jaw dropped. "My god. That's exactly what you did. You offer people their hearts' desires. Then you either deny them what they think they want most of all, or you give it to them in exchange for regret. There is no way to win this game."

"Well put," said the dragon. "Everyone who ever came to me for help arrived in a state of optimism and hope, and found themselves broken by their own objectives. The Scale is not a tool for granting wishes. It is a power whose force lies in the capacity to make people desperate. Kings, generals, even high wizards brought me their aspirations, only to see them crushed. Because I appeared to be magnanimous, they blamed only themselves."

"How does any of that serve you?" said Dorothy. "How does senseless cruelty translate into an empire?"

"It is remarkably easy to persuade others to wage one's wars," said Hypatia. "Given the right state of vulnerability, leaders will fight nearly any battle if they believe it will regain for them what they have lost."

The earth overhead rumbled once more, this time vibrating the ceiling of the tunnel with sufficient gusto to fill the chamber with a deep, brassy tone. Dorothy looked up. "What's happening?"

"An attack, most likely. Things have been set in motion now that cannot be halted."

"An attack? From whom?"

"From the sound, I would guess a European dragon burrowing through the clay. It could be one of your human machines. I don't know those well enough to speculate."

"That's a city up there!" cried Dorothy.

"Burrowing through the city, then. I imagine the people must be in quite a bit of disarray by now."

Dorothy looked Hypatia in the eye, searching for some sense of reason there. "You knew this was coming?"

"Hmm. Yes," said Hypatia. "This is likely my first sacrificial lamb, though he is early. Most inconvenient timing. You don't happen to have an unpleasant history with the wizardess Rosebud you would care to disclose at this time, by any chance?"

"I killed her mentor," said Dorothy. "What does that have to do with anything?"

"It would have been useful to know. I suppose she moved up our timetable in the hope you would die in the confusion. That's the trouble dealing with wizards. Always wheels within wheels with them."

"Wait, are you saying you're working with her?"

"The loosest of confederations, I assure you," sad the dragon. "A simple exchange of favors. I should have suspected she buried a revenge plot in her machinations. Her task was to send me a beast I could make a show of slaying before the masses. You'd be amazed how much goodwill one can generate with such a simple act."

Something pounded the roof of the tunnel, ringing it like a kettle drum.

"Will you stand and fight with me, little witch?" asked the wyvern. "We have an empire to build, you and I, and I regret to admit that will entail no small amount of violence at the outset."

A few dozen yards away, and in the direction of Dorothy's only possible path of egress, a section of the tunnel collapsed. Daylight poured in, as well as distant sirens. Massive reptilian claws moved their way down the rubble.

Dorothy threw her arms in front of her face and shouted, "Fire Shield!" The spell threw an emerald, spherical aura around her body, moments before the tunnel filled with pale yellow flame. Her footing shifted as the coins beneath her softened and melted. She screamed.

The conflagration ceased. Dorothy's shield held, protecting her from the residual heat, and holding her aloft atop the viscous metal below. The wall of flame dissipated around the head of a dragon, snorting and puffing smoke.

Hypatia, unharmed, grinned. "Really, Gustav. Let's take this outside."

[26]

DRAGON BATTLE

Hypatia launched herself at Gustav, pushing off the tunnel floor with her hind legs. As she collided with the newcomer, she bit his shoulder, then spread her wings and catapulted herself upward though the breach in the ceiling.

Gustav stumbled forward, blood flowing from the bite wound. As he struggled to turn around in the enclosed space, his eye fell on Dorothy. Without her sword, she posed no threat to him, and the fire shield still protecting her provided defense only against his searing breath. She could not know how he would treat her given her apparent association with his enemy. Thankfully, she did recognize the name.

"I'm Harrison Cody's daughter!" she shouted.

Gustav snorted again. He turned away from her, setting his sights on the open sky. With a flap of his back-mounted wings, he clambered up the mountain of broken metal and stone, smoothly scooping Dorothy up in one of his forepaws as he went.

The spellbook shimmered into her hand, and she desperately flipped through it to find a magical brace against the expected crushing force of his grip.

His claws locked in place around her, forming a cage. Debris from the surface bounced off this protective shell, and she threw her arms around one of his fingers to hold on as he ascended. It took him at least a full minute to reach the surface. Once there, he set her down in the dirt, well away from the chasm he had dug, and took to the sky.

Sirens blared all around her. The dragon's reappearance in the city triggered a wave of screams, as onlookers pointed or fled. Gustav had torn up a considerable section of city street to reach his quarry. None of the surrounding buildings appeared damaged, but with two dragons facing off that would change soon, and dramatically. In this neighborhood, that could include the NCSA building, less than three blocks away. If the battle extended another mile or so, Dorothy might see her own house flattened.

So far, human activity appeared largely limited to evacuation efforts and treatment of injuries. Gustav's appearance in the city must have been swift, and his destruction of the street as he burrowed had thrown pavement and stone debris dozens of yards from the hole. Several cars lay on their sides or backs, evidence of his haste and disregard for the immediate safety of the people he presumably intended to protect in the long term. Dorothy scanned her surroundings for evidence of fatalities, and found none, for now. It could only be a matter of moments before the number of casualties rose from zero to thousands.

Hypatia sat on her haunches, grinning and patient.

As far as any casual observer would be able to tell, Gustav represented an out-of-control aggressor, terrorizing a city of innocents. His opponent, in truth a despot seeking to regain her control over millions, at the cost of untold lives and destruction, struck the pose of a bystander. Her reputation as a generous benefactor had elevated her to rule a world, once. To renew that, she needed only to allow Gustav to attack. The narrative of Hypatia striking back to defend herself and protect the city would write itself.

"Gustav!" shouted Dorothy. "You can't do this here!"

"Stay out of dis!" bellowed the dragon.

"She's baiting you!"

"You don't understand! You don't know vhat she vill do to your vorld!"

"I do understand!" said Dorothy. "You're playing into her hands! A wizard sent you here! Am I right? A wizard named Rosebud?"

Gustav pulled his lips back in a grimace. A gust of warm air assaulted Dorothy from his nostrils. "Vhat do you know about it?"

"She's working with Hypatia! She sent you here to look like the villain, probably hoping you would kill me in the process. Did she tell you she wanted to help you? Because all she wants is revenge and destruction, and that's what you're giving her! Stand down! Find Harrison! Tell the NCSA why you're here!"

"Dey von't believe me," said Gustav. "Humans lust for power. Dey vill listen to her, and vish on her Scale, and your vorld vill fall to her tyranny."

Ignoring Dorothy's pleas, Gustav took flight and charged Hypatia. His flame already having proven inadequate, he opted for a brute force attack, swinging his claws at her in a roundhouse.

She took the blow, allowing him to rake a trio of blood streaks across her face, then pulled him into a roll to bleed out the momentum of his attack. They collided with a two-story building housing a small grocer and an apartment. The structure collapsed over them, sending up a plume of concrete dust. Hypatia kicked him upward, and he took to the sky.

The white wyvern rose from the demolished building, trails of crimson marring her snow-white albino visage, forming a masterpiece of manipulative art. "Oh, Gustav, you brute! How could you?" She batted her eyes at him and laughed. "Is that all you've got? Let's show these people how fierce and mighty you are. The bigger the show, the more they will cheer me when I throw your broken corpse into their lake."

Gustav roared and tackled her, further demolishing the building beneath her and throwing up a cloud of concrete dust.

Dorothy glared at this attack. "Damn your stupid dragon ego," she whispered.

Apryl Mendoza-Cody appeared in front of Dorothy, startling her. One of New Chicago's resident telekinetics, Apryl possessed a variety of magic-based abilities, teleportation by far the most startling. "Dorothy! We have to get you out of here!" She reached for Dorothy's hand.

"No! Wait!" Dorothy pushed Apryl away and pointed to the dragons. "That white dragon is going to kill Gustav and enslave the world. We have to stop this before that happens! Separate them!"

Apryl looked up. "That's Gustav? Oh, no."

"What's happening? How did you find me?"

"Sparky," said Apryl.

Dorothy grabbed Apryl's shoulders. "Sparky? She's awake? She's all right?"

"She's fine. Came straight to me, then to the NCSA. They are bringing in the mages and the army to kill both of these dragons. We need to go home and let them do their jobs."

"No! Apryl, that's Hypatia! The non-real wizards will recognize her from the legends and take her side! They won't understand everything they learned about her is false!"

Gustav dove down on Hypatia and spat a fireball in her face. Given her immunity to dragon flame, the move could only have been meant to distract, but she turned it around, shrieking and clawing at her eyes with maximum drama. As Gustav reached striking distance she whipped her tail around, sending him crashing into another building.

"Please don't argue with me," said Apryl.

"I'm not arguing! I'm asking for your help!" She looked back at the gaping hole in the street, and back in the direction of the Worm station, too far to see. "Somewhere under this street, Claudia has my sword! Can you get me to her?"

"*Your* sword?" said Apryl.

"Damn it, Apryl! Can you do it or not?"

Apryl looked at the ground and closed her eyes. "I have her. She's running, carrying something heavy."

Dorothy grabbed Apryl's hand. "Go!"

Dorothy had seen Apryl teleport on numerous occasions, sometimes casually, and sometimes in crisis. She had never ridden with her before. The daylight and battle noise vanished like shutting off a loud television. She found herself in darkness, the only light a bouncing beam in the distance moving away from her, no doubt Claudia's headlamp. Fighting a touch of vertigo, Dorothy shouted, "Claudia!"

The beam stopped and spun around, landing in Dorothy's eye. "Dotty?"

"I'm here!"

They ran to each other, colliding in an embrace after a few seconds.

Claudia kissed her repeatedly, and held her tight. "What the fuck happened back there? The tunnel caved in! I thought you were dead!"

"I'm sorry," said Dorothy. "I'm so, so sorry. I'll explain it all later, but we need to move right now. Apryl? Get us topside."

"Apryl?" By the time Claudia finished the word, they had returned to the surface.

Dorothy shielded her eyes against the sudden brightness. In natural light, Strontium's scratches and cracks stood out more vividly than before their journey in the tunnel. In this form, Strontium felt no pain. Only she knew whether the extent of her damage brought fear.

Gustav and Hypatia had taken their battle into the air, but had not strayed far in any direction other than up. Surely Hypatia needed her eventual victory to be seen in the city to optimize the perception of her as a savior.

Dorothy held out her hand. "Claudia. My sword, please."

Claudia took a step back. "Dotty, you can't get involved in that brawl."

"You don't understand," said Dorothy. "Hypatia plans to rule the world. She's going to kill Gustav, take credit for saving the city, and start her empire all over again. The Scale isn't meant to help anyone."

"What scale?" said Apryl. "What are you talking about?"

"It's a long story. Trust me when I say it's the road to Hell. It grants your wishes, but only in exchange for a sacrifice of something you want even more."

Apryl shook her head. "Why would anyone agree to that?"

"Because people are arrogant and foolish! They believe they can live without whatever thing they give up for the wish, but they are always trading down. Or, they foolishly assume their sacrifice is worth more than it really is, and the wish fails. You saw both of those things happen, Claudia. It creates regret and desperation, and that's all it does. We are at a point in history where every nation on Earth is in its infancy." Dorothy looked up to the pair of dragons swooping at each other, exchanging punches, bites and kicks. "If we don't stop her now, she will turn us all into her puppets."

Claudia hesitated, then held Bess's hilt out. As Dorothy reached for it, Claudia pulled her into a kiss. "Whatever you do next, you still owe me a wedding, so don't fucking get killed."

"That's the idea." Dorothy took the sword. "Bess, can you kill that dragon?"

I believe so. We will need to be very close, and take her by surprise. I cannot guarantee you will survive.

"Not good enough. We need a plan." She looked at Apryl. "Can you teleport me right to her?"

Apryl looked up. "No way. I can't hit a moving target, and I'd never be able to stop us from falling to our deaths."

"All right, we won't consider that an option. What if—"

A flash of light followed immediately by deafening thunder cut her off. It took her a moment to regain her wits, at which point she recognized the signature odor of a lightning spell.

Gustav had gone limp. It took an agonizingly slow five seconds for him to hit the ground. He landed on two parked cars, adding the sounds of metal crushing and glass shattering to the soft but brutal *thump* of his flesh meeting pavement. Smoke continued to puff from his nostrils, indicating weak but steady breathing.

Hypatia circled overhead like a vulture.

"What the fuck just happened?" said Claudia.

Dorothy clutched her hair with her free hand. "The wizards are here. Damn it! We're out of time!"

Claudia put her hand on Dorothy's shoulder. "Can't you explain—?"

"Explain what? That everything they know about the legendary Hypatia is a lie? She fooled better wizards than ours for hundreds of years!"

"Where is the scale you're talking about?" asked Apryl. "Can we destroy it before she can use it?"

Dorothy pointed to the hole. "Down there. It's a giant balance scale."

"How does it work?" asked Apryl. "Does it have a power source? Overloading power sources is my specialty."

"The Scale is a tool," said Dorothy. "Hypatia's magic is what makes it work. Can you overload something if the power source is a dragon?"

Apryl shrugged. "I'll let you know." She vanished.

"Damn," said Claudia.

Dorothy shook her head. "I don't know whether that will do any good. Even if Apryl can destroy it, Hypatia will probably be able to make another one while we sit in prison for vandalizing a priceless artifact."

The wyvern descended in a wide spiral. As she neared Dorothy in one of her lowest passes, she said, "That is exactly what would happen."

"Oh, fuck," said Claudia.

Hypatia beat her wings to hover, eventually touching down a few feet away from Dorothy. "I would ask if you have made a decision, but it is clear you have. My hearing is a bit keener than you might have realized."

"Even if I had, I wouldn't have held my tongue," said Dorothy. "You're a monster, and I will do everything in my power to stop you."

"You may want to examine your power more realistically," said the wyvern. "You saw that lightning. Your betters have already chosen to stand with me. Even if they believe your claims about my nature, humans are notorious for believing that temptation and bad judgment are things that happen to other people. They will connive to outwit my Scale, and when they fail, they are more likely to blame you than accept the truth of your words."

"I will prove you wrong."

Hypatia clucked her lips. "Alas, we won't ever know for certain. Do you think an accident would be more convincing, or should I claim self-defense against your pitiful blade?"

Claudia held up her hands. "Whoa! Whoa! What happened to the head start?"

"You forfeited your right to my mercy when you plotted to kill me." She tapped her ear. "Much, much keener than you thought."

Dorothy looked back at her lover and the sad, wooden scraps of her best friend. In seconds they would all be dead, and she would complete her collection of spectacular failures on this quest.

Persuade her to rear, said Bess. *Our only hope is to strike her underbelly.*

Dorothy gulped. This last second shred of hope did not solve her problem. While valuable information, and heartening to come from an ally who even now hoped to save her, she found no immediate way to use it. She would need to buy herself that opportunity. "You want a case for self-defense? You got it!" As Dorothy sprang in her attack leap, Bess asserted control, swinging at Hypatia's wing as she had against Ruprecht. The blade caught only air, as Hypatia dodged the strike with uncanny speed for a creature of her bulk. Dorothy sailed past her in an arc, intercepted by Hypatia's tail, batting her upward and away. The smack stung Dorothy's back, but she rotated midair, visually confirming Claudia had taken advantage of her baiting tactic to grab Strontium and flee in the opposite direction.

Even with the aid of a slow descent spell, Dorothy had to roll as she hit the ground to avoid injury. Bess managed that for her, bringing her to her feet to face her foe. "Fire Shield!" The green sphere rematerialized around her, and she stood her ground for Hypatia's next move.

Media crews had arrived in the wake of Gustav's assault, and they now trained their cameras on Dorothy. Under this scrutiny, Hypatia did not dare roast her alive from a distance. Such an act would never play to her narrative of benevolence. No such constraints bound Dorothy. She threw her left arm forward, launching a bolt of blue-white lightning at the dragon. Unable to maintain two spells at once, she lost control of the fire shield, which flickered out to pale, lime-colored smoke. Though more than enough energy to cook a deranged wolf to death, the lightning attack provided little offense against an opponent of Hypatia's size. Dorothy therefore concentrated on precision in lieu of power. The bolt struck Hypatia on the cheek, scorching a mark on the flesh already bleeding from Gustav's claws, leaving that portion of her face two clashing shades of red.

Hypatia roared. The blast of hot air and deafening sound knocked Dorothy backward even from dozens of yards away. Bess tucked her into a backward somersault, seamlessly returning her to defensive stance.

"You child!" shouted Hypatia. "You speck! You dare presume to elevate yourself to my level? You are nothing! A runty, mundane human, with a bag of parlor tricks! I offer this world riches and glory beyond the most fanciful desires of its noblest kings, and you hope to stop me with sparks? I will crush you, and your own people will celebrate your demise in song!"

"You offer them nothing but subjugation or death!" said Dorothy.

"Which they will embrace with their most obsequious gratitude! You know nothing of sovereignty! Nothing of dominion over the rabble! I reigned supreme for half a millennium offering nothing but subjugation or death, and my subjects begged me to rule them with unwavering joy."

Dorothy thrust the heel of her palm outward, hitting Hypatia with a concussion spell. It clipped her left flank, dislodging two scales and sending them flying. The wound exposed a patch of pink flesh, and triggered another roar. "Is that an opening?" she asked Bess.

Nay, said the sword. *Nothing vital there.*

Dorothy lashed out again, hoping to take out a more anatomically strategic section of armor. A slight pop emanated from her open hand, but it carried no effect to her foe. The first signs of magical fatigue made themselves known to her in the form of a head rush, and she struggled to maintain her balance. Offensive magic taxed her inner reserves in a way more passive spells did not, and she had pushed her attacks for maximum damage against an oversized enemy. Even at her limit, the strikes had done woefully insignificant damage, and she would need rest before she could launch another.

The significance of Dorothy's none-too-subtle faltering did not escape Hypatia. "Oho. Are we tapped out, little witch? So soon? I was beginning to think you presented something beyond mere nuisance."

Dorothy stepped backward as the dragon advanced on her. She rapidly inventoried every spell she could still feasibly cast. Chilling often sufficed to incapacitate or confound a human opponent, but against a creature this massive she couldn't hope for a temperature drop of more than a degree or two. A vertigo curse might prove effective if she could dupe Hypatia into taking flight. No other tactic readily presented itself. Her combat training sessions with Aplomado, ever her least favorite studies in her apprenticeship, now taunted her in their inadequacy to prepare her for engagement with a dragon.

A sound like an axe striking a tree issued from in front of Dorothy, and the wyvern shrieked. Hypatia lurched backward, and towered over her, bellowing in pain, a black arrow protruding from her eye.

Bess seized the moment, assuming Dorothy's motor control, but leaving her enough to execute her magical fighting leap. The sword guided her aim, and she launched herself at the wall of white scales blotting out the sun. Bess found her mark, in the interstice between three plates of dragon armor. Dorothy hit with sufficient force to crack one of them, and to drive Bess's blade into Hypatia's flesh. Her arm advanced into the wound up to her elbow, at which point at least one of her bones snapped.

Hypatia thrashed, her screams increasing in volume and intensity. Dorothy lost her grip on Bess, and the wyvern's spasms flung her away in an arc toward Gustav's burrow. Through the pain of her broken arm,

Dorothy cast the slow descent spell quickly enough to avoid any further fractures, coming to a hard landing on the edge of the debris pile.

Hypatia toppled with a hideous crash, Bess buried in her heart, a scant two feet from Dorothy's face. The ground quaked under the force of her death rattle.

Dorothy rolled over onto her back, favoring the injured arm without looking at it. She looked back to Claudia and Strontium. Behind them, at a distance, Felicia dropped her bow, and ran.

RENEWAL

"Hold still, please."

Dorothy gritted her teeth and made a fist with her good hand against the dirt beneath her, anxiously waiting for the moment to pass. With a loud *snap*, and a flash of piercing agony in her arm, her radius reset itself, and fused into a single piece of bone.

"Ow!" Dorothy yanked her arm back and rubbed it furiously. "Ow, ow, ow, ow, ow, ow!"

"That word is actually pronounced 'fuck'," said Claudia. "You should try that sometime."

"Fuck!" shouted Dorothy. "Nope. Didn't help."

Jonathan, the healer, lifted his hands from her forearm, and stripped off a pair of latex gloves. "Is that the only injury you want treated?"

"Yes, thank you," said Dorothy.

The scrubs-clad young man pointed over his shoulder with his thumb. "You may want to consider getting yourself away from this dragon corpse. I'm not a mental health specialist, but anyone can see this was traumatic."

"Thank you," said Dorothy, "but no. I have something extremely valuable buried in that dragon's gut, and I want to see it retrieved before I walk away from it."

"Suit yourself." Jonathan turned to leave, nearly colliding with Harrison, as he came around the other side of the slain dragon.

"Hey there," said Harrison.

Dorothy waved at him and looked away. A few seconds later, he sat down in the dirt next to her. They both peered down into the tunnel from the edge of the hole. Below them, light from the torches continued to shine on treasure now melted to slag. "How much trouble am I in?"

"We're still sorting that out," said Harrison. "Claudia? Can you take a walk, please?"

"You okay here, Dotty?" asked Claudia.

"I have no idea."

Claudia wagged a finger at Harrison. "We're getting married, you know. Don't fuck that up for me."

"Understood," said Harrison. "Congratulations. Truly."

Claudia harrumphed, kissed her fiancée, stood, and walked away.

"You were about to tell me I am in trouble?" said Dorothy.

"A little bit. I do need to ask you for the sword back before this conversation goes any further."

Dorothy pointed behind her to the body of the wyvern.

"Ugh," said Harrison. "I'm sure we have a team of experts for this sort of extraction. At least I hope we do."

"How's Gustav?" asked Dorothy.

"In more trouble than you are, since you ask. The NCSA has been concealing his existence for a very long time. Now we have to track him. I can't wait to see how he reacts to being tagged."

"He's not hurt?"

"He'll live," said Harrison. "The dumbass. Let himself get played by a wizard like a chump. If he had come to me instead of trying to take out Hypatia on his own, we could have avoided a panic. Now we're on the hook for millions in property damage and medical bills. No one has died yet, so at least there's that. If we do end up with any fatalities it's going to make letting him go pretty damn problematic. Speaking of letting people go…"

Dorothy hung her head. "Here it comes."

"Why didn't you bring Felicia in?"

"That was the plan," said Dorothy. "She even agreed to it. Then it all fell apart when we got to that Scale."

"Did you have a chance to bring her in before that?" asked Harrison.

"No. Maybe. It's complicated." Dorothy sighed. "Yes, we probably could have come to the NCSA instead of going into that tunnel. I was afraid you would try to stop me from using the Scale to restore Strontium. Or you wouldn't understand the situation, and you would treat Felicia like a threat, and someone would die. Or some other damn thing I couldn't predict would happen, and ruin everything." She paused there, to allow Harrison an opportunity to question her further, or lecture her on procedure, or find some other way to make her feel worse.

"Let's start over," he said. "Did you have a chance to bring her in before that?"

"No, sir."

"All right, then. Make sure you state that clearly in your report."

Dorothy looked up. "My report?"

"On the borrowed vault item? You had a study to run under the supervision of agent Sparky, remember? I need a report on your findings. I also still need that report on the incident the day you vanished for several hours."

"You really plan to sweep all this under a bureaucratic rug?" said Dorothy. "For God's sake. I let a known serial murderer escape. Look around you. None of this would have happened if I had brought you in on this from day one."

"Yes, it would have," said Harrison. "It just would have happened differently. Possibly ending with a certain white dragon ruling the world."

An orange streak dropped out of the sky and landed on Dorothy's lap. "Hey! Are you under arrest?" Sparky frowned at Harrison with her hands on her hips. "Is she under arrest?"

"Not at the moment," said Harrison.

"Sparky!" said Dorothy. "I'm so glad to see you! When did you wake up?"

"Wake up?" said the pixie. "You mean shake the wizard-induced funk?"

"Wizard-induced? I thought it was depression! Rosebud said you did that to yourself."

Sparky grimaced. "Did it to... Why, that lying so and so! Of course I didn't do that to myself! This is why I hate wizards."

"Then how did you snap out of it?"

"Oh! That was Felicia. For a killer, she has a hell of a singing voice."

Dorothy's jaw dropped. "I'm sorry. Singing voice?"

"Yup! Sang me a folk song from her childhood over and over until I came around. Well, she said it was from her childhood. It sounded kinda made up, to be honest. Beautiful as all get out, though."

"That's new," said Harrison.

"I know!" said the pixie.

"Why didn't you tell me that when you debriefed?"

"How should I know?" She turned her attention back to Dorothy. "Anyway, once she got me up and running, she filled me in on the bad dragon and sent me to get help."

"How did she know the dragon was bad?" asked Dorothy. "She got her wish."

"Said she figured it out as soon as the curse lifted. That all she wanted to do was beg Hypatia to undo it. That's why she ran. She knew if she stayed she'd offer to do anything if it meant getting your trust back, and she knew she would end up that dragon's slave. Smart cookie. I don't know how she picked up on that so quickly."

Dorothy smiled. "I do. Hypatia finally found a mark who understands manipulation well enough to see it." She turned to Harrison. "You knew Hypatia was the real threat?"

"I did, yeah. The mages apparently had a differing opinion. I just came from a conference you should be glad you missed. Half the council thinks they should have met with Hypatia and seen the Scale for themselves."

"That would not have gone well."

"That's what I said. I think they were a little hurt I didn't trust the fate of the world to a handful of wizards being offered whatever they wanted. And by a little bit hurt I mean they think you and I should both be in prison right now."

"Great." Dorothy winced. "What did Aplomado say?"

"Almost nothing, as usual, but I'm pretty sure that's the first time I've ever seen him smile. I don't think you lost any points with him today. Oh, and the mages want to debrief you on Rosebud, although you didn't hear that from me."

"I can tell them where we met her, but she's bound to be long gone by now."

"Anything you have on her will thrill them, I'm sure. Apparently, they didn't know she existed before today. You may or may not want to rub their noses in that if they give you any shit about how you handled the Scale situation."

Dorothy laughed. "Noted."

"Hey! Dotty!"

Dorothy looked behind her. Claudia jogged toward her, wearing a grin and carrying Felicia's bow, Dorothy's bag, and a white, flat object about the size and shape of a Frisbee. She tossed this latter in Dorothy's direction, and it landed in the dirt a few feet away from her.

Up close, and out of context, a single, detached dragon scale did not present the level of majesty Dorothy had spent a week working herself up to experience.

"Not funny."

"Too soon?" said Claudia.

Dorothy stood, putting a bit too much pressure on her still tender arm. "Ow! Let me see that."

She took the bag and opened it to check for the tortoise skeleton. Aplomado's arbitrary assignment weighed on her in that moment, perhaps from a need to have succeeded at something. Lying on top of the copious contents of her bag, four bands of large bills stared back at her. She pulled them out and handed them to Harrison. "Donate this to Chicago Memorial, please. Make it anonymous."

He raised a brow at this. "That's a lot of money."

"It has a lot of bad deeds to make up for." She dug further, and wrapped her hand around the block of plastic. The tortoise skeleton remained perfectly preserved within. She held it to her face, closed her eyes and sighed deeply.

"Hey," said Harrison. "You have some visitors."

Dorothy opened her eyes. Several wizards and witches from the Council of Mages had arrived, some inspecting the fallen wyvern, othering staring down the burrow, presumably in search of the Scale. They would find it if they climbed down, Apryl's attempt to destroy it having failed, but they would only gain an enormous tool for verifying weights. Without Hypatia, wishing in the Scale would serve no more purpose than wishing on a shooting star or a birthday cake.

"Are you all right?" asked Aplomado.

Dorothy ran to her mentor and threw her arms around him. She had never hugged him before. To the best of her knowledge, no one had. He returned the gesture with the good faith attempt of someone obviously out of practice.

"I'm so sorry I didn't come to you first," she said. "I should have trusted you. I panicked, and now Strontium is lost."

Aplomado pulled back with a worried frown and placed his fingers on Dorothy's temples. "Lost? Strontium is no longer in your mind?"

Dorothy's throat tightened. She shook her head, willing herself not to cry, and pointed to the broken doll. "She's in there, now. For a while she could walk and talk, but she suffered so much damage along the way she can't even move now. I wanted to wish her a new body on the Scale. I thought the Council had given up on her, and I tried to fix the problem myself, and I failed."

Aplomado dropped to one knee beside Strontium's inert form. He stroked her cracked forehead. "This figure is warm." He looked back to Dorothy. "She is still in here."

"I know," said Dorothy. "She's trapped now. I don't even know if she is conscious anymore."

He shook his head. "You don't understand. The transfer of a human consciousness into an inanimate object... It should be impossible. How did you do this?"

"It wasn't me. Felicia hired a dark elf to cast the spell. I didn't recognize the language, or the aura. It's like nothing you ever taught me."

"Dark elven magic? I should think not! Even a non-real human mind would never bear the strain." He leaned over the doll again, picking up its one good hand. "This is wood. Cellular matter. Perhaps... this object might be semi-animate. That would explain a great deal. If it is... I never considered the possibility of a transitional stage. We intended to regrow her body from the ash sample we drew from her remains, but there was too much damage, and goblin blood contamination."

Dorothy bit her knuckle. "You really were working on freeing her? All this time, I thought you had given up."

He stood. "Do you have the skeleton I gave you? Did you keep it with you?"

Dorothy looked at her fist, still clutching the block of plastic. She pulled Aplomado's hand up, placed the preserved skeleton in it, and closed his fingers around it. "I have carried it through deadly perils, and there isn't a scratch on it. Please, please tell me I did well. I need to hear that so badly right now."

Instead of responding, he called over his shoulder, "Mallory! I need you!"

Another wizard, a woman with pale skin and straight, black hair, a little shorter than Dorothy and at least ten years her elder, approached. Mallory, chairperson of the Council of Mages, looked at Dorothy and Aplomado with a blank expression, her patience no doubt taxed by this day's events already. "Yes?"

Aplomado knelt and placed his palm on Strontium's head. "This vessel contains the mind of Strontium. It is still warm. She lives, but cannot communicate. I believe this doll may be semi-animate."

Mallory's eyes widened, shattering her expression of disdain. "Semi-animate? It contains Strontium's mind? That's... We never considered this. How was it even possible?" She turned to Dorothy. "Did you do this? How on Earth?"

"No," said Dorothy. "An elf did it. I'm sorry. If I had any idea she would have ended up like this—"

"You don't understand," said Aplomado.

"How long has she been in this thing?" asked Mallory.

Dorothy took a moment to count backward. "Five days."

"Five days!" Mallory dropped to her knees and held her palms to the wood. "We have hours, at best."

"I am aware." said Aplomado.

"Hours?" said Dorothy. "For what? What's happening?"

"We need vertebrate remains," said Mallory. "Ideally a reptile, dead at least three weeks. If we don't have that in the pantry, we need to hit every magic shop in New Chicago today."

Aplomado held up the plastic block. "Tortoise skeleton. Will it suffice?"

Mallory's jaw dropped. "Should I ask why you have a tortoise skeleton on you?"

"A trial for my apprentice. I tasked her with keeping it undamaged for weeks. It held no other significance."

"I knew it!" said Dorothy.

"Be glad he did," said Mallory. "This will save us time we don't have to spare."

"Time for what?" said Dorothy. "Is there something you can do for her? Can you put her back in my mind? Please! I will carry her again!"

Aplomado looked at her, and put his finger to his lips.

Mallory held the block with the tortoise skeleton in it over Strontium's inert form. As she chanted in syllables unfamiliar to Dorothy, the block glowed pale indigo, then crumbled to dust, which rained down on the broken doll. The fine points of light tunneled into the wood of her body. After a few seconds, buds formed over its surface, by the hundreds. Some bloomed into flowers of diverse colors and forms. Most sprouted leaves, also assorted. New vines curled around her torso, constricting around her one remaining arm until it folded into her and vanished under thousands of expanding leaves.

The doll became a mass of jumbled flora, leaves and fronds stirring in a breeze that did not affect anything else around it. The growth rustled with increasing intensity, then abruptly halted.

Autumn consumed this form, as the diverse leaves cycled rapidly through assorted fiery tones. For a few moments, this figure radiated a comforting visual warmth, before desiccation took hold. The leaves browned and shriveled, finally crumbling to vast amounts of dark, brittle flakes.

Beneath this dust, an infant put forth her first cry.

"Oh, my God!" Dorothy ran to Strontium's side. The leaf fragments dissolved and whisked away in an otherwise unfelt wind, exposing a perfect little girl. An assortment of loose metal pins and hinges lay scattered around her, the only remaining evidence that this child had recently been a doll. Dorothy picked her up, and laid the baby's head on her shoulder. The child cooed, and drifted off to sleep.

Dorothy turned to Mallory, unable to wipe the tears streaming down her face for fear of waking her charge. "Is this her? Is this Strontium?"

"Yes, it is," said Mallory. "This body will grow into the one you knew years ago. She will age rapidly, four to five times as fast as a normal human. When her physical age reaches her chronological age, the aging will slow down to normal. You should know, given her advanced years already, she may well pass away before she reaches that point."

Dorothy kissed the baby's head, feather-soft hairs tickling her lips. "I can live with that. So can she, I'm sure." She looked up at Mallory. "Will she remember anything?"

"I have never attempted this spell before, so please do not hold me to this, but she should remember everything," said Mallory.

"You should know soon enough," said Aplomado. "Once she starts to speak. If everything worked the way it should, the child you hold in your arms will become the same person you hosted for years, with that adult's memories and awareness."

Strontium cooed again, and sighed. Dorothy rested her cheek against the infant's head and drank in the sweet, newborn smell. "You hear that, baby?" she whispered. "I did right by you after all."

Eyes still closed, Strontium nodded.

EPILOGUE

Strontium did a pirouette in her pink flower girl gown. "Can I change out of this yet? I look like a damn child!"

"You are a damn child," said Claudia. "I mean that in the nicest possible way, of course."

Strontium blew her a raspberry.

"I stand corrected."

Guests clinked their spoons playfully against wine glasses. Dorothy and Claudia from their seats at the head table smiled and obliged the crowd with a kiss, to much cheering.

"Hells bells," said Strontium. "How many times are they going to do that?"

"All the times." Claudia punctuated this by dinging her own glass.

Strontium waited for the ritual to play out, rolling her eyes. "And another thing, your bartender carded me!"

"Do we have to have the conversation again about alcohol and young brains?" said Dorothy.

"I'm ninety-nine!"

"In the body of a four-year-old. Please humor me on this one. Hold off on the wine until you hit puberty again."

Strontium put her hands on her hips. "You're not the boss of me!"

Dorothy laughed. "Now you're being difficult on purpose!"

"Damn straight," said Strontium. "Consider it a wedding present."

Melody, three seats down at the table, giggled at this.

"Hey, kid," said Strontium. "Since they won't let us into the grownup stuff, how about you and I have a cake eating contest?"

Melody gasped. Enormous purple butterfly wings—remnants of a spell cast on her six years earlier—fluttered furiously behind her, lifting her from her seat. A napkin fell from her lap onto her plate as she vaulted over the table and flitted straight for the desserts

"Melody!" cried her mother Apryl, too late and with too little conviction. She scowled at Strontium with a barely concealed smile. "You'll pay for that, you little runt."

Strontium grinned and shrugged. "Meh." She charged off to go act like a child.

Harrison, who had left the table earlier to take a call, returned with a businesslike expression that belied his tuxedo and the festive mood of the room. "Dr. and Mrs. De Queiroz-O'Neill? I'm sorry to take you away from your guests, but would you join me for a moment, please? This won't take long."

Claudia gave Dorothy a puzzled look. Dorothy shrugged in return, and they both stood.

Harrison led them to a side room, where wrapped gifts and cards covered a long table. Two metal cases sat on the floor near the display that had not been there earlier, one large and boxy, the other oblong. Harrison handed Dorothy and Claudia each a card.

"What is this about?" asked Dorothy.

"These arrived at NCSA headquarters earlier today, with instructions to inspect them before delivering them to you. I agreed to be present when you opened them."

Claudia opened her card and read it. "I don't get it." She passed the card to Dorothy.

It read, "For Claudia, to complete your collection."

Harrison picked up the larger case and set it on the edge of the table. "Claudia?"

Claudia walked to the case. She inspected it, then undid the clasps and opened it. Both sides of the case held foam inserts with custom impressions, filled with knives in sheaths. One impression lay empty, the exact size and shape of the weapon mounted on the wall in her bedroom, her souvenir dagger. "Holy shit. Does she expect me to use these?"

Dorothy held back a smile. "No." She opened her card.

It read, "Thank you. That is all."

Dorothy opened her case. It contained a single rapier in a scabbard. She removed it and drew the blade. Dorothy ran her finger along the flat, relishing the cold steel, before facing both cases, and raising the sword to her eyes in salute. Then she sheathed the sword, replaced it in its case, turned to Harrison and embraced him.

ACKNOWLEDGMENTS

As always, my gratitude begins with Guinevere Crescenzi, whom I credit with starting my writing career. If you've read my other books (and given that this is book four of a series, I sure hope you have), you already know the story.

Portions of this book were written at the *Highlights* magazine workshop campus in the Poconos, which is starting to become my home away from home. That particular visit was my third "unworkshop" with them, and I offer my thanks to them for creating that opportunity for writers. I strongly recommend looking into it if you have a project you would like to work on in a peaceful environment among other creators. The food is also excellent. Special thanks to Jamie Beth Cohen Schindler for first bringing it to my attention.

A hearty thanks to my beta readers, who have once again risen to the challenge of telling me all the things I am doing wrong. Their contributions range from spotting typos to telling me point blank my entire story makes no goddamn sense (see below), and I desperately value every scrap of input from every single one of them. Many thanks to Dorian Hart, beta extraordinaire, for consistently keeping me on my toes, and engaging in endless debates over style minutiae. Thanks to Ashley Stahle for her pointers and her invaluable fashion advice (if you see any article of clothing in this story described in great detail, Ashley had a hand in tailoring it). Thanks to Josh Bluestein for pacing advice, cliché spotting, and overall storytelling feedback. Thanks to Anne Stinnett for catching errors even after the last round of proof reading. Thank you, Amy Bearce, for your investment in my characters and world, and your general supportive awesomeness.

As with *Mayhem's Children*, I enlisted the aid of a sensitivity reader for guidance on the topic of same-sex relationships, having never been in one. Thank you, Karen Escovitz, for your insights and suggestions, as well as giving me a great deal to think about on the topic of same-sex marriage, and the roll it could or should play in the post-civilization setting of the *Mayhem Wave* series. I am much more pleased with the way that arc plays out than I was before I brought it to you, and I hope I did it justice.

Two special categories of thanks are due to Jeanne Kramer-Smyth. First, the MacGuffin in this story and the nature of its magic are the direct result of a very long conversation with Jeanne, in which I asked for suggestions on how to make that plot twist work. It is also fair to credit her with the title of the book, as it directly pertains to that object. My second cause for gratitude is the annual writing retreats Jeanne has taken to organizing, in which a small group of charming fiction writers gather in a rented house for a weekend and radiate creativity at each other. I finished the first draft of *Balance of Mayhem* in last year's retreat, surrounded by writer-friends, and it was a truly delightful experience. On that note, I would also like to thank Hope Schultz, Rosemary and Tim Blodgett, Ken Schneyer, C.S.E. Cooney, Carlos Hernandez, Anthony Cardno, and my wife Annelisa Aubry-Walton for sharing it with me.

Finally, the lion's share of my gratitude this time goes to my friend Matthew Cox, an insanely prolific and talented novelist who may well have taught me more about prose style than any other individual in my life. Since making his acquaintance, I am now far more adept at spotting double tags, filtering, passive constructions, false urgency, and all the little style glitches that are the bane of every writer. The astute reader may notice that *Balance of Mayhem*, apart from examples in dialogue, was written without a single use of the word "was." That's Matt's influence. I first got to know him well as part of the CQ acquisitions team on the *Mayhem Wave* series, and later as the proofreader for *Prelude to Mayhem*. At first, I took issue with many of his suggestions and comments, to the point of genuine discomfort. However, the more I considered his points, the more I realized he is the very best kind of editor. He tells me what I need to hear without pulling punches, and if it makes me uncomfortable, that is usually just because it is no fun to be caught doing something badly. Because I valued his insights, and because I knew he had already read the rest of the series in his professional life, I asked for his input on *Balance of Mayhem*. To my horror, and eventual elation, he pointed out the central theme of redemption as I had originally presented it did not work. At all. Like, not even close. The resulting discussion included far more examples of him telling me not to be so defensive than I care to count. After a great deal of resentment and complaining, I grudgingly attempted to alter the story in a way that would satisfy him... and ended up with a novel I am proud to describe as one of my personal favorites. Matthew, thank you for kicking me in the rear when I need it, thank you for withstanding the backlash of my irritation, and thank you for not letting go when you are right and I am wrong. You fixed my broken book. I cannot imagine anything for which I could be more grateful on this page.

ABOUT THE AUTHOR

Edward Aubry is a graduate of Wesleyan University, with a degree in music composition. Improbably, this preceded a career as a teacher of high school mathematics and creative writing.

He now lives in rural Pennsylvania with his wife and three spectacular daughters, where he fills his non-teaching hours spinning tales of time-travel, wise-cracking pixies, and an assortment of other impossible things.

Unhappenings

When Nigel is visited by two people from his future, he hopes they can explain why his past keeps rewriting itself. His search for answers takes him fifty-two years forward in time, where he meets Helen, brilliant, hilarious and beautiful. Unfortunately, that meeting has triggered events that will cause millions to die. Desperate to find a solution, he discovers the role his future self has played all along.

The Mayhem Wave Series

On May 30, 2004, the world suddenly transformed into a bizarre landscape populated with advanced technology, dragons, magic and destruction. Now what few humans remain must start over, braving wilderness, dangerous beasts, and new and powerful enemies.

Prelude to Mayhem

Static Mayhem

Mayhem's Children

Balance of Mayhem

Made in the USA
Middletown, DE
09 November 2021